Subversion

Life on the Edge—of Eternity

A paranormal thriller novel by

R. Manolakas

Subversion

Life on the Edge—of Eternity

Copyright © 2013 by R. Manolakas

All Rights Reserved

Library of Congress Control Number: 2013916614
ISBN: 978-0-9898545-1-1

To my mother, Betty Jane Heise Manolakas, and to Sandy Homicz and Pat Sindt—thanks to each for their kind support.

"For they are the spirits of devils, working miracles, which go forth unto the kings of the earth and of the whole world, to gather them to the battle of that great day of God Almighty . . . And he gathered them together into a place called in the Hebrew tongue Armageddon."
Revelation, 14:16, The Holy Bible, KJV

"Humankind is too damned screwed up to be explained solely by chance or logical deduction, therefore there must be a more irrational explanation"—Anonymous scientist working in the Manhattan Atomic Bomb Project, 1945."

"Who knoweth the spirit of man that goeth upward, and the spirit of the beast that goeth downward to the earth?" — ECCLESIASTES

CHAPTER ONE

Georgetown, Saturday morning, March 24:

Dr. Collin De Gise, the surname rhyming with the word "disguise," hunted in the stacks of his favorite offbeat bookstore—The Black Peacock—as though within its dusty shelves he would discover the vital answers to life's dark mysteries. The darkest one by far would present shortly.

Many held that some of its old tomes, like lucky lotto numbers, had the power to turn lives upside down. The Peacock, a literary landmark, drew Georgetown's oddball collectors, occultists, and eggheads. As Collin browsed, the shop's purple, stained-glass window, patterned in black peacocks, rattled and pinged from the morning's violent sleet storm.

Collin, the recent Nobel Prize winner for his groundbreaking work in molecular-manipulation, and the youngest in history at the age of thirty-nine, ambled down the narrow row of books marked "European Wars." As he moved his tall, lean frame in a graceful, fluid manner, he angled his broad shoulders diagonally so that they wouldn't swipe the pillars of books.

Due to mounting stress in his job as the Scientific Director of the infamous vaccine project at the National Health Foundation, he needed an absorbing read to beat back recurring insomnia. His keen blue eyes fastened upon one volume that looked promising.

It lay on top of a pile of out-of-print books—its cover open—as if a surprised browser had quickly abandoned it for fear of detection. Collin bent over to pick it up, pushing a tuft of his wavy, dark-brown hair back from his forehead. He stood straight again, holding the book at chest level to study it, wedging his finger into a dog-eared page.

The spine of the book's binding read: *Faces Behind Shadows*. He peered inside the cover.

The translated Finnish work, copyrighted 1946, smelled odd—like burnt ginger. Moreover, the paper had a strange, woolen texture. On the front cover, he noticed an eerie symbol: a black triangle with solid black dots at the point of two angles, and a small circle at its third.

"Thought I might catch you here, sugar."

Dara—his wife—surprised him with an embrace. He held the book down by his side as they kissed.

Her lithe body filled her yellow, fine-knit dress wonderfully, he thought. She'd been a collegiate swimmer, and, as far as he knew, had never been sick a day in her life. His wife radiated an unnatural abundance of vigor, sporting the tone and carriage of a well-tended athlete.

She pushed him back a bit, studying him with her electric-green eyes, but studied the book rather more. Her gaze peered through him. "Let's grab breakfast," she urged with an unusual note of bossiness. "I don't have much time."

He couldn't remember if she had been in the bookstore before, except maybe once long ago. He also couldn't recall having told her he would be dropping by the store before going to work. He probably had forgotten, he decided.

"How about Grant's?" offered Collin.

"Great. I fancy grits and biscuits." She winked at him. "Let's get out of this horrible place."

"What about your quality management meeting?" Collin had never known her to miss one.

"They can do without me." Dara worked for Weapons Research Logistics, Inc., in nearby Washington DC. Like him, she worked hard and sometimes on weekends, though the stress of her grim job never seemed to bother her.

The US government wanted to mount light warheads on very low flying drones, thus escaping enemy radar and surface-to-air missiles. What the warheads would contain she had never—

6

understandably—shared with him because it was classified. Most of her work, in fact, was classified.

"What's that in your hand?" Her long fingers and bright red nails adjusted the collar of his camelhair overcoat. Dara's eyes flashed back and forth between her husband and the mysterious book.

"Nothing, really." He had forgotten about the book.

"What's it *about*?"

Collin raised the musty tome to eye level. "I just picked it up."

"Whew!" She crinkled her nose, shifting her spray of freckles. "It's moldy . . ."

She looked around. "I hate this place. Plenty of bookstores—why browse here?"

Collin looked around him and at the drab colors and dusty books. "Well, since you asked—."

"—I know," she joked. "*Lilith Green*, the zany owner. She's the mother you never had—and your gonzo sidekick."

"You seemed like you enjoyed her company when we all met at Grant's for breakfast last year."

"When we got home I told you what I really thought of her."

"Yes, I suppose you did."

Collin shrugged. "The real reason I come here? Murder, mayhem, mass destruction—it's all here." Collin, smiling, threw the book down on the pile and drew her closer. He nuzzled her long neck.

"Maybe that's why you're so good in bed. That, and you're really such a damn pacifist." Her eyes sparkled. "You save all your aggression for your taste in old books, and the bedroom." She tweaked his rather finely chiseled nose.

He loved her sassy mouth and whispered in her ear. "Let's just skip the grits and dash back home."

She stepped back, wagging her finger playfully." No time. Better make an appointment sweetie . . . "

Time always seemed short, lamented Collin. He had a hectic day ahead of him, including an afternoon interview at a local PBS-TV station. He faced a potentially confrontational interview about the vaccine project. The public had been up in arms about the "Vampire Virus"—the deadly organism that was sweeping Africa.

The media had claimed that it could possibly get loose from the lab and ravage the Eastern Seaboard. The deadly virus had to be stored at his work in order to develop the vaccine. The First Lady had hired Collin for the job, having been a close friend of Dara's since childhood.

"Let's go—I'm starving." She grabbed him by the elbow to usher him away.

Collin resisted. "I'll meet you in front. I want to put the book away where I can find it later. We'll have to eat fast."

Collin had no time to waste.

Before the TV interview, he also had a meeting at his workplace. The finicky administrator of the project, Frank Seaton, wanted to show him the new "radical" safety features in the laboratory. To make matters worse, that afternoon he also had to squeeze in a family outing to the National Aquarium a few miles away in Baltimore, something that he had been meaning to do for some time but had been too busy.

Collin picked *Faces Behind Shadows* off the pile, and walked with the book to the other side of the stack where he had found it. He noticed that Dara had lingered. "Go on—I'll be just a second, love."

She shrugged, slowly wandering toward the checkout counter at the front of the bookstore.

He noticed a slight frown. "I love you," he called after her.

"Love you too," she said matter-of-factly as she ambled away. "Hurry up. You've wasted enough time in this lousy place." She blew him a kiss over her shoulder.

Collin watched her go, noticing a frown, and her slightly aggressive, forward leaning gait. He loved her very much, but sometimes wondered if he really knew her. He believed many married couples today didn't take the time or energy to stay bonded.

Maybe, you can never really know someone, he thought darkly. Somehow, his relationship with Dara didn't seem quite real. At times, she seemed distant, even in their most intimate moments.

Was it the strain of the home situation, wondered Collin?

Collin and his wife didn't seem to have enough time for their autistic daughter, either. Was that why Dara had been acting a bit peculiar lately?

Maybe she feels guilty about their dear Stephanie?

Their daughter, Stephanie, a twenty-year-old genius with a taste for odd clothes and hairstyles, and a child-like social failure who lived at home, was nevertheless already an icon within her profession as a computer engineer. Her sub-type of autism—a *savant*—although rare, facilitated her singular gift in science. Stephanie's history of hard work and dedication in her field had been an inspiration to all who shared her condition.

When Collin squatted to put the book at the bottom of the stack, the old war injury in his left knee acted up. He had been a Special Tactics commando in the armed services during the second Gulf War. The sharp pain shot up to his hip as he jerked forward.

He dropped *Faces Behind Shadows* on the stained linoleum floor. It lay open at its dog-eared page.

A large, grainy, black-and-white photo stared him in the face. It caught his breath. He flushed. A bead of sweat rolled down his forehead.

He thought he recognized the face in the photo.

Collin rubbed his eyes—*could they be playing tricks on me?*

He picked the strange book up off the ground with trembling hands. As he studied the arresting photo closer, his breath quickened. Swallowing hard, he let his eyes shift from the unspeakable picture to the caption below it:

"The Nazi SS officer Frau Berta Troost: Poland, circa 1943, also known as the 'Butcher of Belzec', beats children with her dog whip as she herds them into Diclon-A poison-gas chambers."

Collin's knee burned—his mind raced.

Rising slowly, his eyes remained glued to the print. They shifted back to the photo. The slim woman that filled the sleek, black SS uniform had large expressive eyes, shoulder length hair under the black cap, and a delicate mouth and nose—it was all very familiar to Collin.

Even the forward tilt of the posture is the same, he thought.

This picture is seventy years old, and that Nazi holding the dog whip must be almost forty in the photo.

The woman in the photograph, realized Collin, would be well over one hundred years old today. How ridiculous—of course it isn't *her*! It can't be the same person.

Nevertheless, there was her double in the old photo, someone he loved dearly.

He studied the horrific image more. Feverish thoughts burned through his consciousness like a raging illness.

That SS officer beating the terrified little children in the death camp looks just like my thirty-eight year old wife!

CHAPTER TWO

Collin took a deep breath and let it out. He smiled at his foolishness. *This isn't possible*, he thought.

There are joke books like this, he reasoned. While in college, a roommate had shown him a very old photograph of Queen Victoria posing with her ministers, one of which looked identical to the American President Calvin Coolidge. He studied the image in *Faces Behind Shadows* for definitive clues as to the identity of the mysterious female SS officer as his mind groped for rationalizations.

Being an experienced virologist and holding a PhD in molecular biology, he was used to working with cold facts. Collin understood statistical theory and probability. He realized that there were bound to be chance look-alikes out there.

There was also another issue that could be affecting his thinking, he realized.

Either I'm not really seeing what I think I am seeing, or I'm blowing it out of proportion.

Collin had been seeing a psychiatrist for his Post-Traumatic Stress Disorder related to his military service. Soldiers are supposed to kill, and he had been very good at it, but the guilt wouldn't leave. He had gone off his medication three months before, under doctor's orders. Technically, the drug was an anti-psychotic, although its main purpose had been to combat depression and not delusions.

The killings had occurred just after his graduate student days, and before his first "real" job. He had been ordered to do it, and WMD—Weapons of Mass Destruction—had been suspected of being harbored within the target's hiding place.

Collin glanced over toward the front of The Black Peacock, observing his wife purchasing a magazine at the counter. He decided against showing her the photo. It wasn't because he thought that she was the one who was really in the old photo, but because it was too revolting—not a proper subject as a conversation piece about a freak coincidence.

Moreover, the photo wasn't conclusive. The image wasn't a close-up. It had been shot at an odd angle. In fact, nothing about it was, not even the partially hidden detailing of the ears, which he knew to be a very important identification marker in a photograph—almost like a fingerprint.

Disgusted with himself for being so impressionable, Collin slammed the book shut. He saw his wife approaching out of the corner of his eye, the forward tilt of her body resembling the posture of the woman in the photo. He shoved the book in the middle of the stack and quickly walked toward her.

"Are you coming or not?" She had rolled up the magazine, whipping it sharply against her thigh for emphasis. The gesture reminded him of the dog whip.

Halting in front of him, Dara looked past Collin to see what he'd been up to. "What's wrong, honey?" She looped her arm through his as they made for the front door. "You all right, Collin?"

"Yes, nothing, really; just daydreaming." As he left, he glanced back at the place where he had left the strange book.

"Well, I'll tell you right now," she said.

"Yes?"

"You look like you've seen a ghost."

Grant's Breakfast Joint, an old dive with a reputation for great omelets, had just gotten more packed as a throng of Boy Scouts streamed through the front door. He and Dara sat at the breakfast counter. The crowded eatery smelled of strong coffee and sizzling bacon.

"More good news," commented Collin. He turned the page of his newspaper from one disaster to another while he leaned over his half-finished fried eggs and corned beef hash.

The headlines punched Collin relentlessly:

"MONSTER VIRUS RAVAGES AFRICA"
"LUNAR ORANGE HALO—GLOBAL WARMING CITED"
"TERRORISTS EYE GERM WARFARE"
"PENTAGON EMBRACES BIOLOGICAL WEAPONS"
"SPREE KILLINGS AT ALL TIME HIGH"

Collin threw his newspaper down on the counter, shaking his head.

"How's the job?" Dara, who had been texting, put her cell phone away and picked up Collin's newspaper. She quizzed him in a nonchalant, throwaway style, while she studied her paper.

"The job?" asked Collin.

"Your virus project. Getting near the end with the vaccine?"

"Yes. I'm meeting Frank later. He's got some slapdash emergency equipment to show me. They just installed it—to muzzle the critics."

"What's the gripe?"

Collin hesitated to talk about the details of his work, even with her. The fact was, though, she already knew about most of it. "We have shoddy disaster controls."

Collin took back part of the newspaper and scanned it as he talked. "The virus is like working with a hydrogen bomb with a hair-trigger." He lowered his voice as his eyes searched the room for prying ears. "One mistake and it's, well—" he crumpled his paper for emphasis "—it's goodbye Eastern Seaboard."

Dara's eyes shifted from her papers to Collin. "How soon 'til you're done?"

"A week maybe. We've done the time-consuming preliminaries. Now—its finesse. Most of *my* work's done. Ten thousand children are dying in Africa each day from this monster. Time is critical. Besides, it can spread here."

"You're altering the Vampire Virus through molecular manipulation, right? How easy is it to introduce a rogue gene into the virus to make it even deadlier than the wild type—to produce a *Super-virus*?"

Collin's eyes flashed at his wife. He was a bit surprised to hear her ask such detailed questions. She'd probably been listening to the media reports, he thought.

"Stephanie's a great help. That mistake won't happen—the Super-virus I mean. I know the press talks about it."

At the mention of their daughter, Dara stiffened. "How's her . . . *condition* doing?" she asked. "Its effect on her job, I mean?"

Collin noticed that his wife spoke in detached terms about their daughter's problem. He thought he had detected a trace of malice.

"Her work quality is great. She's regressed, as usual. The staff wonders why she still sucks her thumb. She calls me 'daddy' in front of them, and so-forth—but they understand," answered Collin. "Stephanie still uses her rocking chair at work for constant motion."

After struggling with the social challenges of rising to such a lofty position of achievement, Stephanie had prepared herself to apply her scientific gifts in the most exalted research labs. Finally, she had chosen to work very closely with her famous father. She had a special interest in helping children get the special vaccine.

"Any new problems?" asked Dara.

The waitress plopped the check on the counter.

"None. Our communication's what's unique. Science is a collaborative art—as you know."

Collin stood up. He was nervous talking about his project any more in public. "You ready to go?"

Dara tossed the paper down and got to her feet. Collin picked up the check off the counter and replaced it with a twenty. He had noticed for some time that his wife had been more inquisitive than usual about the project.

He could tell there was something heavy on her mind. It was probably the concern about their daughter. This was Stephanie's first "star" job, and a critical one.

Collin couldn't get the photo from the Black Peacock bookstore totally out of his head, either. He had tried hard, but there it was.

It haunted him.

As they left, he looked up at the old photo of US Grant on the wall. General U.S. Grant and his wife had eaten there the day before Lincoln had been shot. An old photo hung on the wall to prove it. Some maintained that John Wiles Booth had sat at the table next to the couple as he planned his crime.

Collin mulled over the dark realization that the area his family lived in—Washington DC, Georgetown, and that part of Maryland—a center of technology, government, defense, and intrigue—had its full share of troubling historical events.

The old photo of Grant on the wall fascinated him. He joked to himself. *Come to think of it, that picture of Grant looks kind of like my old college math professor.*

CHAPTER THREE

Northeast of Bethesda, Maryland, Later that Saturday morning:

"I don't know what you mean, Frank. I feel fine," Collin lied. The photo of the female Nazi SS officer still intruded into his consciousness. He knew it was silly, but the thought insertion was too strong to stop.

"You seem distracted. I don't know—off." Frank Seaton, the administrator of the vaccine project, tapped the palm of his hand with his fist. His appraising eyes scanned Collin. "Sleeping problems again? You look a little too thin—and pale." His hand made a new fist. "For the sake of the project—."

"—The project's spot on." blurted Collin.

"Nevertheless," said Frank, "I know you're a big-shot scientist and all, but the buck stops here with me. You've been working too hard, and now we're almost at the home stretch. Most of your work now—except for the final gene splicing—is routine. It's mostly up to your staff. Relax—take a little time off with your family. We'll need you once the vaccine's done. That virus in Africa is bound to mutate wildly."

"Yes Frank, I agree."

Collin buttoned his long, white lab coat—the standard attire at work. He often fiddled with his coat buttons when agitated, and with Frank Seaton that was often. Frank continuously lectured him about the bloody project and the need for adequate rest. The man was single-minded, fumed Collin.

"Glad to hear it, *sir*," retorted Frank. The "sir"—to Collin's ear—always had a little too much emphasis, reminding him of the surly and incompetent tellers at his bank. "Besides, we don't want your *issue* to return."

Collin and Frank's eyes met in a split-second of deep significance. Frank had been informed about Collin's psychiatric problems—governmental policy.

"No, indeed not," agreed Collin.

Frank's eyes, partially obscured by glasses, flashed around the huge lab as the men toured the complex. "First, I like the general look of the place now . . ." His eyeglasses had sturdy, square frames that were made of thick stainless steel—a material somewhat symbolic of his personality, mused Collin.

The administrator's facial muscles displayed perpetual permafrost. Sandy-colored hair in a crew cut, starched dress shirt and black tie Frank, thought Collin. He was the toughest project manager he had ever seen, private or government.

"Notice the pale yellow walls—no pictures, not even a clock. Not even the *flag*." Frank's eyes welled with pride. "Dr. De Gise, I want it pleasant here; but no unnecessary distractions. Agreed?"

"Yes, of course."

Collin actually didn't give a fig about such things, but he did like what he saw. This was not just a safety fix, but also a genuine renovation. Frank knew what to do with free-floating Federal dollars.

There were no enclosed offices, except one, when Collin needed privacy. There was plenty of counter space with state-of-the-art equipment. The critical ventilation, with its numerous large ducts and access grills, appeared top drawer.

"The place is pleasant and well appointed." Collin's tendency to understate seemed to rankle Frank, especially when doling out praise.

Having few windows, mainly due to the original architecture of the building, did give the lab a somewhat claustrophobic feel, however. The National Health Foundation—or "NHF," was older and more hush-hush than its famous twin in nearby Bethesda—The National Institutes of Health—or "NIH." NHF got its real start as a scientific bulwark against the Spanish Influenza Pandemic of 1918.

Collin often cited the little-known fact that more people had died in that catastrophe than in World War Two—including both military *and* civilian fatalities. Three times as many had died in that as in World War One.

By comparison, the Vampire Virus was estimated to be potentially ten times more deadly than the Spanish Flu organism. With a little mutation, Collin had calculated, it could be more than a hundred times more deadly.

What caught Collin's eye as they wandered within the twenty thousand square-foot facility—which occupied the whole second floor of the building—was that the space was divided into two parts by a huge glass wall.

A large, windowed, computerized cooler stood on the other side of the thick glass divider. The cooler—nicknamed the "Fridge," housed the live Vampire "seed virus" under strictly controlled conditions. From this brew, the final "master virus"— and the vaccine—would be made.

Collin was to perform the actual gene splicing, or "molecular manipulation," that would create the vaccine-ready and "attenuated" prototype virus. This should be a harmless twin of the deadly Vampire Virus, but "disarmed." A new science, molecular manipulation was virtually impossible without modern computers.

"You like the Fridge, huh Doc?" Frank pointed his finger toward the giant refrigerated cooler visible through the glass wall.

Collin's eyes shot through the glass to the bulky silver rectangle—itself having a big observation window. He had heard that the Fridge alone cost ten million dollars.

"Let's have a look, Frank."

"The main safety feature is the real reason I wanted to meet you here, *alone*." Frank's eyes drilled though Collin as they walked together toward the glass wall. "Alone, and on a weekend, when it's quiet. That will come later, and it's classified."

As they reached the door to the glass wall, Frank pounded on the clear barrier. It made loud thuds.

"Not glass—space-age, dense plastic developed over at NASA—ten times harder than steel and completely non-porous. There's no place for germs to hide," explained Frank.

Frank Seaton punched some numbers into a code-box on the wall and opened the transparent door. A glass enclosure, which Collin had also never seen before, with a black lever inside, hung next to the code-box.

"Use the standard code that you already have, or the emergency code, Dr. De Gise. The same one to the back and front doors of the main lab."

"Right."

Once inside, they moved to the door of the Fridge and stopped, twenty feet from the adjunct lab area—all behind the protective glass wall.

Collin peered through the large window of the Fridge. "I hope the storage media's working. It took me six months to figure it out. I must've fooled with a million different organic chemicals for that darned seed virus," said Collin.

The pale-green brew within the rows of special, hardened glass beakers—perched upon the cooler's stainless steel shelves—was incalculably dangerous. It would get even more so as the viral strains were developed, thought Collin. Then, the main "attenuation"—or alteration process—would take over in the adjunct lab just a few feet away.

When explaining to Frank the process of "attenuation," Collin often likened it to the biochemical version of defanging a rabid, terminally ill wolf and, instead of euthanizing it, giving it a home in a posh kennel.

Frank stood with his hands on his hips, looking through the observation window into the brightly lit interior of the Fridge. "There's the seed virus." He said that with the tenderness of a father observing his newborn infant through the observation window of a neonatal intensive care unit.

"A monster." Collin, with a different kind of emotion than Frank, felt as if he were next to a leopard's cage—one with the door half open.

"It looks so peaceful," added Frank. He shook his head. " If that gets loose, this tiny town could be wiped out in a matter of hours."

Collin glanced at Frank. His expression was dour. "How about the whole State of Maryland—and DC and Virginia with it, and beyond." Collin noticed Frank's hands all of a sudden made tight fists as the steely Navy-vet clenched his teeth. "That comment's not for general circulation, Frank."

Frank squared off in front of Collin. "Thank God for the radical safety feature I'll show you. Pay close attention when I show you that, Doctor De Guise."

Collin nodded. He looked at his watch. "I haven't time now. I'm taking Dara and Stephanie to Baltimore."

"This is important, Doctor De Gise—"

"You said not to overdo it Frank, you can't have it both ways."

Frank snapped his fingers in agreement. "Right you are. I want plenty of time for that. Meet me here tomorrow morning early, before any one gets here. I'll show you the *Dante* button."

"Dante button?"

"It's a rather unique safety feature. A *paradox*."

" 'Paradox' . . . whatever do you mean, Frank?"

Frank cleared his throat. "Many of us could die."

CHAPTER FOUR

Downtown Baltimore, Maryland, Saturday afternoon:

"THE NATIONAL AQUARIUM"

The De Gise family walked quickly past the sign toward the shark tank. Dara, her bright red hair accented by a red scarf and white-silk blouse tucked into her black, designer jeans, walked several feet behind Collin and Stephanie with her arms folded. Dara had come straight to the aquarium from a busy morning at work. She viewed the sights of the attraction with a blank expression, as if her thoughts were hostage to more important matters.

Collin decided to take Frank's suggestion and try to relax more, and to spend more time with his family. Although nearing a critical stage, the eighteen-hour days in the lab were no longer necessary, and could even be counterproductive. Inspired science wasn't like farming, where every hour tilling the soil may produce a more bountiful harvest. Quality time counted most, especially with the delicate stages of the vaccine process that would soon follow. Besides, both he and Frank had Collin's fragile mental health to consider, the truth be told.

Stephanie stopped at the popcorn booth on the way to the exhibit, and ordered a caramel corn with chocolate sprinkles. She pulled her father by his arm to join her—leaving her mother alone to get in the line for the exhibit. Dara snapped out of her reverie just enough to glare at her daughter, and then shifted her searching gaze to Collin, as if suspecting him of a crime.

Collin felt that something significant must have happened to his wife very lately to affect her already somewhat disaffected attitude. Collin dodged his wife's dark attention as he walked away, trying to understand her shifts in mood. Thinking that his avoidance might be too obvious, he smiled at her, but she didn't smile back.

It had been that kind of day, thought Collin. He ordered two regular popcorns, and then headed back with Stephanie to the long line to join his brooding wife. Collin handed her the treat, which she tried to ignore.

What's on her mind, he wondered? Could it be Stephanie? Maybe it was something *he* had done? Whatever it was, it was big.

As the line moved past the entrance to the show, Stephanie read the posters hanging on the wall next to them. The illustrations explained the violent lifecycle of a shark. Collin looked at the pictures of the huge jaws, the jagged teeth, and the round, cold fish eyes. To him, somewhat amusingly, he admired the up-front, in-your-face nature of their murderous intent, unlike humans, who preferred to put on a charade first.

Stephanie, about the same height and weight as her mother, with similar bone structure and facial characteristics was—at least superficially—dissimilar in nearly every other way. Her red sneakers were two sizes too large. She wore an old Redskins varsity jacket, old baggy jeans, very short, green-dyed hair, and white-rimmed, round eyeglasses that had slightly tinted lenses. The tint was necessary for her condition, her photophobia, and the light hurting her eyes even indoors. She had never worn makeup a day in her life. Her posture was stooped, and not the cadet-like carriage of her athletic mother. Stephanie's gait, unlike Dara's aggressive, forward lean, was lumbering and indecisive.

She chewed her nails, and Dara rather adorned hers to minute perfection.

Despite this, Stephanie possessed an innate vitality that, with her admirable figure, translucent complexion, and perfect white teeth like her mother, radiated a quirky attractiveness.

She looked at her father and, with chocolate smudges around her mouth, made her intentions plain. "Don't want to see the sharks, daddy. Don't want to." She threw the popcorn box into the nearby trashcan. "Don't want to," she repeated.

Collin always tried to accommodate Stephanie's autistic speech pattern—the "echolalia"—an inappropriate repeating of words or phrases. He also navigated her inappropriate affect. The thing to do, he had learned over the years, was *not* to automatically cater to her, but to instead challenge her. Hopefully, he thought, this would expand her scope of experience. He had never claimed to be an expert in autism, but his intuition guided him in much of his interaction with her, and it seemed to have worked.

The situation between his wife and his daughter had also become worse over the last few weeks. Dara didn't look at her daughter when she talked to her. They were growing apart. She had been pulling away.

Unlike his wife, he appreciated Stephanie more as time passed. A child-like genius like Stephanie was a dream companion for him. He considered his daughter a big bonus in life. To Collin, she was as natural as fresh lava or newly fallen snow. With her intellect and boundless curiosity, he considered her the perfect scientist.

Collin and Dara moved into the exhibit as Stephanie followed. Collin, throwing away the popcorn boxes, entered the show with the usher moving them along a narrow hall bordered by a tall fish tank.

The luminescence of the blue water and multi-colored rocks, with the swaying yellow kelp, mesmerized Collin. With the exhibit not being too crowded with spectators, Collin guided his family close to the glass where they had an unobstructed view of the fish.

The huge white sharks undulated, scores of them, randomly darting through the water. Their mouths wide open, they displayed their many rows of gleaming, sharp teeth. Their eyes, cold and savage, seemed to Collin unusually comprehending of their surroundings.

The three family members, lined up at the glass, studied the deadly predators. Collin, his mind wandering for a moment, allowed his eyes to scan the glass in front of him far in all directions. In the glass, he saw reflections of the audience.

In one reflection, where the images were distorted by beveled glass, Collin noticed a tall, somber man standing with two other people. Although they stood together, their retracted body language and silence suggested they didn't really know each other. The young man was drawn—despite his muscular appearance. He wore a tweed jacket over a rumpled dress shirt, the shirt as white as his complexion. Two large, searching eyes . . . Collin, startled, realizing that he was looking at the reflection of *his* family—that *he* was the man in the tweed coat.

Collin took Stephanie's hand as they moved forward, practically pushing their noses up against the cold glass. Dara stood beside them, but slightly back. Collin could sense that his wife felt uncomfortable being there.

Collin tapped lightly on the glass to get the sharks' attention. The sharks then did something that Collin had never seen before. This strange spectacle brought the aquarium attendant close to the glass too. The attendant, and old man with a stooped posture, removed his eyeglasses and cleaned them off. He then looked at Collin, who just shrugged—lost for words.

The old man put his glasses back on and stared at the fish. "Damn me—I've never seen the likes of it. Look at them sharks line up like that."

Collin looked at Dara.

Dara viewed the fish warily. "Let's go." She glanced at her daughter, and then grimaced.

Stephanie let go of her father's hand and slowly backed up from the glass. She looked at her mother suspiciously, and then began to shake. The few other patrons in the exhibit glared at Collin and his family in dead silence.

"Damn me," repeated the attendant, as he shook his head, staring at the fish.

Dozens of sharks had lined up along the glass at eye level—pushing their broad noses against the glass. Their predatory eyes trained on Collin's family, their grey bodies perfectly still. The sharks continued to stare at the three family members, as if it were a mating ritual. Collin stared back, overhearing comments from the audience.

"Damn me," repeated the attendant. "The sharks are still, strange."

Dara walked out and Collin and Stephanie followed her. Collin, seeing Stephanie's fright, put his arm around his daughter. He noticed that as Dara had exited the exhibit, the sharks had started to disburse—almost as if they were relieved by her departure. Before he went through the exit, Collin turned back toward the tank.

The old man—still next to the glass—was looking Collin's way. The expression on his face was palpable: it was not only bewilderment, but also fear.

"Damn me," he said again softly. "Just look. What would make them fish do something like that?"

CHAPTER FIVE

Washington DC, Later that Saturday afternoon:

"If you've just joined us, welcome to *Tech Beat.* The PBS public access television station for the DC area."

Barry Bledsoe, the popular television interviewer, turned from the camera to Dr. Collin De Gise, his guest, who shared the dimly lit television stage. The young black man wore white everything except for a red carnation in his lapel.

"Just to remind you, Doctor, this is a *huge* topic we're discussing today. We'll be taping live on *two* shows—two parts—the second this coming Friday."

Collin, only comfortable speaking in front of his staff—and never in public, let alone on TV—cleared this throat. He took a sip from the glass of water on the small table in front of him. He was too warm in his suit coat and dress shirt with tie. The studio was overheated.

Frank Seaton had set up the interview in order to reap the public relations benefits, and to force him to slow down and enjoy a change of pace—if Collin could control his mouth—that is. He considered the task anything but enjoyable.

It had also been a long day—very long, thought Collin. The shark tank event had troubled him. Then, of course, there had been the look-alike photo of his wife. Now all he needed was a flogging, and he would feel complete.

"Doctor, to recap," Barry looked down at his clipboard, "you're the Scientific Director?"

"Right."

"Director of—'Project *Hephaestus*'—a US Government-sponsored program to find a vaccine for the so-called 'Vampire Virus'. This is the germ that's killing children in Africa, am I right?"

"That's correct. In fact, the First Lady is heavily involved too."

"She even hired you for the Directorship."

"Essentially—Yes."

"And you have some private funding too—from very large health insurance and oil companies?"

"Yes, as I understand it."

Large photos of the capital hung behind them as a studio backdrop—Jefferson Memorial, White House, Washington Monument, and the Pentagon. A small audience was assembled below them, sitting in poorly lit rows of wooden seats. A large screen stood beside one of the three studio cameras, along with the lighting equipment and TV monitor.

Barry moved his finger down his crib sheet. "Let's see, you hold a Ph.D. from Georgetown College, last year's Nobel Prize Laureate in Medicine for your work in viral genomes, born and raised in an orphanage in Maryland until a teenager—and this is very interesting—a Gulf War Two vet; a stint in an elite, international, commando-type organization that was organized by the United Nations?" Barry's voice was soft and his delicate hands—adorned with multiple jeweled rings—moved almost constantly in fluid waves.

"Yes."

"Our research department found out that the paramilitary group you were a member of was not bound by the ordinary rules of international warfare."

"I'm not here to discuss that."

"All right."

This low budget, local program had more substance than the others, thought Collin, but he disliked the experience nevertheless. At least Bledsoe dropped his unpleasant line of questioning and quickly moved on.

Barry looked at his notes. "Your partner, *Dara*—is a physicist. And, this is very *exciting*—you have a daughter in her early twenties who is *gifted*—very gifted. She does have special needs though, right? We've talked about this privately before the broadcast. You seemed very comfortable—"

"—Yes, of course, Stephanie, our daughter. She has a very severe form of autism. Let's get on to the vaccine project."

Collin could see Barry's head nod in obvious sympathy, but, like any father, Collin was not entirely comfortable talking about the condition publicly.

"Back to Project Hephaestus" interjected Barry. "We've already seen some slides of your lab." He waved at the screen next to them. "We talked a little about what you're doing there. I'd like to amplify on that a bit, without getting too technical."

"Right."

Collin leaned forward in his chair and looked sideways into the audience. He could hear aggressive mumbling coming from a large man in the audience. He didn't like the feeling in his gut, and the overheated studio didn't help matters any.

Barry Bledsoe, the interviewer, glanced down at his paper. "Why the name 'Hephaestus' for the vaccine project? I'm intrigued about that."

"Hephaestus was the Greek God of fire and metallurgy—who, using powerful flames, pounded and sculpted amorphous pieces of tough metal into tools and weapons—a fine art. The metaphor holds for our project. We at the lab are also playing with fire, in a way. We are also making powerful tools to defend against a deadly foe."

Collin was playing with fire *indeed*, he thought. He'd better be careful. He didn't want to scare the public about the potential dangers of the vaccine project. There could easily be a panic.

"Gosh . . ." Barry turned his head in the direction of another grumble from a man in the audience. He frowned, tilted his head, and then focused again on Collin. "I'm sorry Doctor, you were saying . . ."

"The Vampire Virus we work with is under control. But, the one sweeping Africa is now potentially much more lethal than the Spanish Flu virus of 1918, and that killed about sixty million people."

Barry looked up to the clock hanging on the wall. Then, he looked straight into the camera. "We'll project a few more photos on the screen for our viewers in a moment. The audience is warned. The pictures are grim viewing." He turned his head back toward his guest. "Go on, Doctor."

"Pandemics today are in many ways much more dangerous," added Collin.

Just then, the images of sick children flashed on the screen in front of the audience. There were audible gasps. Barry, looking up, fixed his gaze upon the screen. "Here we are, the pictures of the victims are on the screen now . . ."

The slides showed emaciated, unclothed black children—dead or dying—lying on gurneys—or sprawled out on the ground or along roads. They lay in their own pools of blood. Their mouths and nostrils had red stains around their rims.

The human skeletons on the screen numbered in the hundreds.

Collin's eyes fastened upon the images—then he averted them. He never got used to the horror.

"My goodness." Barry shifted his gaze from the screen and back to Collin. He wiped his eyes with his sleeve. He was unable to speak for a few moments and then continued in a much lower voice. "I'm sorry Doctor, go ahead."

"No, not at all. This is a real catastrophe." He coughed. "Almost a million dead so far—mostly children—and the body count will certainly rise. Children seem more vulnerable due to a hormone-related difference in their blood clotting mechanism, most likely. The virus may spread to other continents."

"Why do we call it the 'The Vampire Virus'"?

"The virus preferentially attacks the human blood clotting system. Massive hemorrhage ensues upon infection that leads to cardiopulmonary arrest. This happens within a matter of a few hours. So, your blood is almost sucked out of you—hence the colorful reference. I emphasize again that the virus we work with in our lab is slightly different, and under controls."

"I see." Barry shook his head.

Collin left out the technical stuff. With the new molecular manipulation techniques, the lab could grow the actual viral strain responsible—separate its protein coat from its DNA core—then substitute proteins and nucleic acids that will produce an organism that can, after the critical and rapid *recombination* of its altered parts—be introduced into healthy subjects safely. They would then have a very strong immunological defense from infection.

"But, isn't this dangerous?" Barry crinkled his forehead and narrowed his eyes. "What if the wrong gene substitutions are made? I've heard all about a *Super-virus*. It's more deadly even than the Vampire Virus—much more."

28

"You're talking about a so-called 'rogue gene'—the 'Omega gene'—accidently introduced either through molecular manipulation or by unexpected and dangerous mutations. Not likely at all."

"But possible?"

"Well, yes."

Collin paused. Loud coughs came from the audience.

Out of the corner of his eye, Collin could see a large gentleman in the front row causing a commotion. He wore a beard and a long, blond ponytail. He grumbled loudly as he shifted his massive weight in his chair.

Collin turned his head to get a better view of him.

The man's eyes had the gleam of a fanatic. Collin noticed that he also had a bulge underneath his coat.

CHAPTER SIX

Collin ignored the dangerous looking man in the front row. He continued with the TV interview.

He was a bit surprised that the host Barry Bledsoe had so deftly come to the meat of the issue. Collin considered the TV program a welcome throwback to the type of quality and technical discussion he had been used to viewing on TV as a boy, but this was the flip side of that competence.

Barry asked him point blank: "What if the wrong gene substitutions were made on the master virus and a more dangerous Super-virus somehow escaped from the lab?"

Collin didn't answer the interviewer's question directly . . .

"This *art* of sculpting the vaccine—using very advanced techniques in molecular biology, virology, mathematical theory, and computer engineering—literally to shape the deadly virus into a form that suits our goals— will result in complete immunity from the Vampire Virus without illness."

"Yes Doctor, but what if something goes wrong?"

Collin felt uncomfortable in front of the restless audience. "Then we could have a worse situation on our hands. But, think of the cost of doing *nothing*, given that a mistake such as this is unlikely. This virus mutates wildly." Collin coughed.

"But—" Barry tried to interject.

Collin continued anyway: "If the virus spreads for too long, given our modern means of travel and overcrowding and limited public health budgeting, it could wipe out entire nations—even *us*. So, we need to have not only an effective vaccine, but we need to continually change the vaccine to anticipate the changing nature of the wild virus."

"Isn't that hard to do?"

"Yes, it is. Sometimes it seems almost impossible—"

Just then, Collin knew that he had gone too far—way too far.

He could just see Frank Seaton unloading in his pants. The press and the politicians could go nuts with that sound bite.

Damn, am I stupid!

The slide show was over. Collin knew that his words could have alarmed the public even more.

A long silence ensued. Barry took in a deep breath. "We're almost out of time, Doctor. Isn't your idol the late Dr. J. Robert Oppenheimer, who some consider the 'Father of the Atomic Bomb?' In many ways, this project you're working on has many parallels to The Manhattan Project at Los Alamos, New Mexico, in 1943—which Oppenheimer directed. Isn't that correct?"

Collin was thankful for the change of topic. "Yes, Oppenheimer was a patriot, an eminent scientist who had a grim responsibility, and in many ways—later in life—a pacifist, which I admire. He was also misunderstood sometimes."

"Aren't computers critical to your project too? Isn't your daughter heavily involved in that?"

"Sophisticated mathematical calculations—such as those used by the famous and great mathematician Johnny von Neumann—helped to make the Manhattan Project a success. A prototype of his early computer called 'MANIAC' assisted in that effort. More advanced computers are even more important to our project today, and my daughter is key to that contribution."

Barry glanced up again at the clock on the wall, noting that his time was out. "Last, I understand that you attended—as a young graduate student—a seminar at the University of Leipzig in early 2003. This is the same University where the late Dr. Edward Teller—often referred to as the 'Father of the *Hydrogen* Bomb'—studied in the late nineteen-twenties. How well did you know Teller?"

Collin hesitated. He was confused. "I never met Teller. I've never been in Leipzig. He was another great man of science—and a selfless patriot who helped keep the Russians at bay for decades. I would have liked to have met him."

"Well, someone in our research department must have screwed up," offered the interviewer.

Collin was a bit flustered by the last question about the late Edward Teller—a great researcher and American. Not only had he never met Teller, but he resented the implication that his vaccine was like an H-bomb ready to explode any minute . . .

Just then, a loud shot exploded throughout the studio.

Then another as Collin automatically hit the floor. He lay flat.

A third shot rang out.

Raising his head slightly and turning it toward Barry, he witnessed the young host's neck explode into a gush of red goo. His body having been blown out of his seat, he hit the stage floor with a loud thud.

Neither of the two men on the stage floor budged.

The huge blond man with the ponytail rampaged onto the set, screaming and waving his pistol. Collin, not feeling pain, doubted he was hit.

The big guy lunged toward Collin, re-aiming his pistol at point-blank range. Collin swept the man's feet with his long legs and the assailant went down—hitting his head on the edge of the Barry's desk.

The dazed assassin slowly sat up, gun in hand.

He waved his gun again, trying to take aim at Collin, or so Collin guessed, since Barry's body lay partially between himself and the attacker, and so the identity of the intended victim wasn't clear. Nevertheless, Collin rolled on the floor to make a more difficult target.

More shots rang out.

An armed security guard suddenly appeared and emptied his gun into the attacker. Collin knew from his military training to keep flat until the melee had finished. There could always be other gunmen.

As the blood collected on the floor in a huge pool, the hefty intruder squirmed, and then lay still, having absorbed many bullets. He stared at Collin as he lay there bleeding—his pale eyes wide open, barely blinking.

Then he did something Collin had never expected, he did it with his fingers, right on his blood-soaked chest.

With his very last breath, the assassin made the Sign of the Cross. Then, he died.

CHAPTER SEVEN

Georgetown, Saturday evening, March 24:

Collin pulled up into the driveway of his Italianate mansion. It was a sprawling, three story, Siena-red brick structure with a cubical central tower and white stone trim.

The one hundred and fifty year-old house lay nestled behind a row of huge, ancient oak trees that rimmed a spacious lot. His street had been one of the first platted by Georgetown's founders, and the yard space was uncommonly generous.

Dara and Stephanie waited for him on the edge of the driveway, just past the open front gate. Stephanie screamed through the vintage red beamer's front window as the car came to a halt. "Daddy, you could've been killed!"

Collin parked on the driveway, and jumped out to hug his daughter. She threw her arms around him, kissing him on his cheek. Having been badly shaken from the days' trials, he gently untangled himself from Stephanie and hugged his wife.

Her embrace was not so tight or so long. Dara scanned Collins body with appraising eyes. It was as if she couldn't believe he was really in one piece. "Carmen cooked you a nice spread," she said. "It's almost dinner time."

Collin could hardly believe his ears. He had almost been shot, and his wife of twenty years was announcing dinner. All of a sudden, a thunderbolt lit up the night sky. A hard rain started. Collin looked up at the huge, dark gathering clouds and felt a few cold drops on his face. He bundled his family together and they headed for the stately porch.

"It looks like we're in for a big storm," he said.

Since the shooting at the TV station late that afternoon, Collin had been thinking nonstop about his family. Something was out of kilter, and he wanted to make it right again. Frank Seaton's suggestion of taking more time off was sounding better all the time. He might just do that, despite the fact that the vaccine was reaching its final stages. He had been working too hard, and so had Dara.

Soon the germ would be in "recombination," and his work would be mostly left to the staff. As it was, most of the challenging work that remained—the molecular remodeling— was Stephanie's chore anyway.

It wasn't time consuming, but it was tedious. The gene splicing, Collin's remaining task, promised to be quick and routine. It was fortunate that the lab had been closed this weekend, not only to tour the additions that Frank Seaton had installed, but so that he could share quality time with his family.

"Carmen!" As usual, Stephanie ran up the stairs of the porch to be first through the front door. As Collin—with his arm around Dara—moved from the secluded front yard and up the steps of the porch, he glanced at the historic plaque embedded in the front railing. He had petitioned the city to have it removed, but the house—being a historic landmark—had to retain the odious commemoration.

"'*SANFORD HOUSE*': ON THIS SITE IN 1864 COLONEL JOSIAH SANFORD, AND THREE OTHER CONFEDERATE SLAVE TRADERS, WERE HUNG FOR ESPIONAGE AND TREASON FROM THESE VERY OAK TREES."

Collin had heard that those hangings, according to local lore, were not really due to treason, but the strange "lifestyle" of the inhabitants.

He headed straight for the dining room with his family in tow. Dara had broken loose from his embrace and led them to the table. She was more aloof than ever, despite his close call with the assassin that afternoon.

The huge oak table in the dark, windowless dining room was heaped with wooden bowls of hot fried chicken, Spanish rice, fried okra, fresh cornbread, black eyed peas, sawmill gravy, Puerto Rican salad, mashed potatoes, succotash, and fresh green beans from Collin's garden. The china and the cutlery were expensive and Moorish.

Dara and Collin sat next to each other, and Stephanie dined across the table in her usual rocking chair, satisfying her craving for almost continual motion.

Collin heard the clinging and clanging from Carmen fussing with the pots in the kitchen. "Hey gang," he said, "let's get started before Carmen wants to say grace." Stephanie giggled.

The dining room had never been a favorite room of his, due to the lack of natural light and ventilation. He always wondered why the room had no windows. Maybe it was because the original inhabitants had wanted absolute secrecy, with no chance of neighbors peeking in? *What had they been hiding?*

As he sat back in his comfortable chair, Collin recalled the succession of terrible events that had occurred that day. Why should all these things be happening now?

Carmen burst into the dining room from the kitchen door with a huge pan of cherry cobbler and a pile of white napkins, plopping them on the table. "Here, for you, Doctor. You like pie very much." She gave Collin a napkin, and then distributed them around the table, patting Stephanie on her head and smiling at Dara—who ignored her.

Collin watched Carmen as she fluttered about the table, making sure everything had been put in its proper place. Then, he saw her do something very odd.

She removed the chair from the end of the table—the one with its back to the dining room's entrance. She always did that. He figured it must be some kind of superstition from the old country. As she rushed past him and back into the kitchen, he noted her thick, gold necklace with a cross and her tight, black and white maid's uniform that was open wide at the collar. An attractive woman in her fifties, Collin wondered why she had never found someone.

Carmen had asked permission to leave after setting the table, since she had to go church to prepare for an event there the next day. He heard the slamming of the back door, signaling her departure for the evening.

"It's a shame about that nice young man—Barry Bledsoe," mumbled Collin.

Dara put down her fork. "They say the Vatican had once employed the creep that shot him. That guy had a psychiatric history."

Collin caught his daughter dabbing at her corn. Stephanie's plate hadn't been touched. She just stared down at it.

"What's wrong love?" Collin disliked her missing meals.

She shrugged, put down her fork, and wrung her hands. She looked around her absently as she rocked in her chair.

The family continued to dabble at their plates and try to ignore the topic that sat in the room like a huge rhino. That topic was violent death. The sad fact was that a nice young man had just been slaughtered that day right in front of Collin, and they were doing their best to forget it.

Collin pushed his plate away. "Why would that guy with the ponytail want to harm Barry?"

Stephanie's chair rocked faster. "Maybe Barry wasn't the one he wanted to harm," blurted Stephanie unexpectedly in her high, nasal voice. She stared at her plate. "You have to be more careful, daddy."

There was a long silence.

Dara looked at Stephanie coldly.

Flashes of insight by his savant daughter, like this remark that was made in a sure tone, were typical of her, thought Collin. Maybe she's right.

The adjoining kitchen's checkered-tile walls and dark marble floors complemented the black-granite sink over which a large window offered a view of the backyard. A cast-iron gas range and oven stood in the corner as the flaming fireplace beside it popped and hissed.

A mess of dirty dishes sat on the counter next to the sink. Collin wiped the food off the plates and into the garbage can. He methodically stacked the dishes next to the sink as he ran the hot water. The dishwasher had just broken down the day before, and now it was time to wash the old fashioned way.

"I'll wash—you dry—drying's the easy part." Collin winked at Stephanie, who smiled back.

Collin was aware that Stephanie never smiled at anyone except him.

Dara had gone upstairs. The day had been horrid, but something more than that was on her mind, thought Collin. He handed a towel to his daughter as the steam rose in the sink, fogging the window.

Stephanie dried the dishes as she hung her head low. "Is something wrong with mommy?"

"I don't know what you mean, doll," he lied. Something *was* going on—something strange . . .

Collin and Dara had been married since they were eighteen. They had met at a support group for gifted scientists while attending Georgetown College, and had fallen in love instantly. That was the day Dara had followed him out of the meeting and asked him out on a date.

He loved her extraordinary self-confidence—something, socially anyway, he lacked. Being close, she had always shared her thoughts with him. But now . . .

"Mommy's just tired. That darn job—grim work," explained Collin.

"Goodness." Stephanie dried the dish. "Goodness sakes."

Collin was hot from the fireplace. He pushed open the window a crack to let the cool air rush in. He could see through the fogged window that it was almost dark outside. Bits and pieces of the telephone poles and lines in the distance—lit up by the streetlights—ran parallel to the rear of his entire property and behind his neighbor's properties as well.

He noticed starlings sitting on the telephone wire more clearly as the fog on the window slowly began to evaporate, rather like a developing photograph in a chemical bath.

Collin also noticed something peculiar.

The starlings sat lined up on the telephone wires, to the left and right.

He could see the birds in silhouette, resting. There were hundreds of them. Collin took his towel and wiped the rest of the fog away to get a better look, and the strange pattern became clearer.

He saw that behind *his* house—and *only* behind his house—there were no birds on the wire at all. The wire was completely bare behind his property.

Now, what could explain that, wondered Collin? It was yet another eerie thing.

CHAPTER EIGHT

After he exploded, Collin went limp and still.

Dara had reached climax the moment before he had—great timing, as usual. Whatever the horrible experiences he had suffered that day, and whatever changes he had noticed in his wife, it didn't seem to hamper their sex life any. Not that night.

The army had hardened him to violence, and the odd experiences of late had heightened his senses, and, apparently, had done nothing to drain Collin's desire.

Collin's eyes roamed Dara's bright, flushed face and lustrous hair that glittered in the flame-light. He enjoyed the view from his supine position. Sweaty and satisfied—he lay beneath her perfectly still, listening to the master bedroom's crackling fireplace.

"You screamed." She admonished him and then grinned. "You'll scare the people away." She playfully slapped him on his side, as if astride one of her horses.

"What people?" he asked. His hand tapped her lightly on the side of her rounded bottom.

The fire popped.

"*Those* people." She pointed at the wall behind the bed. "The people behind the wall, silly." She leaned forward and rapped the wall behind the bed with her knuckles.

Collin cocked his head slightly. He had no clue what she was talking about.

"The people—*chanting*—and playing the weird music," she said, looking down at him. "You joked about it. Remember? It was almost a year ago."

Collin then remembered.

At the time, he had just awakened from a dream. He had *thought* it was a dream, anyway. He had told her about it, and she teased him.

"Why are we talking about it now?" He picked up the pillow next to him and threw it at her. She ducked.

Dara started laughing. Her mood seemed to have changed miraculously. She arched her back, repositioning her pink hairband. Collin loved the quality of her translucent skin and the suppleness yet firmness of her exquisitely proportioned breasts.

"You should be telling me how great I am in bed," he said.

"You've apparently recovered from your ordeal today."

His eyes narrowed. "Yes—this was just the thing I needed, especially after what happened to Barry." The fact was, he hadn't fretted much about Barry's murder since dinner.

Dara ran her hand over Collin's chest, tracing the indentations of his well-defined muscles. She touched his hand lightly. "Your hands are always so warm—even in the snow—they're wonderful," she said softly as she rolled off him. " Want another sip of wine?"

Collin shook his head. "Austrian wine. It's too sweet."

"*Aber, sehr gut*," she added.

He looked at her with a puzzled expression. "I never knew you spoke German."

Dara climbed off the large king sized bed. "I don't."

She picked up the crystal goblet that rested beside the half-empty bottle on the bed stand. " I love Riesling."

She drank with relish, her searching eyes fixed upon Collin as she swallowed.

Collin had never gotten used to their bedroom's odd shape and feel. It was located in a drafty part of the second floor. He wondered if the builder, long ago, had made a mistake in the blueprints. It also had dark colors and an odd smell to it. He studied the antique, early American furniture—dark, thick, and full of knobs, curves, and uncomfortable whatnots—many of which were original pieces from the mid-eighteenth century.

Dara's body, backlit from the fireplace, glowed perfectly. She turned on some music. Collins's favorite piece filled the bedroom. It was dark but light too, bewitching but uplifting: Vivaldi's Cantata *'Cessate, omai cessate'*.

"Your favorite piece."

"*You* are my favorite piece." She laughed, and then threw an old sock at him that had been lying at the base of the bed. Collin thought how seldom they bantered like this anymore, compared to years past, or even months. It was odd, he felt, how much things seemed different now than just a few hours ago—*why*? It wasn't just the sex.

A small curtained window faced the backyard from their bedroom. Legend had it, ruminated Collin, that Josiah Sanford had been caught in this very room with a "witch." The bloodthirsty townspeople had stormed the house after they had discovered that information. According to Lilith Green, the proprietor of The Black Peacock bookstore, they had tossed the two paramours out of the window before they hung Josiah—not quite dead from the fall—in the front yard. The witch had mysteriously disappeared.

Dara got back on the bed and lay on her stomach—her knees bent and her feet kicking up and down. Collin propped his head up on a pillow and observed the ripple in her hamstring muscles. He loved studying her wonderful physique.

His eyelids grew heavier.

"Heard any lately?" she asked him.

He turned slowly on his side. "Any *what*?" His leg hurt from the fall on the stage that afternoon. He rubbed it.

Dara studied the long scar on his knee. She changed the subject. "The knee all right?" she asked.

"Yeah, just the war wound—acting up from the fall this morning."

"Sweet thing. That was horrible."

Collin furrowed his forehead. "Heard any? Any what?"

She hesitated before she said it. "Chanting . . ."

Collin wondered why she kept harping on that subject. "Yeah, love, just a minute ago, they were chanting for us to take seconds."

She smiled.

Collin kissed her on her smooth, tanned shoulder. "No, I haven't heard any."

He scooted up in the bed and rolled her over on her back. Then he got on top of her. Collin refocused the reading light attached to the headboard into her face. He looked straight into her lively eyes, his face very close to hers.

Her eyes were the most incredible shades of green—deep-sea aquamarine around the pupil—then emerald—and then almost a powder blue bordering the white sclera.

Collin then saw something that he wasn't sure he had ever seen before.

"Do you know that you have a tiny black dot at six-o'clock—on your left iris—just where the white of your eye meets the light blue?" he asked innocently. "Most of the time it's probably hidden by your eyelid."

"Do I?"

"Yes, kind of like a beauty mark."

"Well . . ."

"They say those can be familial—but very rare."

"That makes me even more special," she said.

"Yes. One in about ten million, I'd say."

"That's me."

"I love you. Despite . . . "

"Despite what?" she asked. Then, as if she just remembered something, she frowned. Her mood had transformed again.

Collin looked over at the fireplace—the dying flames sending out tongues of fire in a rhythm that mesmerized him. He was falling asleep. He said nothing more.

Collin realized that when he used to say those words she repeated them back. He felt a terrible sense of loss, despite the great sex and the loving words.

Sleep enveloped him. He now feared the dreams would come again. He wondered which one it would be tonight. They seemed so real.

Collin fell through the sky. Debris circulated around him— pieces of houses, pieces of animals, and pieces of people, too—an arm there, a leg here—a head or two. The heads were of Asian people. Then, the wind that had caught him turned dark, thick, and mushroom-shaped, like a swirling pot of boiling tar.

Collin fell onto a patio next to a bombed-out, ranch-style home. It had redwood patio furniture and a small lawn in its backyard. The boiling tar had disappeared, but he was still caught in a whirling funnel of trash and bodies that framed the horizon.

He had fallen onto one of the redwood chairs with green-striped pads.

Several empty chairs sat next to him. Across the patio sat three elderly men, laughing and talking. One of them, the short one in a white, military uniform, had a thick mustache, and spoke in a strange language.

The other two men—the fat, bald one and the grey-haired, distinguished one—sat perfectly still and silent. Like Collin, they were completely nude.

A young girl came out of the house and served the old men drinks. As she left, crossing the patio, she frowned at Collin.

A tall, very lean young man came out of the house and sat next to Collin. He wore a white shirt and tie, a tan, porkpie hat, and smoked a pipe. His eyes were brilliant blue.

The man with the hat leaned toward Collin. "It's a gentile's house, you know."

Collin nodded. "Yes."

"Do you like it here?"

Collin shrugged.

"They made me wear it."

"Wear what?"

"Why, the blood of course," the man with the pipe looked down at his lap.

Collin stared at him. He could hear the other men laughing and talking over their drinks from across the patio.

"I don't see it."

Collin looked over to the other men. Their teeth were like fangs—and black.

The stranger next to Collin frowned.

The girl came out of the house again with an empty tray. She walked over and stopped in front of the man with the pipe. "Go inside, please, sir." She had a soft English accent. He looked up at her, then at Collin. He rose from his chair.

His eyes met Collin's. "It all makes sense. Doesn't it?"

Collin looked for the elderly men across the patio but they had disappeared.

When he turned his head back toward his companion, he was gone too.

The girl with the tray smiled at Collin.

"It's a pity, but there it is." She had black fangs too. Her eyes were a bright yellow.

This time, instead of her soft English accent, she had spoken in a different voice.

It was Dara's voice.

CHAPTER NINE

Georgetown, Sunday morning, March 25:

"Carmen, are you in there?" Collin pounded on his maid's door. "If you are, open up, please!"

He had been standing at the door for five minutes. He heard noises through the door, which sounded like her walking around—but she didn't answer. She was an hour late in preparing the family's usual Sunday breakfast.

Collin pounded again.

Stephanie appeared down the hall in her yellow pajamas. "What's wrong daddy?"

"Carmen—she doesn't open her door. I think she's in there." The domestic had worked for the family five years, and she had always been punctual in her duties. She had practically become family.

He thought she might be ill. "Love, go get your mother."

Stephanie went upstairs.

Collin pounded on the door harder. All of a sudden, he heard religious chamber music coming from within the room. He heard chanting, too.

Is that sound the same chanting that I'd heard coming through the wall?

Carmen was a devout Catholic. But, he had never heard her play any music at all before, let alone chanting. He decided he'd call the police if she didn't open the door in a few minutes. After all, she could be having a seizure or a heart attack . . .

Then, the door opened slowly—just a crack.

Collin peaked through the opening. He saw several boxes full of belongings. An open suitcase sat on the single bed. Carmen's face filled the top of the crack. Her eyes were bloodshot and her hair disheveled.

She was dressed in her Sunday finery, not her usual maid uniform. There was none of the lipstick and mascara that she wore during working hours. She placed her hand on the edge of the door—the hand trembled.

"Carmen, what on earth's wrong? Why aren't you preparing breakfast?"

Her eyes were wide and darting around, looking past Collin into the hallway. As she spoke in a cracking voice, one hand fumbled with the cross that hung around her neck. "I go to mass. Today—no work. Today, mass—two-time. Here, *bad!*"

Suddenly, Dara appeared behind Collin in her white cotton robe.

Carmen's voice then took on a hysterical quality. "I leave—quit! *Lunes*—tomorrow—I go back—Puerto Rico."

Carmen's large, black eyes shifted wildly between Collin and Dara. The terrified maid then slammed the door shut.

"What's going on here?" Dara stood with her hands on her hips. "What about breakfast?"

Collin, in his jeans and black polo shirt, turned around, facing her. He threw his hands up. "I guess she's angry about something. Maybe someone in her family's sick. I don't know—but she seems frightened—not frightened—*panicked.*"

"About what?"

"How should I know?"

"What about her duties," asked Dara?

"I'll make the darn breakfast."

"Maybe it's best she go. Let's get rid of her while we can—now," said Dara. Collin marched down the hall to the kitchen with Dara closely following. "She's been pouty lately anyway, Collin."

"Well, I don't know, she's—"

"—She's *gone*—she isn't happy here."

Dara and Stephanie sat at the small round breakfast table in the kitchen, eating pancakes as Collin flipped them on the stove's griddle. A tray of pancakes sat on the table next to a jug of maple syrup and a coffee pot.

Collin waved the pancake turner at Stephanie. "Your mother is the real pancake chef of the house."

"Do we have to go to Lilith Green's for dinner tonight?" Dara asked Collin.

Collin walked to the sink and wiped it down. "She's been counting on it."

"Don't you like Aunt Lilith, mommy?" Stephanie peered at Dara through her slightly tinted glasses. The glasses—photo-greys—always seemed to be too dark—even indoors.

Dara put down her coffee cup. "Don't know—she's crazy."

"Pass the syrup mommy."

Collin, having given up on a burnt pancake, worked on more batter at the counter. "There're more cakes coming up." He assembled his ingredients from the cupboard. Dara, giving up her usual chore of making her coveted pancakes from her prizewinning recipe, stared down at the table.

"She's actually a very interesting woman" he continued, "Harvard grad in folklore—her parents were refugees from Nazi Germany—she grew up in Bogota, Columbia—she even had a degree in some kind of jungle medicine—she calls herself a "*good* witch." Collin chuckled.

Stephanie giggled—she loved to giggle.

"She sounds like a nut." Dara took a bite of pancake. "I heard that her dad was on a first-name basis with John F. Kennedy."

Collin, surrounded by bowls, knives, spatula, and a mixer, doled some flour into a measuring cup. "True—the father was a wealthy man."

Stephanie stood up from the table. She walked to the cupboard and opened it.

She screamed.

Dara jumped up from the table as Collin lunged protectively toward Stephanie. A loud hissing sound came from over the counter.

Collin, grabbing a large chef's knife off the counter and then pushing Stephanie out of the way, threw the door of the cabinet wide open.

He saw the shiny, diamond-shaped, black head slowly rising.

The round yellow eyes with the vertically slanted pupils were fixed upon Collin. Two fangs gleamed as the snake opened its mouth wide—ready to strike.

Collin swung at the huge viper in a powerful arc. He severed its head clean off as it gave out an eerie, human-like cry.

Dara shook her head, stunned and speechless.

Stephanie stood in shock—saying nothing.

"It made a strange sound, almost like a hurt child," said Collin.

The body of the snake kept moving, almost purposefully, without its head.

Collin had never seen a snake like that. Could that be why Carmen had been so upset, he wondered? Maybe she had seen one in the kitchen too?

Collin thought the creature was hideous, but there was more to it than that.

The unearthly thing looked possessed.

CHAPTER TEN

Northeast of Bethesda, Maryland, Later that Sunday morning:

Collin guessed that the "radical" emergency feature mentioned by Frank Seaton, the administrator on the vaccine project, must be huge—and perhaps deadly. He was back at the NHF lab at Frank's request for their early morning meeting.

Touring the lab renovations, they stood in the area beyond the glass wall that included the storage cooler—or Fridge—and the adjunct lab area next to it. After briefly discussing the horrible studio killing, they moved on to the main business.

"The temperature controls are phenomenal," said Frank, pointing to the Fridge. He indicated the dozens of silver shower nozzles just below the yellow, ten-foot ceiling. They hung throughout the lab area about twenty feet from where Collin and Frank stood.

"See the metal jets?" Frank looked around the Firehouse, and pointed through the observation window of the cooler. "There too."

"Emergency equipment I should imagine," said Collin.

The meticulous administrator nodded. "If the virus ever gets loose in either the Fridge or the adjunct lab area, "then swoosh," he snapped his fingers, "you're incinerated at one thousand degrees Fahrenheit!"

"What about the staff trapped inside? If the jets activate, is evacuation to the main lab possible?" asked Collin. He noticed there was a smaller cooler in the small lab area across the room, which would be used to construct and store a less dangerous, altered, master virus for the vaccine through his molecular manipulation.

Frank shook his head. "They go down with the ship, of course. They're infected—that's the whole point. The glass wall's just a stopgap." Frank's eyes got more intense. "All staff will sign releases—including *you*, Doctor. Of course, I'm talking *big* accidents. For the small ones, we have the usual emergency showers and other primary procedures. Don't forget, a major spill is unheard of—in my lab anyway."

"I see." Collin nodded as he pondered the grim prospect of being burned alive.

"I know this all seems harsh, but look what we're dealing with?" said Frank plaintively.

Frank was right, thought Collin. The whole project, and the virulence of the virus and its eerie ability to spread and mutate, was unchartered territory. Plus, they had little time. "Where's the control unit for the burn?" asked Collin.

"Outside the door on the wall. The black lever encased in the glass enclosure. You just pull it for incinerating inside the Fridge *only*—or rotate it first to incinerate the adjunct lab area *and* the Fridge—the whole darn Firehouse."

"Are the jets the radical emergency feature that you wanted to tell me about?"

Frank continued the tour as they moved on to the lab area next to them. "Not entirely." The men stopped.

Frank waved his hand toward the lab counter. "This, of course, is where some of the real tedious work is done—*your* work, Doctor."

"You mean the biochemical attenuation of the master virus—taken from the seed virus?" offered Collin. Frank, although having received a degree from the Naval Academy in chemistry, wasn't a scientist. Therefore, Collin summed up important parts of the project in convenient sound bites to emphasize the important scientific hurdles they must face.

"Yes—that's it," agreed Frank.

"The molecular manipulation and gene splicing—the crucial step before *recombination*—the last step in producing the vaccine," added Collin. "It should be routine. If we start it Wednesday as planned, we should be done by Saturday evening."

"What does recombination mean again, Doctor?"

Collin had been all through this before, but such reinforcement was essential. "The new DNA core recombines with the new protein coat. It's mostly the new coat that makes the attenuated virus less lethal—but more immunogenic—and a better vaccine."

"You mean more easy for the children's immune system to recognize the Vampire Virus as alien? This helps the body's defense arsenal—right?"

"Yes, essentially, antibodies plus white cells."

"Then what?"

"Growing the final vaccine only takes a matter of hours in the proper media—it turns over logarithmically," Collin droned almost automatically.

Collin glanced around the work area. He found it similar to the main lab beyond the glass wall, only better equipped: workaday sinks; cubicles; stools; test tubes and beakers; centrifuges; gas chromatography machines; gene splicing equipment, and electron microscopy. All this was in addition to the space suits, more temperature controls for the smaller cooler, and other safety equipment.

"Questions about the additions?" Frank cracked his knuckles.

"No; quite interesting. The scope of the work—and how fast you accomplished it—is astonishing Frank."

Collin had already seen some of the changes in the lab, and the staff had continued its vital work through the renovations—some hidden behind partitions. However, this final tour had brought it all together.

Frank beamed. "Follow me."

Frank led Collin out of the Firehouse into the main lab area, where they had started the tour. They walked thirty feet to a huge metal desk with a leather swivel chair, and paused. Collin could smell the ammonia of the recently scrubbed, white-tiled floor.

"Your new desk, Doctor." Frank motioned to the chair, and then sat down opposite Collin.

As Collin took a seat, he studied the huge, black microprocessor unit sitting beside the desk, and the black, forty-two inch monitor sitting on top of it. Frank waved his hand at the equipment as if he were the star salesman in a Mercedes dealership showroom. "The new Ultra-666 Super-computer I promised, with holographic, 3-D, goggle-enhanced graphics."

Collin pointed to the red goggles on the desk. "Handy to simulate the molecular manipulations—and gene insertions." He glanced at the twin setup across the lab about thirty feet away.

"Yes, identical desk and equipment for your daughter," offered Frank, anticipating Collin's next question." The only difference is that Stephanie's computer is purple, yours is black."

Their eyes had met fleetingly at the mention of Collin's daughter. Frank had at first resisted hiring Stephanie, but was won over by her brilliant proposals. "This new equipment will make your collaboration with Stephanie even more powerful," he added. "Of course, her chair is different than yours."

Collin glanced at the white rocking chair sitting next to the purple desk. "It looks comfy." Frank had thoughtfully accommodated his daughter's need for perpetual motion.

"Do you confide in Stephanie completely?"

"Why yes, of course. Why not? She's a key player." An odd question, thought Collin. Stephanie's complicated mathematical calculations and computer simulations assured the safety of the live virus used for the vaccine. This lessened the possibility of introducing a dreaded "rogue," or Omega gene.

Frank's expression became grim. "Stephanie is not to know about this. Look under your desk, Doctor. You'll see a black button—with a silver covering. Look—do *not* touch."

Collin bent over and looked underneath his desk. He saw the button. He looked at Frank. "What does it do?"

"We're the only two people on earth that'll know about it—that's aside from a dozen or so construction workers brought in from Mexico. They've already been transported back over the border as rich men—and lost to the wind. Of course, they had to know about this—but not its entire purpose."

"Go on."

"The black button under your desk is code-named 'Dante'."

"Yes."

"If there's ever a big spill that goes beyond the Firehouse—especially if it's a dangerous viral strain—then one of us activates the Dante button."

Collin pointed down through the top of his desk. "What does that burn?"

Collin suspected what was coming. Frank stood up and nervously circled the desk with his slow, pacing gait. This was the "radical" safety feature that Frank had mentioned.

Frank cleared his throat. "Everything."

"Explain."

"The whole building erupts in flames—then explodes." Frank pointed to a few metal canisters rimming the walls of the main lab near the ceiling. Meant to resemble smoke detectors, Collin realized that they really concealed fire jets and probably explosives.

Collin sat up straight in his chair. "You mean—"

"—There's nothing left except charcoal."

"What about an escape? We're talking maybe hundreds of lives, Frank."

He glanced over at Collin—finally making eye contact. Collin sensed that the stress was finally getting to Frank. "Yes, there's an escape. You have two minutes to get out—after the button's pressed."

"Get out? Where?"

"Remember all that construction on the road outside; lasted about six months?"

Collin nodded.

"We said it was to put in new sewer pipes. That was bull. There's a secret passageway in the basement of the building."

"Leading to?"

"It leads to a new tunnel under the road. It's makeshift—but good enough. You crawl a hundred feet or so under the street to a little toddler-park. Behind some bushes is a secret hatch, and you're out. You'll get a special red emergency key."

Collin pondered this monstrous scheme, but then another, more trivial detail for some reason consumed his attention.

As Frank stood very close, Collin got a good look at him from a different angle. He noticed something odd about him.

Collin noticed that Frank seemed to never blink his eyes.

What an odd thing? Of course, it probably has no significance.

Collin nevertheless wondered what strange physiology would cause a person to never blink. He had read that psychotics had this tendency, and some drugs may cause it was well. But, he'd never personally seen this peculiar trait in anyone, let alone his administrator.

CHAPTER ELEVEN

Georgetown, Later that Sunday morning:

"Collin my dear, what *on earth* are you searching for?" Lilith
Green stood over Collin as he rummaged through a stack of books
in the "European History" section.

"*Faces Behind Shadows*—an old Finnish translation—I saw
it here yesterday."

Lilith narrowed her eyes at the mention of the title. "That
book's never been in *this* store." She hugged him. "You have no
idea how I worried. That maniac at the studio—"

"—I'm lucky to be alive—I know."

"I've been calling you."

"Sorry."

"Who was he?"

Her high-pitched, patrician, Yankee intonations reminded
Collin of a pedantic Kathryn Hepburn rather than a South
American expatriate. She released him from her embrace, peering
into his eyes as if she were directly reading the synapses in his
brain that lay behind his ocular retinas.

Collin shrugged. "The police questioned everyone—me
too. No proven connections that makes sense."

"It's that awful work you do, isn't it, darling." It was a
statement, not a question.

Of course it was, thought Collin.

Flash insights—the ability to grasp what Collin considered
obvious and not just probable—was the basis of their initial
friendship. They were always on the same intellectual plane.

"I suppose that's it," agreed Collin with typical
understatement. He hadn't wanted to admit it—especially to his
family, so as not to alarm them.

Lilith picked up a stack of books she had left on a shelf and
sorted through them. "I know I'm a pest, but I'd bail out of that job
if I were you." Tall, rail-thin, horn-rimmed glasses studded with
tiny diamonds, black designer jeans, grey cashmere turtleneck
sweater, and salt-and-pepper hair wound in a tight bun, she had the
look of a stylish but pesky librarian. "Take the short cut."

"They need me," he reminded her.

"Oh yes, the vaccine, well, you're right, I'm sure."

Collin turned back to the stack he was searching in. "How about the book I was looking for?" His eyes combed the rows of titles.

"I told you precious, we never had it."

Collin turned back toward her, placing his hands on his hips. "I'm telling you *precious* that you *did* have it."

Lilith put down her books. "Let's go look it up on the computer upstairs, dear." She led him up to the loft.

At sixty, Lilith was what Collin would consider a solidly attractive and mature woman. Their relationship had been on the level of an eccentric and young at heart aunt attending to a mischievous but gifted nephew. As time went by, Collin had recognized the brilliance of this reclusive woman, and her passion for truth.

Words like "darling," "dear," and "precious" were nothing more than part of her sophisticated lexicon. She had never been married, and had no romantic interests that he knew of, except for one or two that many in her stuffy and distant family had tactfully labeled "non-traditional" matches.

Collin couldn't have cared less. At any rate, he knew that her real union was with nature, the stars, and the undercurrents of human experience.

Lilith led him past his favorite genres: "Scientific Milestones"; "Historical Mysteries"; "Paranormal Wars." As he passed them, he noticed the wide variety of patrons browsing within the bookstore: men in three-piece suits; housewives in curlers with kids in tow; scruffy students with backpacks; scientific types with lab coats and calculators sticking out of their shirt pockets; Satanists; Wall Street mavens, and even the occasional politician and cop.

Collin followed her up the stairs. "Maybe someone bought it."

"Is that book why you're over here?"

"No, actually, I wanted to re-confirm dinner tonight at your place. Dara and I will be there at seven."

"You don't like phones? Something's wrong, tell Auntie."

Collin knew she was pumping him. The depth of her inquisitive mind had no bottom. "I don't know exactly. It's just a feeling."

"You wanted to talk. What's bothering you, dear?"

"The book. Other things too."

"Tell."

Collin went into most of it: the strange incident with his family at the aquarium; Carmen's nervous breakdown; the horrendous snake in the kitchen; the gunman in the TV studio crossing his chest in prayer before he bled to death; the growing estrangement between himself and his wife and between Dara and Stephanie; and even the birds lining the telephone wires behind his home in that strange pattern.

The biggie, the Nazi photo, he'd prefer to slip in a little later.

Unexpectedly, Lilith seemed to fluff off those uncanny happenings as being unlucky happenstance or strange coincidence.

Fine, thought Collin. But why is this all happening right now—and so close together?

As they ascended the stairs, Collin looked through the store's stained glass. The morning sky was still dark and forbidding from the gathering storm clouds. "You come clean too, Lilith. What do you have against the *Faces Behind Shadows* book?" Collin asked.

She didn't answer. He kept at her.

"Lilly, you frowned when I mentioned the name of the book—*why*?" As far as Collin knew, no one called her by that nickname except him.

"Did I?"

"You know you did, love."

"All right, you asked for it, darling. The old Finnish codger that wrote it—rumor has it—died a horrible death."

They reached her dimly lit loft area. Collin passed old paintings as they walked toward a small desk, chairs, and a computer at the other end of the loft.

"What do you mean?" asked Collin.

"Do us a favor, don't ask."

Collin scanned the scores of old paintings lying around the perimeter of the area.

54

Some were dark portraits, some grim landscapes, and a few of buildings or shrines. Many were religious pieces in various states of disrepair. Special ones hung on the walls with price tags—big numbers. What struck Collin was how many depicted war scenes and wholesale slaughter.

Lilith sat behind her desk as Collin took a seat in front of her.

"I'm *asking*. How did he die?"

She fired up the computer and then punched a few keys. The glow of the screen accented the features of her intelligent face—distorting them slightly.

"Well, it was nothing unusual. His throat was cut; he was hung by the neck; and then lit on fire later, that's all. You might say natural causes."

Collin couldn't help but grin at her witticism.

He noticed one piece in particular. It looked ancient. The subject was a fierce looking angel in armor chopping off the head of a Roman centurion.

She glanced between the screen and Collin's face, as if reading his mind. "Yeah, some interesting stuff here." In her best throwaway style, Lilith finally asked the question Collin was waiting for. "What did you see in that book, anyway?"

Collin hesitated. "You'll think I'm nuts."

"You're too late."

"Something in it . . . that reminds me of . . . someone I know."

Lilith broke a nail on the keyboard. "Hells Bells!"

For a woman who never touched makeup, she wore very loud fingernail polish. He noticed the bright silver color with purple moons, stars, and planets. She sucked on her finger for a second.

"Someone you know? You mean Dara, of course."

"How did—"

"—How could I *not*? "

Lilith and Dara didn't hit it off very well. It was fox and hare at its worst. Lilith continued to punch the keyboard. As she searched, she mumbled some stuff about different books, the volumes, the prices, how many . . .

"Let's see here," she said. "Yes, we *did* have one copy of *Faces Behind Shadows*—that *dunderhead* Jonathan—I didn't know about it. He's my new assistant. I don't know where he came from—mysterious young man. But . . ." Lilith's eyes shifted from the screen to Collin.

"But what," prompted Collin?

"There's no record of a sale. It seems to have disappeared."

"Very recently—it would seem," added Collin.

"Could be pilferage. It happens frequently. *That* book only has two copies in existence—it's out of print. That one was ordered from Romania. The other copy is in Israel. "

Collin shrugged. "Can we get it?"

"I can try if you really want it."

"All right. Why not?"

"Because it scares the crap out of me, that's why not. But for you . . . "

Lilith wrote down some information and peered at Collin over her glasses.

"Let's have it, dear boy. How much did this photo look like your wife? What was the old photo about?"

"I don't know."

"How old?"

"Old enough."

"Tell," she said.

"This is sort of silly, really. I mainly want it for a conversation piece—how did you know it was a photo that interested me?"

"It happens all the time, darling. I had one young man who swore his that wife was really Lillian Gish."

There was a subtext going on in the conversation that Collin felt uneasy about. He leaned forward in his chair. "So, the author died a horrible death—a murder, as it were. That's terrible, but why blackball his book? It seemed to have caused a splash— might be interesting. Many people die horrible deaths," said Collin.

Lilith ignored the question buried in the statements. That signaled to Collin that maybe the book was too disturbing for Lilith to dwell upon.

"Collin, so many old photos look like somebody or another. What of it?"

Their eyes met. Hers had a question in them.

Collin felt compelled to answer the unasked question. "I know . . . of course, I'm not suggesting . . ."

"*Of course* you're not."

But, the sub-text was still there—and only between old chums like them would it exist at all, realized Collin.

Did Lilith really imagine that I thought the woman in the old photo and my wife could be the same person?

"Besides," taunted Lilith, "you want the book as a joke—a conversation piece—isn't that it? Nice choice. How fun."

"Shut up and get me the damn book." They both laughed—but the laughter, to Collin, had a certain strained quality to it.

"The Finnish author had just announced a new edition the day before he was murdered." Lilith turned off the computer and frowned. "How about a painting instead? I'll cut you a real deal." She stood up and grabbed an old oil painting off the ground next to her.

Collin looked at the piece. It must have been hundreds of years old—crusted paint—faded colors—decaying frame. The red robe on the bearded man next to Christ was now light pink.

"You like this one of Judas? You always talk about Judas, and you're not even religious. Why?"

"I don't know. Everyone likes a story about a turncoat."

Lilith turned her attention back to the paining. "I bought it from an old Russian officer—he and his buddies looted Dresden at the end of the war."

"Lovely."

"Tell me what the photo in the book was about—what was the lady up to?"

"Lilith!"

"Look Collin precious, you told me about all that weird stuff happening, and now the photo. What are you trying to say?"

"Nothing."

"The lady in the photo was doing something awful, really awful, wasn't she?"

Collin had known he wasn't going to get out of there without answering that question. He got it over with.

"She was no '*lady*' at all," said Collin. Then, he explained how he found the Nazi photo, and what it showed in detail.

Lilith brushed off the painting and hung it on the wall. "Frau Troost—a monster."

"When all is said and done, I guess that's why I'm here," said Collin gravely.

"All right, darling, consider the damn book ordered."

CHAPTER TWELVE

Georgetown, Sunday afternoon, March 25:

Peering through the windows of his greenhouse, Collin could see that the telephone wires running through his back yard were bare, and in his neighbors' yards too. All the starlings had moved on.

The branches of the bare oak trees jostled in the wind. The gusts, forcing their way through the crack in the door of the greenhouse, produced a low-pitched whistle, with a crescendo and decrescendo that assumed a strange melody.

There had been a few days of unseasonably sunny weather in the middle of the month, producing green buds on the trees. But, winter had shunned death.

Dressed in his dirty overalls and denim shirt and short hiking boots, Collin moved his water can over the rows of flowers as his wife and daughter labored at their oil paintings next to the herbs. Stephanie and Dara—in their paint-crusted smocks—silently stroked their easels. He noticed that the women were quieter than in months past, and smiled much less.

Collin lovingly spread the fertilizer among his prize roses—reds, yellows, whites, and pinks—a veritable ocean of early spring colors whose buds were delicate and required careful nurturing. His eyes shifted to an even more happy sight—his favorite flower. It greeted him in a small plot of soil by the window.

The Royal Catchfly embodied the marvel of creation, and, to him, symbolized all that was good and pure in the wicked world. Indigenous to the area, it had a strikingly beautiful Royal-red blossom shaped in a five-petal star. He loved to carry one around in his pocket for good luck, usually in a film of clear plastic.

"I'm going in the house," said Dara. "Someone's got to keep an eye on Carmen." Her manner was abrupt—and angry. "She's still holed up in her room. I'll be glad to see the end of her butt tomorrow." The problem with the maid had set Dara off most of the day.

Collin put down his fertilizer can. "I thought she changed her mind and was going tonight."

"She couldn't get a flight," said Dara as she left.

When she disappeared through the door, Collin noticed—hanging on the wall by the exit—an old photo of Dara and Stephanie.

He had taken the photo five years earlier. Collin studied the smiling faces, the shining red hair on both of them, and the sunny backdrop. He thought it remarkable how much alike they looked in that heart-warming image—the high cheekbones, bright green eyes with a dash of blue, and the narrow, slightly upturned nose with the freckles.

That had been a happy time, he remembered sadly. His daughter had been functioning better with her condition—or so it had seemed. She had dabbed at dressing more normally, even stylishly like her mother. In fact, the pink blouse Stephanie had worn in the picture had been borrowed from Dara.

Collin walked across the greenhouse over to Stephanie, who was busy at her easel. Collin approached the canvas Dara had been painting on, which hadn't been covered. As he walked past, he glanced at it. The picture depicted a house in flames. Fire was everywhere—and people were running out the front door. They were on fire.

"What's wrong?" Stephanie glanced at him as she painted. "Daddy, what's wrong with mommy?"

Collin stopped behind his daughter and studied her work. It was an innocent picture of roses in bloom—red roses.

Collin noticed the other paintings leaning against the wall. One, partially hidden by another, looked strange. It had a frame similar to Dara's piece—the one he had just seen.

"Oh, it's just a little trouble with Carmen again, that's all."

"Why is Carmen leaving?"

He walked over to the odd painting. "Her English isn't too good, so it's hard to understand exactly what's going on."

Collin moved the painting so it stood on the ground in full view. He studied the odd but familiar geometric shape. Collin picked up the painting, studying it at eye level.

"What's that you have, daddy?"

He looked over at his daughter. "I've never seen anything like it," he told her inaccurately. Collin's eyes shifted back to the oil piece.

Dara's work made him feel unclean.

Collin couldn't remember where he had seen that weird symbol before. Then it hit him like a gun blast between the eyes. The diagram was a black triangle with dots attached on top two of the angle points, and a small circle at the third.

He remembered.

He had seen the same dark symbol the day before on the front cover of that wretched book in The Black Peacock—*Faces Behind Shadows*—the one with the Nazi SS photo of a woman who looked like his wife.

He shuddered as he realized that the symbol on her canvas, and the symbol on the book, independently connected his wife to that horrific photo.

It must be another coincidence, he reassured himself.

But, how could it be?

CHAPTER THIRTEEN

Washington DC, Later that Sunday afternoon:

"Well, I believe that killing a lot of people—especially people you don't know—is wrong."

That left the thud of silence around the luncheon table that only very loud flatus could equal. Collin rarely expressed an opinion like that, but he felt he had been provoked. Dara sat next to him, dressed in a pink pantsuit, and across from them sat Gordon Givens, his wife Camilla, and the elegant First Lady—Shonda Rice O'Neal.

Shonda sat silently as she held court in the expensive eatery—her keen, grey eyes weighing each comment—looking at those who had not spoken as a signal to weigh in with their opinion. The fact they were talking about germ weapons astounded Collin, not only because it seemed to taint his professional achievements, but also because none of those present influenced policy anyway, with the notable exception of the First Lady.

Gordon Givens, the hawkish Assistant Secretary of Defense, his face flushed, grabbed the last word with his eyes targeting Collin. "If the terrorists have germ warfare, we damn well had better have it too. That vicious crowd locked up in Cuba means business." Gordon waved his hairy hand at his wife without looking at her. "I know, we've—uh, *I've* been there, haven't I Camilla?"

Camilla nodded dutifully.

"I agree with you Gordon." Dara searched around the table for consensus as she spoke. "The vaccine project will stop the pandemic in Africa. Then, we can use the Vampire Virus to develop our arsenal."

Collin didn't look at his wife as she spoke. He was pissed. "I can see my husband's point too. After all, he went through a lot in the second Gulf War." She looked at Collin, expecting a reaction from him and receiving none.

Collin didn't mind the free expression of her opinions, but her venue had troubled him. At that moment, he reflected upon the strange symbol he had found on her painting stored in the greenhouse, and the odious photo of the female SS officer. Now, she was talking about mass death.

Gordon nodded to Dara in appreciation. A powerfully built ex-jock in his early forties with piercing brown eyes, he sported a dark crew cut. He had overdressed for the luncheon in a brown suit that was too small for his bulky frame. The rumor around town was that he and his wife Camilla weren't getting along. Gordon, said to be a religious man, had led a prayer at the table minutes before.

Shonda Rice O'Neil's commanding gaze shifted to Camilla.

Camilla swallowed hard, hesitating to talk as she swiftly gulped her morsels of food, recognizing her boss's signal. As Social Appointments Director for the First Lady, she was used to catering to Shonda's ways. "Well, it's a tricky situation. I'm not really qualified to talk about such things," she sheepishly offered in an uncertain voice. She glanced at Shonda, then at the others, like a puppy who'd been scolded once too many times for pooping on the carpet. "Our first consideration might be to help the kids who are sick." Her tired eyes searched the stone-like expression of the First Lady for a clue as to how her carefully constructed opinion had been received.

Camilla, a pale, fading person—including her almost albino shade of white-blond hair and pinkish skin—could be a real looker if only she would jettison the frumpy clothes and wear some makeup, mused Collin. He suspected that an unusually fit body hid underneath that polka-dot parachute that hardly passed as a dress. A suppressed woman with low self-esteem, Camilla wrung her hands—a nervous habit that complemented her cracking voice and husband's aggressive fidgeting.

The First Lady took a bite of her club sandwich, and then put it down. Surprisingly to Collin, she spoke with a near-full mouth. "Maybe we shouldn't be talking about this. But I think healthy debate is good." She put three sugars in her coffee. "I want to make one thing clear."

It had been no accident, Collin thought, he had been thrown together with the likes of Gordon Givens. The luncheon had been Dara's idea. He looked around the table at the faces of the other guests in the trendy, sky-high restaurant that looked down on the Lincoln Memorial in the far distance.

These minions were assembled like animals during feeding time at a zoo, mused Collin. Gordon's eyes were dull, like a caged monkey, but followed the First Lady's every move and gesture. Dara's, disturbingly to him, were sharp like a hawk's. Camilla's had gone from frightened puppy to those of an overfed stable mare. Shonda's large, clear grey eyes, however, were regal and complacent. Collin wondered how Shonda perceived his.

"First, I respect all points of view," continued Shonda. Her tapered, bejeweled, elegant fingers circled the cup as she drank. The restaurant, having been cleared of most patrons, was perfectly quiet. "This is how I *feel*." She went on to talk about facts that really had nothing to do with feelings at all.

Collin thought her very easy to look at as she addressed them around the table. She wore thick golden hair in a sixties flip; the bridge of her nose was narrow and straight, and the high, smooth forehead imposing. She was very tall—almost six feet— and gazed *through* you at times with those aristocratic eyes, rather than at you. "The vaccine project is the most important thing in my life," she intoned. "Bless the little black children." Everyone at the table nodded.

Mrs. O'Neal's yellow-silk blouse shimmered in the light from the window. Her neck was adorned with a diamond necklace—the one Collin had seen her wear during interviews on TV. Her soft, but sharply enunciated words flowed on. "Collin and his daughter Stephanie are central to the mission to save thousands of innocent little lives. I got them their jobs—they were gracious enough to accept."

Her eyes landed upon Gordon. "I welcomed this luncheon. I had heard some rumors, and I wanted Collin reassured. The vaccine project is for the children—and that's it."

Collin looked at Gordon. Gordon's face was impassive, but his hand strangled his napkin.

Collin then looked back at Shonda as her eyes met his. "I want to reassure you, Collin," Shonda continued. "Not only because your wife and I grew up together as army brats and are dear friends, but because I honor and respect you as a scientist, and a *human being*." Collin smiled. Her voice had been resolute and rang with strong, mid-western resolve. She concluded. "Your work will never be perverted into making tools for killing."

Collin felt that for some reason Gordon Givens hadn't given up on his plans for the Vampire Virus. He wanted a catastrophic weapon, and Collin's astounding scientific expertise was the best way to get it.

Despite the First Lady's beneficent words, Collin realized that this problem wasn't going to go away.

CHAPTER FOURTEEN

Georgetown, Sunday evening, March 25:

The cold winds had become stronger as night fell.

Collin and Dara strode along the sidewalk from the car to the corner of Caine and Abel Street, where Lilith's plum colored, Federalist row house came into view—one of the oldest in the city.

When the dinner guests ascended the rickety wooden steps of Lilith's front porch, Collin observed the conical towers of pastel houses. They fascinated him with their gothic, almost medieval style, symbolizing the raw power of that bygone era.

As Collin knocked at the front door, he noticed a historical, brass plaque fastened to the railing. He had only been to Lilith's home once before, and had not noticed the plaque. Maybe a story lay behind it, thought Collin, just like the one at his house. It seemed that this area had attracted more than its share of dark historical events.

"We're not staying long," commented Dara. "I'm only going because . . . " She stopped in mid-sentence and reconsidered. " Never mind."

Collin had not seen such overt hostility toward Lilith before. He wondered what lay behind it.

"It rather reminds me of digging into a sublime, boysenberry tart," said Lilith. As the hostess escorted the dinner guests to the dining room through a dark, winding hallway, her true addiction to simplicity was displayed in her monochromatic color scheme. Lilith informed Dara that almost her entire interior had been painted in "scorched berry."

"Do you like stories my dear?" Lilith asked Dara.

"Stories? That depends on who is telling them," retorted Dara.

Lilith took her by her arm as they entered the dimly lit dining room. She sat her guests around the dinner table, with Collin and Dara taking their places at center table, facing each other.

Collin looked around. Nothing hung on the walls. No dressings covered the one small window. Lilith detested drapes or shutters, which interfered with her "imbibing the earth elements" while indoors. Collin noticed that, just as in his house, the room seemed to been built around the concept of intense privacy. Her cherry-wood dining chairs and table were cheap Korean imports. In contrast, the "warrior's urn"—the centerpiece—looked to be a priceless collector's item from the Ming Dynasty.

Black candles hung over the table in a circular chandelier, which shed soft, flickering light, slightly distorting the shadowy faces seated beneath it. Lilith stood at the head of the table. She picked up a large knife and started chopping vegetables on a cutting board, preparing the Greek salad from the ingredients spread about the table. " I hope you darlings like my salad."

Lilith fit the part of the sophisticated, boutique occultist perfectly, mused Collin. Her black poncho hung down almost to the floor; a stone amulet dangled from her neck; and a red scarf— that displayed a moon design—was wrapped around her head.

Dara sat with her arms folded, looking vacantly across the room into the crackling fireplace. The firelight played upon the shiny antique silverware, pewter goblets, and wooden plates and bowls that didn't quite match.

Aside from the salad, crusty white bread and stuffed grape leaves filled the large wood serving bowls. Mounds of tangy Feta cheese beckoned next to bottles of bitter, Greek wine.

"Collin, you may serve the vino, precious."

"Everything looks fantastic," said Collin as he reached over the table to Lilith's glass with a bottle and poured her some wine, after he had served Dara.

"I believe everything should be absolutely fresh— preparation of quality ingredients right under your noses is the best appetizer." Lilith chopped black olives and pink lettuce.

"I saw your historical plaque on the porch, Lilith" said Collin, not intending to steer the conversation. "We have one on our porch too." Lilith had never been to their home.

"I'll have to tell you all about that," said Lilith as she crumbled some of the Feta cheese onto the huge bowl of salad. She took a long gulp of wine. "This house was built by a man named

Thaddeus Hawthorne in eighteen fifty-five. He knew President Lincoln."

Collin poured himself more wine. "I've never heard of Hawthorne. I've read practically everything on Lincoln—what did Thaddeus do for a living?"

Collin held the bottle up to Dara. Dara nodded. He poured, noting his wife was at least paying attention to the hostess, instead of ignoring her. She seemed interested in the story as she gulped her wine much faster than usual.

Lilith chopped three colors of olives—orange—black—and a strange white one that Collin had never seen before—as she responded to Collin's question. "He made a fortune selling repeating rifles to the Union." She drained her wine glass. "He was one of the first big munitions moguls in a long line of death merchants. The new rifle was a huge technological innovation." Lilith pointed to another wine bottle. "Pour me some of that, won't you dear?"

Collin poured. "Go on about Thaddeus Hawthorne."

"Oh yes, he died tragically."

Collin looked at Dara, who, normally bored or revolted by Lilith, hung on her every word. She leaned slightly forward in her chair.

"He was quite a ladies' man, and apparently seduced his house maid." Lilith shook her head. "Too bad for him she had discovered the Black Annex—in this very house—on my third floor. It was destroyed—."

"—The what?" Collin started feeling lightheaded from the wine.

Lilith's dark eyes darted between her guests. She paused.

"Lilith—'*Black Annex*'—what's that?" asked Collin, keeping her on track.

"In those days the townspeople called it that—sort of a chapel for witches. It's where they formalized their evil plans for the world. The word was out that every Black Annex had to have a skylight, so the covens—the congregations of witches—could view the moon during their night rituals. Apparently, they imbibed their dark energy from the moon. They did it naked, too—which I'm sure helped their membership drives, but didn't endear them to the god-fearing town folk."

Collin glanced at Dara. Her eyes were fastened upon Lilith.

"That's the way it was." Lilith closed her eyes, "I'm having a hard time remembering," and then she opened her eyes slowly. "Oh yes, so when the maid reported the Annex to the Union soldiers, they climbed on the roof one night and found the skylight—and used it to spy on poor Hawthorne. Apparently, he did all his evil planning there too. They caught him red-handed, worshiping dark forces, which in those days was a virtual death sentence."

Collin put down his goblet of wine. "What do you mean by 'dark forces'?"

Lilith dipped a pinkie in the salad dressing and stuck it in her mouth. "Not bad." She answered Collin's question but looked at Dara. "Something about 'Disciples of Satan', and the 'Apostate' from hell. The Apostate—a gifted but troubled renegade to their cause—had various concubines throughout history. These women were used to accomplishing dark deeds."

"'*Dark deeds*?'" interjected Dara, to Collin's surprise. She was actually asking questions.

Lilith's eyes intensified. "Subversion of history, my dear, to a wicked end. Surely you've noticed reading the papers." Her droll humor elicited a smile from Collin, but not Dara.

Collin, not enchanted with the turn the conversation had taken—especially in light of recent events—remained silent. He offered Lilith no more encouragement.

Lilith mixed the dressing into the carefully prepared salad bowl and picked up her pepper mill. "Legend had it that the Apostate didn't even know that he had been part of this *Dark Army*. He apparently had a little good in him, and that made the good side in him hard to recall the bad side."

Collin hadn't been quite able to follow Lilith's story probably, he thought, because of how much wine he had drunk. "Where did you learn all this, Lilith?" He took another drink of wine, then offered more wine to Dara, who motioned to have her glass refilled.

Dara continued to closely study Lilith in spellbound silence.

"From a book entitled: *His Dark Army*. A Greek Orthodox theology student wrote it and then died under mysterious circumstances."

Collin noticed that at the sound of the book's title, Dara had coughed nervously.

Lilith hesitated and then continued. As she rambled on about Hawthorne, she served the salad onto the plates and then handed them to her guests. "I read the book about thirty years ago. The book disappeared shortly after. I've never seen it since and I can't remember much of it."

Lilith then asked Dara something very curious. "That small Austrian town—the hamlet that you and the First Lady grew up in together when your parents were stationed with the military; what's it called again, my dear?"

Dara shifted in her chair. She cleared her throat. Her response was slow.

"It is called Teufelheim."

Collin could see by his wife's expression that she wondered why Lilith would blurt such a *non sequitur*.

"Interesting . . . " Lilith passed around the grape-leaves and bread, and then took her seat. She took a long gulp of wine as they started on their salads. "Back to Thaddeus Hawthorne—would anyone like to hear about how he was slaughtered?" Lilith framed the question playfully as she raised her hand—as if teaching grade school.

There was stone silence around the table. No one raised his hand. Collin looked at Dara, but his wife's eyes were still on Lilith.

Finally, the spell was broken.

"Yes, I think I would like that," said Dara. "Very much, in fact."

70

CHAPTER FIFTEEN

Lilith drank more wine as she described the grisly death of the munitions mogul Thaddeus Hawthorne, more that one hundred and fifty years ago.

Dara, rather than revolted by the tale, immersed herself in it. Collin wondered if the recent horrific events might have had something to do with Dara's unexplained fascination with Lilith's dark story.

As Lilith continued her story, she sat at the head of the dinner table, serving herself more salad and wine. "So, the angry Union Soldiers had pegged Thaddeus Hawthorne as a warlock—or a male witch. It was said that he was really a thousand years old, and that his string of concubines—some of whom had dark powers themselves—had worked their evil among humankind for centuries."

"So what about the Union soldiers?" Dara asked.

"Well, when they caught Hawthorne practicing his magic in his Black Annex, they dragged him and his female cohorts out to my front yard. It didn't help their case any that some of them had no clothes on."

Lilith stood up and walked down the table to reveal a small mound of baklava pastries. "By that time the good folk of Georgetown had assembled in front of my house with their torches and pitchforks." Lilith loaded two small dessert plates with pastry and placed them before her guests. "They screamed for blood."

Dara took a drink of her wine. "What happened to them?" The fire hissed and crackled. Collin looked over to the dark branches pounding against the window.

Lilith sat down. "The Union soldiers, who had the prisoners in custody, looked the other way while the townspeople strung up the women from the trees. The citizens played the fiddle and danced under their kicking and thrashing legs."

Lilith's eyes landed upon Dara, as if she were testing her reaction to her next morsel of information. "Some said that the knots of the hangman's noose were deliberately set to malfunction—for a slow death of strangulation instead of their necks snapping."

Collin studied Dara's reaction to the violence. She seemed unperturbed.

"And Hawthorne?" asked Dara. "What happened to him?"

"He didn't have it so good." Lilith put down her fork, sat back in her chair, and stared at the ceiling. "As the lore of the day went, there was a sure way to rid yourself of a warlock. It's the last thing I remember about this story."

"Well?" asked Collin.

"His throat was cut with a dagger. The knife was from the 'Holy Land'—a necessary item, as rumor had it. Then, Hawthorne was hung in the front yard—for all to see. They made an example of him. Oh yes, burning alive was a preferred method too."

"Those were the good old days," joked Collin.

No one else laughed.

"You know Lilith, our house is supposed to have a similar history attached to it, although I don't think we have any skylights." Collin chuckled while he looked at Dara, but Dara wasn't smiling. She was glaring at Lilith.

"Lilith, do you really believe in witches? Aren't you a witch yourself?" Dara's question wasn't a question at all, but an accusation.

Lilith's eyes narrowed as she ignored Dara's rude question.

Collin didn't like the tone of the conversation. Somehow, despite Dara's apparent fascination, there was an undercurrent of aggression in her tone. The wine hadn't helped improve her attitude, either.

Lilith cocked her head and leaned toward Dara. Her eyes smoldered. "Dear, I worship the moon, the stars, the wind, and the water—as to the rest—I'm as lost as anyone. I guess I'm the proverbial 'good witch'—a star-gazing agnostic with an old broom that doesn't fly."

"But you believe in black magic, right?" Dara seemed set on defrocking Lilith down to the bottom layer of her skin. Collin decided to remain neutral, as long as no goblets or dishes went flying.

"I can tell you what I *don't* believe in," responded Lilith. "I don't believe in harming anyone. How about you, Dara?"

"Let's cut the bull, Lilith—darling, precious, *dearest*. You don't really think Hawthorne was a warlock—do you? That he had supernatural powers?"

Lilith, caught for words for once, demurred.

Collin wanted to go home, but he also wanted to hear the answer—in a perverse way—to his wife's question. Collin had never had that kind of conversation with Lilith before.

"You sweet thing," said Dara sarcastically to Lilith—"you're just about sales—to a bunch of wooly-minded eggheads who get off on *Twilight Zone* and *Star Trek* reruns."

"I like those reruns," threw in Collin as he smiled.

Dara scowled at him.

Lilith took a long draught from her goblet, then plopped it down on the table. "Well, since we're waxing philosophical tonight, I'll have to say again that I just don't know—no more than I know whether the Red Sea was really parted or the lepers were really healed. But whatever Thaddeus Hawthorne was or wasn't, there's no less or more evidence to support that than any other belief system."

Dara rose from the table. She looked at Collin. "Let's get out of here."

"So nice to see you again, my dear." retorted Lilith.

Dara's cold eyes stabbed through Lilith like a sharp icicle. "I think you're a bad influence on my family. I think you're sick. Thank you for your charming story, Lilith."

Lilith's eyes just twinkled. She smiled. "Any time, *darling*."

Collin got to his feet. Embarrassed, he moved around the table and took Dara gently by the arm. "We've had a lot of wine tonight," he interjected, turning his head toward Lilith. "*All* of us. Thank you for the dinner, Lilith. It's early yet. I have things to do in my study to prepare for work tomorrow."

Dara marched out of the room.

Lilith watched her carefully as she left.

She lowered her voice. "Collin, I want you to watch the History Channel tonight. You have that on cable, don't you?"

"Yes."

"There's a documentary starting in about an hour—I read the program—it might interest you."

"All right."

Her eyes searched Collin's. "You're a scientist. You deal in facts and evidence. What do you think of all this? I may have to know."

Collin was puzzled by Lilith's comment, but he tried to answer her.

"Well," said Collin, "as I see it, it's not a matter of thinking—*feeling* is what's important. That might surprise you coming from me, a researcher."

Collin put on his coat that had hung on the nearby coat rack. He looked nervously in the direction of the door where Dara had just left in a huff.

"The truth is that I'm torn," explained Collin carefully. "Sometimes I feel there's a force for good in the world. Sometimes I feel the opposite. I contradict myself. "

Collin looked into the flames of the fireplace as it crackled. "Take a flower, for instance. Man can pervert people—we can pervert science—sometimes, even nature—but not a flower."

Collin pulled the Royal Catchfly out of his shirt pocket and held it up to the light, admiring its crimson loveliness.

"A flower is just good," he said softly.

"But the fact is," he looked intently into Lilith's eyes, "a flower's a gift from something we can't explain, but we can feel."

CHAPTER SIXTEEN

Georgetown, Later that Sunday evening:

"Otto Han and Fritz Strassman were the first to split the atom in Hitler's Berlin in nineteen thirty-eight. When they conducted the famous experiment, the beginning of the nuclear age was at hand . . ."

Sprawled over his green leather couch in his terrycloth robe with remote in hand, Collin turned up the volume of the cable program as he listened closely. He was watching the History Channel documentary, *The Road to the Arms Race*, as Lilith had suggested at the end of the dinner party.

Enjoying a pint of lager with potato chips in his knotty-pine paneled den, he couldn't figure out why she had recommended this rather elementary science program. He watched the old footage of the two middle-aged men in lab coats, working with their beakers, slide-rules, and test tubes. He noted the absence of computers, and remembered that precursors of early computers were used in the later development of atomic and hydrogen bombs, with the Mike Test of October 31, 1952 being the first successful test of the hydrogen "Super-bomb."

The somber voice of the narrator of the documentary program droned on: "The lab was fortunate enough to have two women scientists who made substantial contributions. One was Greta Heiss, who grew up in Teufelheim, Austria, and would hold scientific retreats at the imposing Teufelschloss Castle in her hometown. Heiss had served as the laboratory director until the war broke out in nineteen thirty-nine . . ."

So, thought Collin, this woman Heiss was from Dara's hometown.

No wonder Lilith had brought up the name of the village during dinner. True, it was a co-incidence—but, so what?

Just then, the image of Greta Heiss came onto the screen. He sat up and leaned forward.

It was a distant shot, and at an angle. She had her hair up in a bun, and wore a long, baggy lab coat. The grainy, black-and-white film of her wandering though the laboratory flickered on Collin's huge screen. The woman also wore eyeglasses.

Nevertheless, the resemblance of Greta Heiss to his wife was impressive. He quickly pushed the "record" button on his remote.

Collin's eyes fastened on the next images.

The documentary footage showed an aerial view of Teufelschloss Castle.

The castle was an imposing, medieval structure whose walls were shaped in a triangle, with one large circular tower at one point with an interior circular courtyard at its center. Two smaller, solid turrets stood at the other two points. A swastika flag flew over one of its towers. Somehow, the image of the castle looked familiar to Collin, but he couldn't quite place it.

Collin dropped his glass of lager on the floor.

The last image of the Berlin laboratory seemed to suck the oxygen out of his body. A close, group-shot of the scientists in the laboratory flickered on the screen. This split-second view of Greta Heiss was clearer, and then it was gone.

It seemed to Collin that she had her hand near her face, perhaps trying to hide it, but he wasn't sure. It was plain that the scientists had been surprised by the camera shot.

Collin considered the cheekbones, the nose, the ears, and the slight forward lean of the female researcher. He had seen a hint of the familiar eyes in a flash, for in this shot there were no eyeglasses.

The eyes were critical. Greta Heiss had large, radiant, beautiful eyes just like Dara's eyes.

The documentary then switched to the nineteen-fifties and nuclear tests in Nevada. Collin pushed the buttons on his remote, switching from live to playback mode. He found the last images of Greta Heiss, playing them on his screen forward and backward, going over and over the images of the strange female scientist who appeared to be Dara's double.

He pushed the zoom-in button and studied her face minutely. Yes, this image, though grainy, sure looked like Dara all right. This was from nineteen thirty-eight, ruminated Collin. With the image he had found in the book *Faces Behind Shadows* yesterday, the whole mess seemed truly unbelievable.

The first photo was a fluke thought Collin, but a second one?

He produced the best zoom-in image of her face that he could find while he advanced the film frame by frame. He recorded it. Then, he hit the mute button while mulling over his discovery.

It was like yesterday all over again only this was another damning photo.

But, it still wasn't *conclusive*, he finally decided, looking down at his hand that held the remote.

It shook.

Collin's cell phone rang. He turned off the TV. He didn't bother to look at the caller-ID number.

"Yes Lilith."

It was Lilith all right. Collin closed his eyes. "I saw . . . yes, the castle too." Collin reclined on his couch—staring at the ceiling. "Yes, it's all a bit strange—but that's all it is. I see now why you mentioned the Austrian town during dinner."

All of a sudden, out of the corner of his eye, he could see the tall figure of Dara standing at the doorway—her arms folded.

He turned off his cell phone and glanced over at Dara.

There was a long silence.

"You spilt your drink." She was looking down at the floor—with those same eyes that he saw on the program. He hadn't even noticed the spill.

Collin sat up. At that instant, he knew that he wouldn't discuss the matter with her. Not yet, anyway.

"Yes. I did spill it."

"Who was that?"

"Lilith."

"What did she say?"

"Since when do I have to report my phone calls to you?"

They had never had an argument before, not about something like that.

"What's the big secret?"

"I don't like an inquisition, that's all."

"Are we quarreling then?"

"I don't quite know—are we?" Collin decided to button up.

Dara let it alone. "Come on—let's go upstairs to bed. I'll clean up the beer tomorrow morning."

For the first time in their marriage, Collin wasn't quite sure that he wanted to go upstairs. At any rate, he would return downstairs soon to erase the images.

He had the horrible feeling that a lot more than that in his life was being erased.

CHAPTER SEVENTEEN

Northeast of Bethesda, Maryland, Monday morning, March 26:

The tarnished silver emblem set in the wall over the entryway read: "NATIONAL HEALTH FOUNDATION: ESTABLISHED 1849—'THE SCOURGE OF DISEASE'."

It was the big meeting in the main lab. A huge milestone had been reached with the vaccine project after almost two years of toil. It was time to take stock and regroup before the major final event: *recombination.*

Dr. Collin De Gise, in dark suit and tie, was at the front of the room next to a large screen as his two hundred and five staff members sat before him. All were dressed in neat white lab coats and sat in neat rows of chairs. Each participant had a yellow pencil and small tablet in his hand for notes. Frank Seaton had meticulously arranged the details.

The lab workers on the project included the cream of the molecular biology community, as well as the ancillary sciences. There was even one Nobel Prize winner in the audience. Key government officials were also present—most with Ph.D.'s. They represented the FDA, the Surgeon General, the Navy, the Department of Defense, and even the Department of Homeland Security.

As Collin lectured, slide projector remote in hand, he indicated the images projected upon the screen with his pointer. A small microphone hung from his lapel.

Collin walked among the first couple of rows of his audience as he talked. "As we speak, hundreds of children are dying in Africa. You all know me, and you know my reputation. I'm telling you that the Vampire Virus vaccine will work, and we'll bring it in on time."

Collin's eyes landed upon Dr. Stanley Chu, siting in the front row. The FDA liaison—with his trademark yellow bowtie—was assiduously scribbling down notes, no doubt, surmised Collin, to facilitate his perennial ball busting. Chu, the voice of doom representing the Food and Drug Administration, relished the role of naysayer.

"As you know, the general strategy in making the vaccine is to reproduce this deadly organism in our lab in a form that triggers the maximal human immune response, without the deadly symptoms. We must have a *live* virus for maximum immune response in this case—and this means there are dangers. We have minimized those."

Collin moved his pointer over the different steps in the process. "First, we purified the seed virus from the African wild type Vampire Virus. Two workers were killed in that difficult process. Then—through our viral factory—we grew and separated the strains and selected the best ones. Through painstaking biochemical processes, we *attenuated* the selected organism—or chemically altered it—to make it relatively safe for our master virus. But alas, with this vicious killer, it's not enough."

After lowering the room's lights with his remote, Collin put the molecular images of the virus on the screen. The images, multi-colored, some craggy, some globular, and all bizarre looking, resembled huge chunks of rock. "We succeeded in separating the virus's DNA core from its protein coat. Here it is under the electron microscope with computer reformatting . . . "

Collin's eyes rested upon Frank Seaton in the second row, arms folded, and eyes narrowed. He knew that Frank's job was on the line with this vaccine, and he knew that Frank thought that too much sensitive information was being shared with outsiders.

" . . . Last Friday, we completed the time-consuming work of sequencing the amino acids and nucleic acids from these components of the virus. Now, it's on to molecular remodeling and manipulation—scientific techniques that are in their infancy. This is the last step before the *gran finale*—recombination—which starts Wednesday and must be completed by the end of this week, Saturday, the last day in March."

Collin could see his dear Stephanie in the middle of the assembly, wearing her immaculate white lab coat. "When complete, we will have our final virus. As most of you know, from this comes the actual vaccine."

His daughter's green hair stuck out like a beacon. He could even see her swaying slightly in her chair, her need for perpetual motion almost incessant.

"We all know how critical computer modeling and mathematical calculations are in our work."

Collin flashed upon the screen a computerized model of a critical gene—globular in appearance. Part of the grey bundle of molecules was labeled bright red, forming a small valley in the digital simulation. "I have the pleasure of working with my dear daughter—Stephanie—on remodeling. It demonstrates that there's zero tolerance for nepotism in the project."

A burst of laughter spread throughout the audience. Collin laughed too.

Collin pointed to the image on the screen. "We have succeeded in isolating the vital functions of the Epsilon gene in the Vampire Virus. Without going into much detail, the red portion here is the Epsilon gene of the wild virus. It produces the so-called "inhibitor protein" that inhibits the function of the "interferon alpha"—which is the host's anti-viral defense when infected with the Vampire Virus. So, in simple terms, if you knock out the enemy's missile defense system with your missiles, your *other* missiles can get through to make the kill. The Vampire Virus is of course the enemy."

Collin looked around the auditorium. "In this way the children will have their missiles."

The auditorium erupted in applause. Collin turned off the light on the projector and turned the room's lights up, clearing his throat.

His eyes avoided Frank Seaton. "Now for the bad news."

CHAPTER EIGHTEEN

Collin hated to give his assembled staff the bad news, especially since Dr. Samuel Chu of the FDA and Dr. Winfred Astaire-Adams, his comely attack dog, were sitting almost front and center, on the lookout for any chink in his armor.

"The latest word from our contacts in Africa is that the Vampire Virus is killing even faster than we think. It mutates faster than any virus on record, making HIV look like Old Faithful."

Frank Seaton sprang out of his seat. "The press isn't aware of this—*yet.*" He looked around at the staff members. "So, keep it under your hats."

"None of us wear hats, Frank." Collin tried to keep it as light as he could, and got a few chuckles out of his rejoinder.

Dr. Stanley Chu shot his hand up. Collin reluctantly nodded to him. "I'm sure you all know Dr. Chu of the FDA," said Collin.

Chu stood up, placing his hands on his hips. As he talked, he searched the faces of the participants for reaction to his comments. "What about the *other* bad news, Dr. De Gise?"

His yellow bowtie didn't make him more lovable, thought Collin. He walked over toward Chu, so he could address him more directly. "And what news is that, Stanley?" He was used to the FDA liaison trying to embarrass him.

"What would happen if you were to make the enemy's—or the Vampire Virus's— missile defense system *stronger*—not weaker? What if it became more able to neutralize our immune system—we would have a *Super-virus* on our hands—right?" Dr. Chu plopped down on his seat.

"And how would that happen?"

Instead of Chu, Dr. Winfred Astaire-Adams—his assertive colleague—stood up to complete the assault. To Collin, this duo had been rehearsed.

As a black woman who had been, it was rumored, considered by the Nobel committee five years before, she was respected—and a celebrity of sorts—in the scientific community. At forty-five, tall, urbane, and well dressed and well-spoken, great things were expected of her in health administration—especially in the government sector.

"First, Dr. De Gise, you're working with your daughter on the Epsilon gene—through an untried molecular remodeling and manipulation protocol. This violates our culture here. Second, neither of you has any experience with pathogens of this complexity and virulence—."

"—*Nobody* has, Dr. Astaire-Adams," interjected Collin. He felt slight resentment for her mentioning his daughter in this context.

"I didn't interrupt *you*, so I'd appreciate it if you would please allow me to have *my* say."

"Go on."

"Third, if through your daughter's mathematical calculations and computer simulations she should make a mistake in the nucleic acid sequences or protein molecule compositions, then she might inadvertently introduce an *Omega* gene into the virus instead. We would then have a deadlier *Super-Virus* to contend with. This is what my esteemed colleague Dr. Chu is concerned about. If that virus ever got out of the lab, it could, theoretically, kill almost *everyone* on this planet!"

There were loud murmurs in the audience—voicing general agreement with Astaire-Adams. Collin had considered this remote possibility long ago, but the risk of doing nothing had been far worse that the very minimal risk of the alternative. Stephanie's computer simulations had confirmed this conclusion.

Collin answered directly. "Yes, I realize that the Epsilon gene and the Omega gene are very much alike. And yes, if I should splice in the wrong gene based upon a faulty model that could be horrible. This is a very remote possibility. We also have safeguards—and millions will die *for sure* unless we push on."

Astaire-Adams, with her patrician profile and attractive but penetrating brown eyes, turned her head around the room, looking for consensus. The murmur went away just as it had months ago when, at a similar meeting, the same topic had been broached on a more simplistic level. She sat down.

Collin glanced over at Frank Seaton, who was mouthing obscenities at her under his breath. Frank was gung ho, and he didn't give a rat's ass about the dangers.

Chu stood up again, to offer his overall bureaucratic recap on the discussion, also like the last time. Collin then predicted to himself that Chu was going to spout something like: "We should pay more attention to quality control and the FDA approval process."

Chu cleared his throat. "Then, we should pay more attention to process during these last days of the project: FDA approval and quality control."

"Yes, of course," chimed in Collin.

Collin knew he hadn't heard the last word from either of them, but he did know that a major hurdle to the development of the viral vaccine had been avoided.

He was free to move on to complete the critical project, but was prepared for last minute disasters.

CHAPTER NINETEEN

Washington DC, Later that Monday morning:

"We have folks locked up in Cuba that will stop at nothing. We need any deterrent we can get."

Gordon Givens—the Assistant Secretary of Defense—pointed to the huge statue of Abraham Lincoln—sitting and observing his visitors in all his righteous might. "If Lincoln were alive today, he would agree. He would say that God's on our side."

Gordon and Collin walked around the Lincoln Memorial viewing the great President from every angle with quiet awe and respect. Collin looked up at Lincoln. Gordon Givens' choice of a meeting place was carefully planned to impress him. It did. He had not taken the time during the last few years to visit the area's famous attractions, and now, thanks to Frank Seaton's prodding to take more free time, he planned to redress this neglect.

"I think you have that wrong, Gordon. Lincoln hoped that we were on *God's* side—not the other way around, and he said so about the Civil War." Collin kept walking briskly, touring the historic site. He was infatuated with Lincoln, and had read about him extensively.

Gordon, wearing a brown suit again and a tie with an American flag on his lapel, locked his very intense brown eyes onto Collin's. Collin didn't want to discuss such a charged topic as germ warfare with him face-to-face, even informally and unofficially. So, he kept up his pace.

"Lincoln was at war, and so are we!" Gordon's voice hardened.

Collin, having shed his lab coat, and wearing his jeans and tan Polo shirt, had planned to leave the lab directly for his psychiatry appointment.

"Look," said Collin bluntly, "I won't stand for my scientific research being perverted—I don't care how just the cause may be."

"You may have no choice." Gordon interrupted.

Gordon stopped walking so that he could square off, but Collin just kept going. He deliberately moved toward some tourists, hoping that the lack of privacy would force a change in the conversation.

Collin studied Lincoln's face carefully. "No *choice*?"

He still felt Lincoln's determined expression and steady gaze upon him. He thought he knew how Lincoln must have felt.

"Yours is essentially a government project, Doctor," Gordon Givens continued in a lower tone, "the White House is coming around to our point of view."

"The First Lady would never allow it," Collin countered. "You were there."

Gordon's tone softened even more. "We have a sacred duty, Collin. To our country, our wives, our children, to protect this nation and our allies with any means possible."

"Gordon, aside from the technical difficulties—"

"—Screw the technical difficulties."

Collin realized that the conversation was hopeless. Gordon had played the patriotism card, and how can you discuss that rationally? It was like arguing about religion or your home baseball team. In fact, Collin felt that Gordon *had* been arguing about religion all along. That had been the undertone of the conversation.

"Nice to see you again, Gordon. Sorry we couldn't have the tour of the lab. This is a busy time." Collin walked away.

As he left the Memorial with his back turned toward Gordon Givens, he heard the man blurt, "We never had this conversation, understand Dr. De Gise?"

Collin thought about what had just taken place. He would have been more blunt had Gordon not been connected to the First Lady—Dara's childhood chum. Gordon was also a high government official and Collin had to use discretion. Nevertheless, he resented being pressured, and hated being used.

After Collin had walked a good distance from the Lincoln Memorial, he glanced back at Gordon to see if he were still there— and he was.

Gordon was now talking to another dark suit with sunglasses. The conversation appeared to be more than just casual. Gordon had been up to more than Collin had thought.

Collin had the distinct feeling that their conversation had been tape-recorded, or, was this just his latent paranoia again?

CHAPTER TWENTY

Washington DC, Monday afternoon, March 26:

"Collin, it seems from our discussion that you feel guilty about killing those children in Iraq."

"Of course I do."

"You shouldn't. It was an accident, after all. Well, not an accident. You were ordered to inject yourself into a situation where collateral damage was possible."

"Is that it?"

"Yes, you didn't know that the target would be a children's hospital. My years in the Navy, in Viet Nam, taught me shit happens."

"We burned everything down, then blew it up."

"Your platoon was ordered to do it. You told me it was a clandestine, international asset, and the chain of command was blurred."

"We shouldn't have even been using the damn flamethrowers. Is that why I'm fascinated by fire, Dr. Firestone? The power?"

"*Bridge*stone."

"I beg your pardon."

"My name is Dr. Jonas Bridgestone—not *Fire*stone."

"I'm dreadfully sorry. Is that why I'm fascinated by fire— or is it because the children all burned to death?"

"*Are* you fascinated?"

"I rather think I must be. It's in most of my dreams."

"Is your sleep any better?"

"No, only three for four hours a night—sometimes less. I try to read, exercise, watch my caffeine, sex, nothing works."

"Should we try the anti-depressants again?"

"I don't know—I'd have to report that to the government."

"I said anti-depressants, not anti-*psychotics*."

"It doesn't matter to them."

"How's that job going Collin? Any closer to a viable vaccine yet?"

"You've never asked me specifics about my work before."

Pause . . .

"There's something else, Dr. Bridgestone."

"What?"

"I think . . . my wife Dara is not who she says she is."

A slight chuckle—"Welcome to the club. I didn't think so either before my divorce."

"No, I mean it *literally*."

A longer pause . . . "I see, then who is she, Collin?"

"I'd rather not say—not right now. I don't know, really."

"I see."

"For instance, I called my wife Klara yesterday, and her name is Dara."

"Oh well, we've all done that. Once I called my ex-wife by our dog's name by mistake. I guess as a psychiatrist I should say it had a deeper meaning."

A long pause ensued as Collin heard papers shuffle across the room.

"Have you . . . had any more of your delusions?" asked Dr. Bridgestone.

"Which—?"

"—Your strange belief systems that people are conspiring to harm you, or that they are out to get you?" A cough . . . "We did have you on anti-psychotics a few months ago, remember? You seemed to improve."

"I do have solid reasons."

"I'm sure, Collin."

"There's more."

"Yes—all right. Tell me."

"I don't like telling you this. Sometimes I'm not sure who *I* am."

"Collin, you're an intelligent man. Think through these things with me. Do you remember what I said about the term '*depersonalization*?' "

"Yeah, I don't mean that exactly."

There was the sound of the keyboarding on the desk opposite Collin.

"Bits and pieces of things sometimes intrude into my mind, Doctor. These things are strange to me. I don't know quite what to make of them."

"We call that in psychiatry, 'thought insertion'—it's not uncommon with your condition. Do you still have those objects in your study—the ones in your locked closet? That you had brought back home from the Middle East—and the Gulf War? "

"Those things left over from the army?"

"Yes, Collin. You know what I'm talking about. What do the authorities say about that?"

Collin shifted his weight on the couch. He opened his eyes. He looked at the photograph on the wall. It was a younger picture of Dr. Bridgestone.

"They don't mind."

"Why?"

"They don't know about it."

"How'd you ever manage to get them there?"

"Army transport—not hard for a junior officer. Then, the trunk of my car."

"Why keep them?"

"Why on earth not?"

"You know it's a sign of paranoia, don't you. "

Collin thought that it had been strange that he had just visited Lincoln—the statue. Now, it seemed that he was talking to him.

The bearded man in the old photo on the wall—in the Navy uniform—looked just like Abe Lincoln. Collin was now talking to an older version of what was in the photograph on the wall in the psychiatric office—Dr. Jonas Bridgestone, his psychiatrist. What an irony, thought Collin—another photo look-alike—this time of Lincoln, but not so alike to make him suspect . . .

"Why keep the weapons?" asked Bridgestone.

Collin thought the Doctor's voice was rich and deep, probably the way that Lincoln had sounded.

"I don't know. To remind me, I guess."

"About what?"

"That—it's wrong to kill."

"Yes."

"Doctor, other things are bad."

"Other things?"

"With my family."

"Tell me."

"Dara—my wife, is acting strange toward our daughter Stephanie."

"How?"

"I don't know—just strange. Different; secretive—cold—hostile—suspicious."

"How so?"

"Well, she doesn't like to be around her anymore. She acts like Stephanie has a horrible disease."

"Any *physical* abuse—?"

"No."

"How's Stephanie doing otherwise, her *condition* I mean—her autism?"

"Better, but she's still regressed. She calls me 'daddy'—giggles too often—no interest in dating. She'll be twenty-one soon and she doesn't have a car, or even drive at all. She still lives at home and still sucks her thumb."

"All that is actually not that peculiar, especially these days. She's a child prodigy, right? Math genius? I read about her the other day in the *Washington Post*. Besides, I suck *my* thumb. Nasty habit. How's her job doing?"

"She's phenomenal."

"She works with you in a very special capacity, doesn't she Collin?"

"Yes."

"How does she react to Dara? Does she have any unusual ideas about her mother?"

"I don't quite know what you mean."

Collin turned his head and glanced over to the other side of the dimly lit room. Dr. Bridgestone, sitting behind his desk, busily took down notes. He looked austere, with a heavy dark beard and disheveled hair, his eyes were continually sad. He had on an expensive navy blazer with a white dress shirt and open collar. The hair on his head was almost completely grey, not black like in the photo.

Collin frowned as he lay on the couch. "Stephanie's afraid of Dara."

Bridgestone was silent for a few minutes. He closed his notebook.

"Aren't you afraid of her too?"

Collin glanced at Bridgestone. Their eyes met. The insightfulness of the question stunned Collin.

Dr. Jonas Bridgestone got up from his chair and put away the things on his desk.

"I see we're out of time."

"Thank you, Doctor."

"Next time, I want to spend more time talking about your dreams." He stood up from his desk.

"Yes, all right," said Collin.

Collin lay still. He thought about the children.

There was something important that he had had not told Bridgestone, but he had forgotten what that was.

It was very important.

CHAPTER TWENTY-ONE

Washington DC, Later that Monday afternoon:

Collin De Gise studied a finger-painting on the wall, decorated by an American child, one of thousands of youngsters that had donated a painting of remembrance to the Painting Wall at the Museum of Hate and Intolerance in Washington DC.

This picture had a lone teardrop painted on its white background. As he looked at the other graphics on the lower level of the museum, he strolled past a sign: "FIRST LADY DEDICATES NEW WING ON THIRD FLOOR TODAY."

Shonda Rice O'Neal had requested to see Collin as soon as possible about an important matter. She had set their meeting time just after her dedication, at three o'clock in the museum's cafe—the only time open on her calendar all week.

Collin had about thirty minutes to kill before the meeting. As he strolled the other floors, he soon found himself engrossed in the exhibits, artifacts, and emblements of genocide and mass human destruction. The museum was not only a testament to an unspeakable train wreck in the human experience, but offered inspiring stories as beacons of hope for the future.

He walked over to the directory near the elevator, and scanned the numerous offerings. Then, he saw something that he had not expected—and indeed, he had not even been aware of until finding the book *Faces Behind Shadows* in The Black Peacock.

There was a temporary exhibit on the development and use of Diclon-A, the poison gas used to murder millions of victims in the Nazi death camps. It was the gas mentioned in the caption below the seventy-year-old photograph of the Nazi Frau Troost—the double of his wife Dara.

Collin walked to the second floor. He strode past the other exhibits and soon came upon a setting that turned his stomach. A huge circular stage presented—with three walls and a ceiling that had a small round opening in the roof. It was the simulation of a primitive metal shower-room used in one of the extermination camps.

In front of the stage, on a long mural, were photographs, reading materials, and a continuously playing digital film with headphones. Putting on the headphones and viewing the grim documentary footage of death camp victims being gassed, it only took Collin several minutes to learn that thousands of unsuspecting prisoners—fully disrobed and expecting to receive showers—were summarily gassed to death instead. Diclon-A gas had been dropped from the opening on the ceiling.

Collin, moving on to the booklets, turned the pages, hoping to find another photograph of Frau Troost . . .

"Can I help you?"

Collin looked up. He saw a very old and bald man with a thin grey mustache.

"I'm looking for something."

"What?"

The old man had no eyebrows, but his brown eyes were luminescent, radiating youthful energy. Short, dapper, and wiry, he was dressed in a dark suit. His wrinkled skin, stooped posture, and labored breathing were offset by his quick manner and the vitality of his German-accented voice. Collin sensed that he was a Holocaust survivor. The only abnormality that betrayed the horrendous mental trauma of his past was a nervous tic—he intermittently closed his eyes for about one second, for no apparent reason.

"I need information." A close race ensued between Collin's need for more information and his reticence in drudging up horrific memories for this kind stranger.

"Perhaps I can direct you," he responded.

" I'm sorry, but—you're a—survivor—of the camps, right?"

"Yes, but do not be sorry—this is the reason I am here."

"I'm Dr. Collin De Gise. I need information about the gas chambers." He found it incredible that these eyewitnesses could talk about those times at all, let along conduct exhibits. He figured it was their unselfish sense of mission.

"Ziggie Einbaum." He held out his hand and Collin took it. "What is it about the gas chambers you would like to know?"

"I'd like to know more about a Nazi woman who worked in them."

The sagacious eyes narrowed. He looked around, noticing other visitors. He moved closer to Collin, taking his arm, and guiding him toward the corner of the room where there were less people.

"Who?"

"A war criminal; she worked at the Belzec extermination camp in Poland during 1943."

The old man frowned. There was a pause. "I was there then. A woman? The name of this war criminal?"

Collin, strapped for time, and not really knowing how to start, decided to just plunge in. "Have you ever heard of a female SS officer named Berte Troost? She was supposed to have been an attractive woman—but very sadistic. She would have been in her late thirties at the time. She supposedly developed Diclon-A—the same poison gas in your exhibit."

Einbaum's pale forehead grew bright pink blotches. His face flushed. He tried to talk at first, but couldn't form the words. The sympathetic eyes turned dark as his old hands shook. "'*Supposedly!*'" He raised his voice to a harsh pitch. "Supposedly nothing! She did indeed invent the gas! She was very good at sciences."

Ziggie grabbed Collin by his collar. "We called her 'The *Butcher* of Belzec'".

Collin looked around him. People were starting to stare. "I didn't mean to—"

"—Belzec was one of the worst camps. How do you know about this woman?" He took his withered hands away from Collin. His breathing became more regular, his voice more even.

Out of the corner of his eye, Collin saw a uniformed security guard rapidly approaching them. The armed man stopped about three feet away. "Everything good here, Mr. Einbaum?" the guard asked the old camp survivor.

Ziggie pushed his hand in the air toward the guard. "Yes, yes fine." The guard left.

"I read about her," Collin continued.

The old man was silent, and just stared at Collin.

Collin let out a deep breath. "Please tell me about her. It's very important. Where was she from?"

"From hell!" Ziggie's eyes became moist—his manner subdued. "I did not mean to frighten you, young man. It is just . . . " He shook his head.

"I fully understand. Please."

Ziggie looked around the exhibit and then started walking. Collin walked along with him.

"She came from hell—and at the end of the war she vanished—some say in the bombing. Her records were destroyed. Not even the great Wiesenthal could find much about her. Like Mengele—she was physically beautiful. She had lovely red finger nails to match her red hair—she had a thing about them."

Collin felt his knees weaken.

He thought about Dara's lovely red nails and hair.

CHAPTER TWENTY-TWO

They stopped in front of the educational film at the Diclon-A exhibit. They viewed—without the headphones—the grisly footage of the victims being herded into the "showers" to be gassed.

Ziggie—the old death camp survivor—lost himself in history, as his eyes seemed to go blank. "That bitch from hell would strip the women herself to get their jewelry before she pushed them into the showers. She enjoyed it—even in a sexual sense, I believe."

His words gushed out as if a dam inside him had broken. "She collected painted nails—of the victims—*red* ones only—she yanked them herself using her pliers—right on the train platform—after she selected those who would die."

Collin was speechless.

"She wore a necklace of red nails as a souvenir."

As the old man spoke, Collin studied the horrible images on the movie screen of the concentration camp inmates being herded into gas chambers.

"Where was Troost from?" asked Collin.

Einbaum thought for a moment. "No one really knows. The rumor was—she came from a small town—you would not know it."

Collin, not wanting to ask the next question, already felt that somehow he knew the answer. He started to sweat.

"Was it named—Teufelheim?"

Einbaum's eyes smoldered like red-hot coals. "How did you know that?"

Collin ignored the question. Berte Troost and Greta Heiss—the Nazi SS officer and the atomic researcher in Berlin, were both from the same small Austrian town and both resembled Dara. Could that really be only a coincidence, wondered Collin?

"Please tell me about *Teufelschloss*—the castle in Teufelheim." Collin turned his head away from the images on the screen. He suddenly felt sick. He hated asking the old man these questions.

In his mind, Collin grabbed at rationalizations, probabilities, and unlikely but possible scenarios to explain away ugly facts. *Troost and Heiss could have been related, and therefore looked alike. If related, being from the same town wouldn't be that unusual. Their resemblance to Dara could remain a fluke, and maybe it was.*

Ziggie Einbaum answered Collin's question. "That lair of the wolves—Heinrich Himmler and Reinhard Heydrich—conducted SS meetings there in that castle. Camps belonged to the SS—and so did that evil castle. Himmler even had a round table in the castle, like King Arthur. They thought they were knights."

Collin sensed that a profound sadness had overtaken his new friend. "My little daughter loved to paint her nails red. That day we got off that cattle-car train that stopped at the camp." The old man cleared his throat. "My wife had already died in the train. Frau Troost grabbed my little daughter's hand on the train platform. She took the pliers to her little fingers, then . . . " There was a long silence. His lip started to quiver.

Collin's eyes welled. "I see." He put his hand lightly upon Ziggie's shoulder, and then removed it.

"After my little one was gassed, Frau Troost's gruesome necklace had a little red fingernail on it! She paraded it in front of me before she hit me with her dog whip."

Collin said nothing for a while. He didn't know what to say.

"How do you know about these things, Dr. De Gise? Why do you care about Frau Troost?"

Collin had a goal in mind. "My wife's from Teufelheim. Her father was an American army officer stationed not far from there. He died in a military transport crash when my wife was very young—along with her mother. They were leaving on vacation."

"Your wife is from that town?"

"Yes, from the American base right next to it."

"The German word '*teufel*' means 'Devil'. The town's name means 'Devil's home', and the castle's name means 'Devil's castle'. The area is known for its grand military history and brave warriors," explained Ziggie. "Not all were Nazis, of course. Many were decent officers and fought hard for their country throughout the war."

Collin looked at his watch. He had to meet the First Lady. "I have to leave. We may have information for you about Frau Troost."

Ziggie nodded. "Yes, not many are from that wicked place. Your wife is. I'd like to meet her"

"Maybe we can have lunch soon?" suggested Collin.

He felt as if he were playing a dirty trick on the old man. When he sees Dara, who knows what will happen? But, concluded Collin, it needs to be done.

It sounded crazy to him, but he couldn't help himself. What better way to find out if his wife and Frau Troost were indeed the same person? It's the best way to show that they are *not*, thought Collin.

They can't be!

Arranging a meeting between his wife and the old man seemed the best way to prove it. Despite his hopes, Collin cringed at the thought of how an encounter like that might turn out.

CHAPTER TWENTY-THREE

Washington DC, Later that Monday afternoon:

"I think of those poor little people being murdered. It makes me ill. I want to bawl my eyes out." The long, elegant, bejeweled fingers of Shona Rice O'Neal wiped her moist eyes with a napkin. "Never again."

The wet, very pale-grey eyes of the First Lady peered through Collin. "I'm glad I dedicated the new wing here at the museum." She pushed back the edge of her blond flip hairdo, which had encroached a tad bit too much upon her smooth neckline.

Collin put down his fork in his half-finished macaroni and cheese. "It was good of you to do that."

He felt uncomfortable being alone with the First Lady during their late luncheon. This was the first time he had ever been alone with her, without Dara present. Shonda had chosen the cafeteria in the museum in which to dine, and it seemed an odd choice. He understood, however, she was rushed for time.

Mrs. O'Neil wore a beaded cashmere sweater over a black sheath, with a Tahitian pearl necklace and matching earrings. In his jeans and casual shirt, Collin felt their life experiences were as far apart as their dress. It wasn't, however, the setting or attire that bothered him. It was rather the fact that she was so intense, and her gaze—to him—always seemed too searching.

Collin watched her devour her velvet cake dessert, her appetite seemingly intact despite her sorrow about the victims of Nazi crimes. Her sweet tooth was famous, but she never seemed to put on a pound.

"Don't you like your mac and cheese?" she asked him.

"It's all right. I'm not very hungry."

"Incidentally, the museum's food isn't too bad—a cute little cafe—isn't it Collin?" She looked over at the next table, where three dark suits and sunglasses sat devouring their burgers.

The Secret Service never disappointed in looking obvious, thought Collin. A few other patrons also were eating in the pink and white, parlor-decorated restaurant. The decor seemed to be a deliberate attempt to provide light relief for the grim content of some of the museum's exhibits. A few tables and chairs around their table were kept empty of guests by the Service to provide a safe perimeter from dangerous intruders, surmised Collin.

Her fork dabbed at the white icing. "You visited with Gordon Givens this morning at the Lincoln Monument. What did he say to you?"

Collin was a bit surprised at her hubris. It had been a private conversation with Gordon, after all.

How did she find out so fast?

"Frankly, he wants me to use my research at the lab to help the Department of Defense build a germ warfare program," he answered.

"Is that so?" Shonda Rice O'Neal—as classy a lady as one might find, thought Collin—was actually busy licking the rich white frosting from her elegant fingers.

"Yes." Collin took a drink of his iced tea. "He's concerned about the terrorists in Cuba getting that capability. He thinks the United States is dragging its feet."

"And what did you say?"

"Well, what I've said before. I won't participate."

"I know." She stuffed the last piece of cake in her mouth, and then smacked her lips as she chewed. "Well, good. The children come first. I'm glad you straightened him out." She then wiped her mouth.

"The Vampire Virus won't become a weapon. I'm morally against it."

"I'm glad you said that. Of course, you're right."

Collin hesitated. He didn't like getting involved in politics. "Gordon seemed to hint that that your husband may not see it quite that way—."

"—Nothing to it."

She looked around the room, obviously wanting to change the subject. That was fine with him. Shonda smiled. "You're progressing rapidly. You should be done soon with the vaccine."

"By Saturday, I should think. We'll have the altered master virus in hand—the template for the vaccine. The rest is quick—if—."

"—If what?"

"If the FDA—Dr. Stanley Chu and his colleague Dr. Astaire-Adams—don't cause too much trouble. Actually, she's the one I'm most concerned about. They both seem surprisingly resistant to the idea of our success."

"Don't worry about Astaire-Adams." She leaned forward in her chair. "I heard about your lecture and how they sounded off. There's no reason for concern."

"Glad to hear it. Speaking of the project, I'd better get back to the lab. Stephanie is working out the molecular sequences—the main work that's happening now—and I'd like to observe." Collin knew there would be many opportunities left to do that, but he felt eager nevertheless.

"What about *after* the vaccine?" asked Shonda.

Collin was a bit miffed. These *political* people, as he called them, like Gordon and the First Lady, didn't seem to value his time. It was almost as if they were trying to get him out of his lab for some weird reason.

"After? " It then dawned upon Collin what she may have been talking about. He was impressed by her acumen. "We must keep making different variations of the vaccine—because the serotypes of the wild virus in Africa will change due to rapid mutation. A moving target is hard to hit."

"I think I understand Collin. You're a useful man to keep around." She laughed.

"I hope so, First Lady."

Collin's thoughts then switched to Ziggie Einbaum and on the Teufelschloss. He wanted to ask Shonda Rice O'Neal about her hometown. On second thought, he thought it might be inappropriate.

"What's on your mind?" It was uncanny how she read him, he thought.

Collin's curiosity then got the better of him. Besides, she seemed to be in an informal mood. "What did you think of the *Teufelschloss*?"

She motioned to one of the Secret Service agents without even batting an eyelash at the name of that strange castle. Collin asked the waitress for the check.

"It's on me—or rather the taxpayers," she said in her calm, even voice. "I've got to scoot. Been a pleasure—give my regards to Dara."

Collin looked around him, glad to be averting his eyes to anywhere but hers.

She smiled, but Collin sensed reserve. She had forgotten to answer his question.

It had then occurred to him that this grand and generous lady didn't quite trust him to do his very important job at the laboratory. He didn't know why.

CHAPTER TWENTY-FOUR

Northeast of Bethesda, Maryland, Late that Monday afternoon:

Stephanie rocked in her rocking chair behind the desk at the lab.

Having discarded the traditional white lab coat for a more comfortable, and warmer, Redskin's varsity jacket, she smoothed back her short green hair and looked up at her father through goggles. "It's done, daddy."

She pointed to the green, globular structure on the computer screen. " I sequenced it."

"Great job, love." Collin pointed out to Dr. Astaire-Adams the unusual configuration of the molecule. "The red portion in the middle of the green—the location of the Epsilon gene—is a big reason why this baby's usually so deadly. Beautiful, isn't it?"

Frank and Collin stood next to each other—also wearing the goggles—as they looked over Stephanie's shoulder at the strange figure.

"Deadly things can come in pretty packages," said Collin.

Collin's witticism drew a quick rejoinder from Frank. "It *should* be pretty. It cost me millions," added the administrator. "And I like the goggles."

Collin felt as if the molecule would jump out at him from the screen.

Chu and Astaire-Adams stood off to the side of Stephanie's desk, glum and silent. They took off their goggles and scowled.

Stephanie enlarged parts of the image while she pushed some buttons on her keyboard. The red patch, on closer view, resembled a spiral staircase with hunks of craggy rocks resting on slanted steps.

Dr. Stanley Chu then surprised Collin with his praise. "Congratulations, Stephanie, I know what hard work this was. What I don't understand is how you worked out the sequences with just the information you had. You even had to do the permutations of PH and temperature and electrical charge . . . well, it's a *tour de force,* that's all."

Stephanie turned red with embarrassment.

Collin wondered about the real reason behind Chu's compliments.

"That red thing then—that's the Epsilon gene, right? I just want to confirm." Frank Seaton marveled at the structure as Stephanie changed the computer images to show various orientations of the molecules under different media-bath conditions.

"That's it all right," said Collin.

"Good going. This is a milestone in our project." Frank lips parted, his imitation of a smile.

Collin looked around at the group. "Now behold this."

Stephanie tapped a few keys on her purple computer keyboard and the red clump reappeared, only slightly different. The spiral stairs now had different looking steps—there were no craggy rocks on them. She hit another key. The before and after images of the Epsilon gene both filled the screen, with yellow shadows highlighting the difference in shapes.

"The second image on the screen is our new gene," continued Collin. The molecular remodeling that we're doing will produce the second image—and it'll render the virus harmless after I splice the gene into the master virus. It'll produce a new protein coat." Collin's eyes lit up.

Chu and Astaire-Adams stood with their arms folded, visibly skeptical. Collin noticed this negative body language.

"So, what does all that mean?" asked Frank Seaton.

Collin nodded to Stephanie. "That's enough for now."

The computer screen went blank. He took a seat on the corner of Stephanie's desk, sitting beside her as he faced his three colleagues. "I'll tell you what it means, Frank." They removed their goggles. With each point, Collin bent back the fingers of his right hand as he enumerated them. "I'm splicing the new gene you saw on Stephanie's screen back into the master virus DNA—I can finish that tomorrow by end of the day. Then—*recombination.*"

Frank and Stephanie nodded in agreement.

Dr. Chu and Dr. Astaire-Adams were stone-faced and silent.

Collin noted the depth of their subdued reactions. "Any questions?" His wary eyes frisked the skeptical FDA representatives.

"All right," interjected Dr. Astaire-Adams as she took down some notes on a pad, "let's see what kind of final result we have. It's too early to start celebrating."

"No one is celebrating—yet," said Collin.

She scribbled as she continued talking, not looking at the others. "The FDA took the unusual step to imbed us within this project not so that we can be loved. We ask the tough questions." Her eyes then shot to Collin. "I've done fresh calculations. The chance of a rogue gene is much greater now. If you take the time to examine the chemical baths in the Fridge it will prove this."

"We've been over this before," said Collin.

"What about the *seed* virus," asked Chu? "Any evidence of increased instability?"

"Soon, we won't need it anymore—or the Fridge." Collin looked at Frank Seaton. "I'll be storing the master virus in the adjunct lab area—just outside the Fridge. We have temperature-controlled enclosures there that are just as good. All my gene splicing equipment is there."

Collin stood up from the desk. He looked over at Stephanie and winked. She smiled back. "All right Stephanie?"

She nodded to her dad.

"We have to be absolutely clear about our timeline here," admonished Collin.

"We're almost there—" Frank Seaton's animated eyes searched Dr. Chu's, "—we all need to pull together. Collin has trained a great, highly skilled team here, and the goal post is inches away. "

Chu nodded. Seaton's eyes narrowed as he shifted them to Dr. Astaire-Adams.

Collin also knew that she would be ready to cause trouble.

CHAPTER TWENTY-FIVE

Georgetown, Monday evening, March 26:

Carmen had her bedroom door bolted shut.

She had been hiding in her small room since the day before, until her planned departure. She would have left sooner, but she couldn't get a flight, and she had no extra money to get a hotel despite Collin's generous severance pay. That had gone to pay off her debts, such as her generous pledges of money to her church and the new pairs of expensive shoes she bought on a regular basis.

Her bible was open on the bed-stand while her choral music played softly from the CD player on her dresser, next to the burning candle. She kneeled by her bed in her cotton nightgown, fervently praying. Modest clothes lay on the bed. Her thick, lustrous, dark hair had been neatly pinned up on top of her head in a bun.

A can of gasoline and a barbeque lighter stood in the corner of the room.

Tears ran down her cheek as her hands shook with fear. Then, she looked down at her bed, and gasped at what stuck out from under her pillow. At first, she thought it was her dark belt.

A hissing sound came from the belt, and then it moved.

She realized, to her horror, it hadn't been her belt at all, but a long, black snake.

It moved toward her slightly and raised its large, diamond-shaped head. Its mouth opened, displaying its two curved fangs. The fusiform, yellow eyes peered intensely into hers. They had a human quality—a malicious glint to them.

As her mouth opened wide to scream, the snake's jaws seemed to open more too, as if it were human—mimicking her.

The viper enjoyed her fear, she thought. But when Carmen cupped her mouth and tried to scream, no sound came. The terror had paralyzed her—the yellow eyes had control of her—to do very horrible things.

Movies played in her mind, and she knew that the snake had put them there. Evil, moving images of murder and destruction played on and on. Carmen put her hands over her eyes but the images still rushed into her thoughts, because she saw them only in her mind, which she no longer controlled.

She only knew that she must put an end to it all.

Collin, dressed in his silk pajamas, entered his kitchen and walked to the sink, drawing himself a glass of water. He looked out the window and saw that the sky was pitch black except for the glow of the moon, which was just over a quarter full. He detected the very faint orange halo that everyone had been talking about it.

Moving over to the kitchen table, and saw the note from Dara: "Working late, D."

He went quietly upstairs and walked along the creaking hallway until he came to Stephanie's study. Slowly opening the door and seeing that the room was empty, he crept farther down the hallway.

Collin found Stephanie sleeping peacefully in her bed, buried in her quilt covers. He headed downstairs to the kitchen to make something to eat, detouring past Carmen's door. He noticed that her door was ajar.

Slowly approaching it, he peered through the opening. No one seemed to be in the room and he thought that odd, since he had not seen her anywhere in the house. At that hour, it would be unlikely she would be out for a walk or on an errand.

Pushing the door open further, he saw that the room was deserted. But, music played and candles burned. Carmen had been around recently—or *someone* had. Then, he noticed the note lying on the bed.

Collin entered the room, and picked up the note, written in Carmen's broken English.

"SHE EVIL."

What could Carmen mean? *Who* could she be talking about? Could it possibly be Dara? Collin tucked the note into his pocket.

Then, Collin smelled the gasoline. He looked over into the corner of the room, and saw a gas can—the top was lying next to it . . .

The door creaked behind him.

Collin spun around.

Stephanie stood in the doorway, wiping her sleepy eyes.

Collin embraced his daughter. "Honey, go back to bed."

"Daddy, what's the matter? Where's Carmen?"

"Don't know, love."

He took Stephanie by the hand and led her into the foyer. Noticing a draft, he glanced toward the end of the dark exit and discovered the front door was slightly open.

"Baby, go back to bed, all right? Everything will be fine." As Stephanie went up the stairs, Collin moved slowly toward the front door. That's when he heard the loud scream coming from the front yard . . .

At first, Collin had thought that it was the neighbor kids next door igniting some type of peculiar fireworks. Then he noticed that the flaming statue was actually running through the front yard. It screamed.

It was no statue. It was Carmen!

She was on fire—burning alive—as she dashed across the lawn under the huge oak trees. Collin sprinted after her. He tackled her on the lawn. He tore off his silk top and frantically tried to smother the fire with the skimpy material.

It was no good. The fire had progressed too far. He dashed for the garden hose and turned it on. Then he ran back toward the flaming body thrashing in agony on the grass. The hose was too short. The stream from the nozzle missed its burning target by two feet.

Carmen rolled over in agony as she burned, screaming at the top of her lungs.

Collin dropped the hose and ran to her, trying to get hold of a leg or an arm to drag her closer to the hose. The flames were too powerful to gain purchase. Collin looked around for something bigger to smother the flames with. There was nothing in sight.

He tore inside the house and called 911.

When he returned, Carmen lay completely still and silent. Her clothes had been burned off and she was charred all over her smoking body. Except for her right hand, which she held in a tight, burnt fist, all her fingers and toes were only black stubs.

Collin couldn't detect breathing movements from her chest. The gasoline had done its work all right, he thought. It had been a quick but horrible death.

"In my twenty years on the force—I've never seen anything this bad." The hefty policewoman pushed back her cap and shook her head as she took notes on a small pad. "She has no relatives living in the States, as I understand it?"

"That's right," answered Collin as he stood in the moonlight, his sweaty, muscular body glistening. "But she does have relatives somewhere in South America." Collin, tired and wet, was shivering in the cold night air.

Dara was still working the late hours. That left him alone with Stephanie to contend with this horrific mess. Given the string of recent, horrible events and now this shocking development with Carmen, Collin felt completely drained.

He spotted his charred shirt on the lawn next to the covered body. "She was our maid."

"Yes Doctor De Gise, we know." The three squad cars flickered their bright lights as the other officers milled about, taking photographs and measurements. "Did she say anything peculiar to you—to give us a clue as to why she would do this to herself?"

Collin thought for a moment. "No, nothing."

"She left no note?"

Collin glanced over toward the charred shirt lying on the lawn.

"No," he lied. He rationalized that it had only been gibberish anyway.

"Do you know anything about her medical history?"

"No."

"Sir, my name is officer Mendez. I shouldn't tell you this, but between you and me, Carmen had been down to the station recently—several times, in fact."

Collin looked from Carmen's body to Officer Mendez. Past Mendez, he could see the red, blinking lights of the red fire-truck parked next to the squad cars. Collin's eyes narrowed. "Why?"

"Well, she was saying some crazy things. Things that make us wonder about her mental capacity—if you know what I mean?"

"Like what kind of things."

The officer looked around her. "Well, I can't say. However, we looked in her room, and in her purse, and we found *this*." She held up a little red pill with tiny black letters squiggled on it. The letters formed a word that Collin knew to be psychiatric medication.

"Well, unofficially sir, it appears to be some sort of antipsychotic."

"I see."

"Did she seem—*normal*—to you?"

"I don't know—her English wasn't very good—yes, I think so. She seemed upset about something, though."

"Do you know what?"

"No."

"What?"

"No. I said no."

Officer Mendez nodded her head. She looked at Collin doubtfully. "Oh, there's one other thing."

She pulled a very small, labeled envelope out of her pocket and emptied its contents into her hand. She held it up for Collin to see.

"We found this on her body. She was clutching it in what was left of her right hand."

Collin looked at the charred object.

"Is that a—?"

"Yes sir, that's right, it's a burnt crucifix."

After the body had been removed and the police had left, Collin walked over to the remains of his shirt. He picked it up. Inside the pocket, he felt the piece of paper that, surprisingly, was still there. It was her note.

"SHE EVIL."

CHAPTER TWENTY-SIX

"Did the police say why they think she might have killed herself?"

"No."

"Do they suspect foul play?"

"No."

Collin was half asleep. Dara was still sitting up in bed, talking about Carmen.

"Did she leave a note?"

"Like I said, they think she just went off the deep end. She didn't leave anything." Dara then snuggled next to Collin, who rolled over—turning his back to her.

She made his flesh crawl.

He wanted sleep, and that's all he wanted. She stared at his back for a moment, and then flicked off the light. It seemed to him that she wanted more than sex anyhow—she wanted information.

Collin felt like his head was floating. He didn't want to be next to her. He knew she sensed it. The events of the last couple of days had piled up on him.

It seemed like his head melted into the wall. He heard strange voices. One voice sounded familiar, but he couldn't identify it. Everything was bright, and solid objects were becoming translucent. The voices were young, and soon he suspected that the voices were children's voices, talking in a strange language.

He was flying through the air, high above the ground and into the clouds again. Collin sat on a roof—a big, flat roof on top of a building many stories high. The bright sun burned. There were white buildings down below. Mosques dotted the landscape.

The sign in front of the building upon which he stood had a red cross on it. Ambulances parked near the entrance to the building. Collin wore battle fatigues as he crouched on the roof, checking his combat equipment.

A large metal canister was strapped to Collin's back, along with a machine gun. He wore a helmet that housed special lenses within its visor—including infrared capability. The service pin attached to the lapel of his tunic displayed the motto: "DARE."

Three huge helicopters, equipped with heavy guns, dropped more special-forces commandos from hanging tethers onto the roof. The men readied their weapons after landing upon the sizzling hot roof. Many held long metal wands, which were attached to the canisters on their backs—flamethrowers.

Their orders were simple: kill every living thing that moved on immediate contact. " W. M. D." —Weapons of Mass Destruction—were suspected to be within the target structure. Since they were thought to be chemical weapons, then an airstrike without ground forces had been ruled out, since explosives from missiles or bombs could spread toxic material for miles.

Simultaneous with the commando infiltration onto the roof, infantry had assaulted the ground floor of the hospital. Tear-gas had been introduced through the windows and the inhabitants couldn't breathe. The children in the hospital were trying to escape through the fire exit on the roof.

Two soldiers dashed to the fire exit on the roof and forced open the locked metal door. Collin joined them. He heard screaming coming from inside the building, on the stairs leading up to the fire exit. He removed the wand clipped to his ammo belt, and stood ready to "toast" all contacts.

Collin looked down the dark stairway and into the interior of the building. The other commandos crowded next to him at the entrance. Suddenly, people were running up the stairs from inside the building, trying to escape though the exit door.

A commando screamed. "Burn!" The commando activated his flamethrower. He incinerated one of the insurgents running up the staircase.

Collin pulled his trigger too, unleashing a huge plume of fire.

Then, Collin saw that the moving targets scrambling up the stairs were children. More commandos activated their flamethrowers. The children wore nothing but white hospital gowns. Some still had IV needles in their arms. Adults were mixed in the crowd, some wearing white coats. Some couples—wearing street clothes, looked to be visiting parents, led their children by the hand.

They all coughed, struggling to get fresh air in their lungs. They all burned well.

112

The ones closest to the door caught fire first, while still running, turning into human torches that burned brighter as wind from the outside fanned the flames.

Collin became intoxicated with the excitement and the scent of the propellant. It almost seemed that a guiding hand led him to activate his flamethrower with the other commandos. As he pulled the trigger again and again, the huge plumes left his wand, incinerating a screaming young girl and her father.

The scent of searing flesh sickened him. In a few seconds, there was noting left of the girl and her father but a black heap. He pointed his wand at another target, pulling the trigger again, then again, and . . .

Waking, and drenched in sweat, Collin looked over at Dara lying in bed, her back turned to him, apparently asleep. He threw the covers off him and sat up. His pajamas were soaked. He quietly left the bedroom and walked down the hallway to his study.

He walked up to his desk and took a key from under the green pad. He unlocked the door to his closet, turning on the light and entering.

He pushed back the old coats and pants hanging on the hangers and there they rested: his khaki uniform and beret; a tarnished metal wand and canister with a can of fuel; his grappling hook with a long rope attached to it; his 0.40 caliber Beretta revolver with ankle holster; and his red-sheathed, Middle Eastern dagger with the long curved blade.

He let out a deep breath, looking at the photo on the wall from his old army days.

It was a shoulder shot of him with two chums, standing in their khakis, smiling into the camera, their heads shaved under the red berets.

Who is that man, really, wondered Collin?

CHAPTER TWENTY-SEVEN

Northeast of Bethesda, Maryland, Tuesday morning, March 27:

Dr. Astaire-Adams marched back to her cubicle in a huff. She had just talked to Dr. De Gise and he seemed uninterested in her concerns about the safety of the vaccine project. She was sick of his aloof manner. This morning, he had seemed unusually preoccupied.

    Although a brilliant researcher and a Nobel Prize recipient—and terribly good looking, she had always had reservations about him—his *stability* that is. In fact, she had heard through the grapevine that he sees a shrink, and that he had marital problems. Moreover, she had seen the story about his housekeeper on the late-evening news—weird! Not that he had been at fault, but . . . At any rate, she resented the fact that he hired his strange daughter to do key research in such an important government project, when she had worked her way up the professional ladder by merit.

    Typical white crap, she thought.

    While at her computer, she looked down at the tile floor, and then screamed. Two coworkers ran to her cubicle, finding her nearly frozen—trembling—her eyes fixed upon the long black object lying on the ground.

    Collin, hearing the scream, sprinted to her cubicle. Standing over the distraught woman, other researchers pointed at the floor. The peculiar shape of the object was disturbing to all. He scooped it up off the floor.

    Collin held up a long black snakeskin. The creature had molted, and its fleshy contents were long gone.

    "No worry—it's just an empty snakeskin without the snake." Collin said to his distraught colleague, Dr. Astaire-Adams. He carefully picked up the skin and threw it in the trashcan. "I'll have the sanitation engineer pick it up right away. I'm sorry you had a fright. It'll be all right."

    She had her face buried in her hands as she sat at her desk. She slowly lifted her head and glared at Collin. "No, it's not all right!" Her eyes were narrow slits of rage. "This lab's a mess!"

"You're overreacting—"

"—The ventilation system in this place is vital to safety! How did the damn thing get in here? If *that* could get *in*, maybe a virus could get *out*!"

Collin finished for the morning. He looked forward to lunch. He wanted the chance to be alone, so he decided to go to his favorite Thai restaurant—a little hole-in-the-wall that sat only a few patrons. He had a lot to think about. For one thing, he had noticed that the snakeskin felt warm—strange indeed.

He decided to peek into the Firehouse before he left—the small lab and Fridge area behind the glass wall—to see if everything was in order. He saw his colleagues laboring over their equipment through the glass.

He had spent a lot of hours there, and would be spending more in the next day or so until the critical recombination began.

Collin's eyes wandered over toward the Fridge.

To his astonishment, he thought he saw a white lab coat moving inside the Fridge. Had some fool entered without clearance? He hadn't seen a "space suit," or even the heavy sterile protective clothing or the airtight oxygen helmet that was required for entry.

Collin recalled what this meant.

It meant that should even a moderate accident with the virus—or "spill"—happen, this would automatically require the activation of "catastrophic incineration" within the Fridge, rather than the routine, less lethal emergency procedures. It meant, in short, the black lever. It meant a fiery death to whoever was trapped inside.

As Collin sprinted to the door of the glass wall to see just who the unauthorized person in the cooler was, the general alarm sounded. He could see that the woman in the Fridge was trapped inside, the automatic locking door having been activated. He could also detect that within the cooler a beaker of virus had fallen from its perch on the security shelf—thus triggering the closure.

The intruder, trapped within the cooler, had her face pressed against the glass of its window, pounding on the hardened-glass with her fists.

Collin saw that it was Dr. Astaire-Adams.

115

Having no clearance, she had entered the cooler illegally. As she pounded, blood started to ooze out of her nostrils, then her mouth. Her fists then opened.

The force of her blows against the glass tapered as her strength vanished from a massive hemorrhage. Collin watched the spectacle in disbelief, as he stood—petrified—at the glass wall. The Vampire Virus—even in a weakened state from the attenuation media—had taken only a minute to murder its victim. What was odd about it, though, was that it took so short of time to kill an *adult*, indicating to him that some bizarre transformation of the virus might have occurred while being stored within the Fridge.

He punched the security code into the box hanging on the wall. A strong hand then restrained him. Frank Seaton had arrived, and was blocking Collin's entrance. Frank then broke the glass enclosure on the wall next to the code-box and pulled the black lever. Collin instantly realized that Frank, having not rotated the lever first, would incinerate only the interior of the Fridge—and not the small lab area as well.

Collin could see fire erupting within the huge cooler. Frank then punched in the entry code and both he and Collin entered the Firehouse. They ran up to the window of the Fridge as Dr. Astaire-Adams burned like a marshmallow at a summer bonfire.

In seconds, she was consumed in the fiery inferno—along with the entire contents of the cooler. Collin and Frank moved very close to the window, witnessing the carnage inside as if it were a horror film.

Collin's wondered again if some even more monstrous form of the Vampire Virus had somehow taken hold.

Frank grabbed Collin by the arm. His eyes were savage. "Doctor. I want to confirm. You *did* transfer the final master virus to the adjunct lab area, right?"

"Yes," don't worry Frank, its was moved this morning."

Collin knew that Frank Seaton was right.

His concern about the virus rather than Dr. Astaire-Adams did seem a bit callous, but the project was all-important. Millions of lives depended upon it. There had also been nothing else to do but activate the black lever—they couldn't risk either the spread of the Vampire Virus or the danger to the project.

Now that she was gone, the project was on a sure course to completion—a cold fact but true.

Collin nevertheless felt guilty about the death of Dr. Astaire-Adams.

Then, he thought about the warm snakeskin.

CHAPTER TWENTY-EIGHT

Georgetown, Tuesday afternoon, March 27:

As Collin walked through the historic campus of the Georgetown College, its gothic towers, ivy-covered brick buildings, and tall campanile in the central courtyard failed to impress him—his mind being consumed by the horrors of the event in the lab that morning.

Somehow, he felt that the tragic death should have left him more shaken. Maybe, thought Collin, like the society that raised him and suffered world wars and genocide in recent history, he had become acclimated to death and destruction?

Dr. Charles Childress, Professor of Modern European History, maintained his office on the top floor of the five-story building just behind the new student quadrangle. As Collin walked through the campus on the way to his appointment with the professor, it seemed that nobody else at the lab cared much about the loss of Dr. Astaire-Adams either.

At any rate, he also had distanced himself from her grisly death. Due to the importance of the vaccine project, and its connections with government authorities and important people, the official fallout from the death had also been surprisingly mild. After all, work lay ahead and nothing should get in the way.

The police had showed up but were not admitted into the lab. Instead, the FBI and the Department of Homeland Security took over, and went through the motions of a minimal investigation. Astaire-Adams had known the dangers of the project. She had signed numerous release forms. No crime had been suspected. She had broken procedure. That was it.

Frank Seaton had already been in touch with the project attorneys about a generous out-of-court settlement for the family. The lab had been restored to its working order after a major effort working in first priority mode.

As Collin passed below the gambrel roof of the Faculty Office Building and through the front door, he left behind the gathering dark clouds and light sprinkle of the early afternoon. He walked along a dim hallway and climbed a narrow staircase until he reached Childress' office.

The man specialized in the study of totalitarian societies.

"As I said on the phone, I need research on two historical figures. I tried to Google these people, but didn't get much back." Collin had decided that he wasn't going to go into anything about the "why" of what he was seeking.

He wasn't exactly sure himself. "I'll be glad to pay a private consultant fee, Professor Childress—or donate to the college."

Childress looked at Collin's hands. "Your fingers are shaking, doctor."

The day's events had taken their toll. "Too much caffeine," he fibbed.

Childress nodded in agreement. His eyes questioned. "Sure, I have that problem too."

Collin had taken a liking to the big academic. After Childress had greeted Collin at the door to his office and the usual pleasantries had been exchanged, Collin took a seat across the desk from the professor, who sat in his commodious leather chair, assembling the rusty marine parts on an old, outboard motor that rested upon his large oak desk.

Childress, a portly black man with a shock of grey hair and dark eyebrows, had initiated the meeting by explaining in a very soft voice that he loved boating.

Then, Collin had turned to the business at hand with his shaking fingers.

"I'd like hard copies of primary documents," said Collin. "The faster you can get the information the better."

"Who are the historical subjects?" Childress held a rusted propeller in his hand.

"There are two. One is named Greta Heiss. In nineteen thirty-eight, she was in her late thirties, lab director of the project that first split the atom in Berlin. She's from Teufelheim, Austria. Ever heard of her?"

"Yes, as a matter of fact. She worked with Otto Hahn, right?"

"That's the one." Collin was impressed.

Looking nervously around the office, Collin saw no other evidence of devotion to marine pastimes. He did observe, however, numerous prints and photographs hanging on the walls depicting important individuals in European history. Joseph Stalin, Winston Churchill, Adolf Hitler, Charles de Galle, Bernard Law Montgomery, Margaret Thatcher, and Chairman Mao were only a few of the luminaries represented.

The Professor took his screwdriver and tinkered with a carburetor. "Who's the other person?"

"Her name is Frau Berte Troost. She was a Nazi SS officer—would be born about nineteen hundred—also from Teufelheim. She's a war criminal."

Childress gazed at Collin—raising his eyebrow. He then put down his screwdriver and put his hands together—the fingers intertwining. "Did she work in a death camp?"

"Belzec—she was known as the 'Butcher of Belzec'." Collin took out of his pocket the typed summaries of what he knew about the women. He placed them on the desk in front of Childress. "She developed a poison gas. All I know about them is on these papers that are in front of you."

"Is the gas Diclon-A?"

"Right," answered Collin, leaning forward in his chair and making solid eye contact with his consultant. "Have you ever heard of Frau Troost before?" asked Collin with a strong note of hope in his voice.

"No—and I thought I knew them all." Childress threw his pliers down on his desk and buried his chin in his hands. His eyes shifted thoughtfully.

Collin leaned back in his chair, disappointed. "I'd like to have photos—especially close-ups—also copies of birth certificates, medical records, school papers—anything that may show evidence of birth marks, scars, or other unique physical identifiers. A very close shot of the ear would be helpful as a marker." He emphasized the next sentence with a slightly higher volume to his voice. "The eyes too, of course."

"This won't be easy." Professor Childress pushed the partially assembled motor away from him. "A lot of bombs fell between then and now. Records of these events were purposely destroyed so as not to leave tracks. Besides, we're talking seventy years or more." He coughed. "Of course, the principals are dead, or are very old women."

Collin was silent.

He dug into his pocket and pulled out a recent photo of Dara. He reluctantly handed it to Childress. "If you see anyone who looks like the woman in this photo, be sure to let me know. That was taken six months ago."

The professor stared at the photo. "A looker." Collin could see in his eyes him wondering why Collin had handed him the contemporary picture.

"Dr. De Gise—this will take a while."

"Yes, of course. I'd be grateful for anything you can do for me."

"May I ask why you're doing this?"

Collin stood up to go.

He held out his hand—his answer was soft but firm.

"Let's just say, to settle an argument with myself."

CHAPTER TWENTY-NINE

Northeast of Bethesda, Maryland, Late that Tuesday afternoon:

Collin worked on the master virus in the Firehouse with his clinical staff. Through Collin's expertise, he and his staff had already rendered the master virus less harmful using conventional techniques. This made the hands-on work that remained during the molecular manipulation process slightly less dangerous.

Outfitted in their space suits with safety helmets and special gloves, his three colleagues joined him in carefully manipulating the hardened-glass beakers and tubes of solutions in order to splice the altered Epsilon gene into the perfected master virus DNA. Some new safeguards had already been put in place in the lab since the Astaire-Adams accident, such as padding on the tile floor and a more efficient ventilation system.

"Excuse me Dr. De Gise. There's a man named Gordon Givens on the phone. He insists on talking to you. He sounds very upset." Collin turned up the volume of the emergency cell phone embedded within his "space helmet" that he answered by nodding three times. The lead operator of the lab had rung him through their wireless connection.

"*Who?*"

"He said his name is Gordon Givens. I'm sorry. He's insistent. Should I put him through to you?"

Collin, holding a beaker of trypsin solution in his gloved hands, cussed under his breath. "He's called before. Tell him I'll get back to him."

Three minutes later Collin heard the same three soft tones sound within his helmet. He nodded three times.

"Yes?"

"Gordon Givens says it's an emergency. He wanted me to also tell you that it—and I quote—'involves someone near and dear to you'."

"Tell him to call back in thirty minutes. When he does, put him through to my private office line. I'll be done by then."

Exactly thirty minutes later that is exactly what Gordon Givens did.

"Yes, Dr. De Gise speaking." Collin could hear heavy breathing on the other line. "Yes, who is it?" He pressed the receiver harder against his ear. He had closed his office door and been ready for the blasted call.

The pause was long.

"This is Gordon Givens." Collin noticed a profound change in the cock-sure tone.

"I know. What do you want?"

"I don't blame you for being pissed at me." Collin felt that something was terribly wrong with Gordon. "Is anyone else listening?" he asked.

"Certainly not." Fact was, Collin wasn't sure.

"I mean, are you alone?"

"Yes."

A pause.

"Pray! Find God—get on your knees—and pray."

"What's all this about? Have you lost your senses?"

"You're in danger—we're all in danger! Kill the project!"

"What? Just the other day you wanted germ warfare—."

"—Forgive me. I was duped. We *all* were. They're after me." Collin could hear Gordon's voice crumble with fear.

Gordon's gone off the deep end—some paranoid delusion perhaps?

Collin knew the feeling.

"What are you raving about, man?" asked Collin.

There was only silence.

Collin recalled the message about his loved ones.

"What's this about 'someone near and dear' to me?"

"No . . . no . . . no—not over the phone."

"Why?"

"Because—*your phone is tapped.*"

"My phone's bugged!" Collin was stunned. *Could the Government be spying on me?* The anger welled up within him. "You bastard!"

"I'm sorry. State made me do it, Dr. De Gise. Meet me in your lab parking lot in thirty minutes—the main parking lot next to the highway."

"Tell me *now* you—."

"—I can't talk. The bug in the phone isn't the only reason. They're watching me. I have to go now."

Collin thought that he had better lead him on. He wanted to know if his family was in any danger—and he wanted to know *now.*

What produced this kind of desperation in Gordon—this kind of terror?

"Hello Collin . . . are you still there?"

"Yes Gordon. Tell me about my family, please."

"Be waiting . . . a red sports car. "

"Listen!"

Then, the phone went dead.

As Collin put down his phone, he walked softly over to the door of his office, and quickly opened it. No one had been listening by the door.

But, standing next to the Firehouse, he saw Dara talking quietly to Frank Seaton. They seemed to have a lot to say to each other. He walked toward them. Dara abruptly turned toward him and smiled.

"Hi," she greeted him.

Frank waved and walked away as Collin faced his wife. "I just talked to Gordon Givens," he said.

She tried to give him a perfunctory hug. "What about?"

Collin noticed that Dara was dressed in casual jeans and a light turtleneck sweater—not her usual work attire. She never missed work. He ignored her question.

"Have you talked to Gordon today?"

"No. Why? What's the matter?"

Collin looked over to see where Frank had gone. He had disappeared.

"Nothing, he just seemed upset, that's all. He just called me on the phone." Collin decided to not say anything about the meeting in the parking lot.

Dara nodded. Her eyes flashed with some sort of recognition that Collin couldn't understand. "I've got to get going to work."

"Sure thing."

He noticed that she left without saying goodbye to their daughter.

Collin passed by Stephanie's desk. She was busy rocking, looking at the genetic sequences on her computer screen. Collin stood over her. "Hi love. I'll be gone for about an hour if anyone asks."

Stephanie continued looking at her screen. "What's wrong?"

"Nothing, dear. Things are strange, that's all." He caught himself. She wouldn't understand, he thought. "I've got a meeting. A man I know is upset, and I have to know why."

"Who?"

"No matter."

Stephanie looked up from her screen at Collin. She smiled at him.

"That was mommy. Mommy."

"Yes."

The smile faded. He loved her smile. It seemed all knowing and calm.

Collin thought about his meeting in the parking lot and why Dara might have shown up—and about the timing of the two events.

Collin also wondered what Dara and Frank Seaton had been up to. Frank Seaton had wanted him to take more time away from the lab since work was being accomplished through staff using routine protocols and because vital contributions from him might be necessary later.

Were those the real reasons, or does Frank want me out of the way for some underhanded purpose?

Mostly, Collin wondered what the hell was wrong with Gordon Givens.

In few minutes, he'd find out.

Gordon Givens burned his red Porsche down Wisconsin Avenue. Two other cars swerved to get out of his way. His brown eyes—darting about frantically—glanced back and forth between his rear view mirror and the road.

After racing around corners, he came to a stoplight. Quickly looking both ways into the intersection—he ran the signal and sped off down the road in a crazed fashion. It turned into the two-lane, winding National Health Foundation Highway.

Gordon sped along the tree-lined road parallel to the long parking lot in front of the lab. He could see Collin in the distance in his white lab coat, waiting for him in the parking lot. Gordon, being a crack member of the National Rifle Association and handy with a gun, was prepared for any eventuality. Therefore, as he reached a curve, Gordon took his eyes off the road for a split second to open his glove box and grab his revolver.

The black snake with the yellow eyes greeted him.

The troubling gaze of the creature paralyzed Gordon, as his startled eyes locked onto those of the hideous viper. Gordon hadn't been able to see the huge truck that had passed a car just before the bend. The driver had tried to get back into his own lane, but failed.

Speeding at ninety miles per hour, the huge rig tried to swerve off the road to avoid a head-on collision with Gordon's red Porsche. It was too late. The truck smashed into the sports car and flattened it against a gigantic oak tree on the side of the road.

Both vehicles melded into one massive, fiery, metal junk heap, the red car getting the short end of the encounter. Gordon Givens—still conscious as he lay dying in the flames within the cab—screamed in agony as the inferno consumed him.

Collin, witnessing the horrendous crash, sprinted toward the flaming spectacle to try to help Gordon, even though he knew it was no use. When he got there, he pulled his cell phone out of his pocket and called 911. It seemed he was getting used to this task.

Taking a seat on the curb at the side of the road, Collin watched the flames of the burning wreck.

Gordon disappeared into the fire.

CHAPTER THIRTY

Washington DC, Later that Tuesday afternoon:

"Dr. Bridgestone, I'm sorry. I needed to see you fast. I know you have other patients."

"No, that's what I'm here for. I told you to call whenever you needed me."

"You heard about Gordon Givens, the Assistant Secretary of Defense?"

"Yes, it's all over the news."

"I knew him."

"Oh? What did he tell you?"

Collin was a bit confused by the directness of the question. "You mean, about *what*?"

"Obviously you brought him up in reference to his violent death—the tragic accident. Did he tell you anything in connection with that before he died?"

"No, nothing specifically." Collin had to lie. Gordon Givens had been terrified. He wasn't an easy man to scare, either. He'd also been crazed—maybe about something personal. What could Collin tell the doctor?

"Strange things are happening to me, Dr. Bridgestone. I'm not sleeping well. My work is demanding and in its last stages. People are dying."

"Dying?"

"Yes."

"Tell me about your work first." Bridgestone's voice sounded animated. "What do you mean by the 'last stages'?"

"The end of the project is rapidly approaching and we are close to the goal." Collin thought it odd that Bridgestone wanted to hear about his work first, and not the deaths. "I admit that we've had to cut corners. But, kids are dying."

"Yes. Is that what you meant by 'people are dying'?"

"Not entirely. There's been another accident. One of my colleagues—in the lab—she spilled some virus. She's dead—a horrible way to go."

127

"I understand your concern. After all, she was someone you worked with. Any damage to the lab?" Collin was a bit taken aback by the callousness of the question. The doctor hadn't asked him more about the woman who had died.

"Yes. It could have closed us down. We just managed to escape that."

"Tell me more about the virus itself—your progress. I'm sorry about your colleague, though."

Collin shifted his weight on the couch as he lay there in front of Bridgestone. He glanced over at the tall psychiatrist, his Lincoln-like persona appearing even more so due to the heavy bags under his eyes.

"We're inserting a critical gene into the virus."

"This is stressful—*very* stressful, right? The pressure of perhaps failing." The smooth voice of the doctor was mesmerizing. "Do you feel you'll be successful?"

"Yes."

Collin couldn't understand why Dr. Bridgestone asked about the project so much. Then, he figured that the pressure of the job could be worsening his symptoms. Naturally, that would concern the doctor. Collin felt that, in fact, he might be getting more paranoid. As his sleep deteriorated, perhaps he'd even become a bit delusional.

"We're nearly done with the gene insertion. My staff's handling the technical details."

"Wonderful. So you aren't too worried about failure?"

"Bizarre things have been happening, Dr. Bridgestone."

"Tell me about the bizarre things, Collin."

"I don't know. They seem to center around Dara. I feel like I don't know her anymore. I told you about this last time."

Bridgestone looked down at this notes. "Yes, you said that you've grown apart."

"Yes, and what really concerns me is . . . " Collin sat up from the couch and stared through the window. He could see the laurel tree swaying in the strong wind. He hesitated to bring up his daughter.

"What really concerns you?"

"Somehow I feel that Stephanie's in jeopardy."

"What kind of jeopardy?"

Collin couldn't put it into words. He couldn't yet place it. But, he knew things were terribly wrong. "I don't know really."

Collin knew that he would do whatever necessary to protect Stephanie.

"Do you feel Dara is responsible for these strange things?"

"I don't know."

"How bad is your sleep?"

"Real bad."

"How many hours do you get?"

"Three."

"That's not enough."

"Sometimes it's two. I try to read, do the other things, nothing seems to work."

"Is it affecting your work?"

"Maybe." Collin saw Bridgestone write something down as he sat at his desk. "I had the dream again, doctor."

"The children's hospital?"

"Yes. I didn't like something about it. It reminded me about how I felt at the time it happened—about the murder of the children."

"Yes of course, it was a horrible business, naturally you felt bad at the time—."

"—No, that's not it."

"About your sense of guilt now?"

"No, that's not it either."

"What is it then?"

Collin stared at the tree. Now, a hard rain was hitting it.

"Burning them—I think I liked it."

There was a long pause.

"Nonsense, Collin. Guilt can play odd tricks."

Bridgestone put down his pen and held up two pieces of paper.

"I have two prescriptions. One for you to help your sleep, and the other is for Stephanie. The one for her is the old medicine. I'm starting her on a new one at less dosage very soon—but I want to see her first again before I do."

"How's she doing, doctor?"

"Fine. I don't see her much anymore, as you know. Her regressive, child-like behavior's improving a bit—but she's still very much isolated socially. She's still very non-communicative," said Bridgestone.

"Yes. She is."

"As for you, Collin, I'm glad your project is almost done. You've been working too hard. You need to slow down a bit, or you'll be no good to anyone."

"I've heard that before."

"I'm sure you have."

What do you suggest?"

"Do you have a place to get away? From people, traffic, noise?"

"No, not really."

Bridgestone held up a key with the prescriptions. "He's a key to my cabin in Maryland—actually not far from your laboratory. Well stocked—nobody uses it much. Try it."

The doctor leaned forward over his desk, his hand reaching out to Collin with the key and papers. "I'm writing down the directions."

Collin got off the couch and walked over to Bridgestone to accept the items. He got a good look at the doctor's face—close up. A surprise hit him even though he knew these days anyone could be seen wearing such strange things.

Dr. Jonas Bridgestone had a tiny silver ring though his left eyebrow.

As Collin put the key and papers in his pocket, he stared at the pierced eyebrow.

"Are you surprised?" Bridgestone, noticing Collin's staring, touched above his left eyelid. He blushed slightly.

"I'm sorry—I didn't mean to stare." Collin knew he had a bad habit of over-analyzing physical details of others.

Bridgestone smiled sheepishly. "All the rage!" Bridgestone winked at Collin. He stood up from his desk. "I'm recently divorced. An old, ugly guy like me needs a little fashion. I'll do anything to get laid!"

The doctor laughed heartily as he escorted Collin to the door. "This time I'll see you out."

They shook hands. Collin left.

As Bridgestone's smile faded, he stood by the door for a moment to make sure his patient had really left. He sat back down at his desk and picked up the phone.

"Connect me please to Frank Seaton at the main laboratory. Tell him it's important that Jonas Bridgestone speak to him right away."

CHAPTER THIRTY-ONE

Countryside Northeast of Bethesda, Maryland, Tuesday evening, March 27:

Bridgestone's little A-frame cabin sat on the edge of a very small and rare pine forest in some shallow hills. Surrounded by office buildings, new subdivisions, and strip malls, the rustic oasis neighbored the National Health Foundation laboratory.

Legend had it that this historic area—not far from Washington DC—briefly harbored John Wilkes Booth after he had gunned down Abraham Lincoln in Ford's theater. Dressed in his old jeans, a Washington Senators baseball jersey, and hiking boots, Collin rested on the leather couch in front of the roaring fireplace. Opposite, on a beige-cloth recliner, sat Dara.

"There's something happening, isn't there Dara? Something terrible." The only clue on her face that Collin's question had registered at all was the slight crinkling of her forehead.

"It's something that I don't want to talk to you about. Not now, maybe not ever," she responded with icy finality.

Her voice had been as neutral as if she were discussing whether she preferred milk or cream in her coffee. She looked elegant, even in her old jeans and cotton pullover jersey. "Not until things shake out."

Collin thought that she had the look of someone who was possessed by something, rather than indifferent.

But possessed by what, and to what purpose?

Instead of looking at each other, they both stared into the huge flames—their faces illuminated, casting shadows against the wood-paneled walls. The only other light source in the combined living room and kitchen space was one bare light bulb hanging over the potbellied stove, next to two closed doors that led to the two bedrooms.

"What about Stephanie?" Collin asked. At this juncture, he was more concerned about his daughter. He didn't know exactly what was going on with Dara, but he couldn't tolerate her growing hostility toward Stephanie.

"What about her?" Dara glared at Collin. He saw a look in her eye that he had never seen before. "Has she told you anything that I should be aware of?"

Collin wondered what exactly Dara was getting at. "No, she hasn't."

"I want to ask you a question."

"Yes?"

"What does *Alois* mean to you?" She studied his reaction closely.

What a bizarre question, Collin thought. "Nothing at all. What's that?"

Dara's piercing gaze cut right thought him before she looked away in disgust.

Collin looked around the room at the deer antlers and bearskins hanging on the walls, ugly reminders—to him anyway—of the violence against innocent animals. He was tired of violence of any kind, even mental violence that happed all too often in families—even his family.

Stephanie—dressed in a yellow ski-jacket and black nylon pants—came out of one of the bedrooms. For her, thought Collin, this was high fashion. She had borrowed those clothes from Dara. She glanced at Dara, and then walked up to her father.

Dara, squirming in her chair at the sight of her daughter, got up and abruptly marched out of the room and into the other bedroom. She slammed the door behind her. Collin could hear the lock click.

"Daddy, mommy's not well."

Collin rose from the couch and put his arm around her. "We'll be done with the project soon. Then we'll all take a nice vacation. It'll be fine, you'll see. Let's enjoy the outdoors here."

Collin could sense that she didn't believe him. He didn't really believe what he had said either.

"What did mommy say to you?" she asked. "Say to you?"

"Nothing." Collin looked over at the kitchen. "Let's drive down the road and get something for dinner. I noticed a little market coming up here."

They went down the dirt pathway to Collin's old, red beamer. The huge birch trees around the perimeter of the cabin gave off a strong scent that reminded Collin of his hunting days as a boy. Even though he was a crack shot, he had long since given up that sport. His commando days—and sniping— had put him off anything like that.

"Look daddy. The moon. How odd. It's got an orange glow around it." Twilight had given way to darkness. Collin studied the strange halo.

It had turned into a clear night. The stars were bright. The moon, between a quarter and half-size, had a brighter orange rim than the previous night.

"Strange—isn't it?" Collin stopped at the car door. "They say the ozone layer and global warming are causing that," said Collin.

Just as Stephanie opened the door on the passenger side, she screamed at the top of her lungs. Collin dashed around the car. His daughter's eyes were fastened upon the small creek running beside the cabin.

In the soft, shining light of the moon Collin could detect a large black snake slithering along the rocky creek bed. Stephanie screamed again as Collin embraced her, keeping an eye on the snake. It disappeared under a large boulder.

"It's just a snake honey."

Her arms were fastened around her father's neck, and she wouldn't let go.

"That's all right, honey. It's gone now."

Stephanie released her grip and looked around, making sure that the snake had indeed vanished. "Daddy, let's go home. That's the same snake as was in the kitchen!"

"Love, it was just a plain old snake. It wouldn't harm you." Collin hadn't had a good look at it, but doubted that it had the same strange qualities.

"I want to go home, daddy. I have to work on my calculations for tomorrow. My calculations need work."

"All right."

"Now!"

Stephanie shook from fright.

"Let's pack up. I'll go tell your mother."

Collin didn't think about the snake as he walked back into the cabin. He thought about his crumbling relationship with his wife. He thought about the weird question that Dara had asked him just minutes before. "Alois—what could that be?"

It hurt him deeply, but he suspected that his marriage was doomed.

CHAPTER THIRTY-TWO

Georgetown, Later that Tuesday evening:

At home, Collin labored over his calculations for the next morning's lab procedures. The computations were tricky. Vivaldi's haunting cantata, *Cessate, omai cessante,* played softly from his CD-player as he worked. It helped him to think.

Sitting at his desk in the study, Collin tapped his computer keys to bring up the necessary mathematical equations on his screen. His cell phone rang. It was rare to get a call at that hour, even from his lab.

He pulled the phone from the drawer of his desk, and looked at the number on the register.

The number belonged to Professor Childress.

He took the call.

"I've been at it all day. It's . . . bizarre, Dr. De Gise." Childress sounded like a doctor who had found an interesting but potentially dangerous spot on his own chest x-ray. "I get a strange feeling about this research."

"Please tell me what you found, Professor."

"Frau Troost is connected to Reinhard Heydrich of the Nazi SS, who was also known as 'The Blond Beast'. Heydrich attended the infamous Wanssee Conference in Berlin in January, nineteen forty-two, at a Nazi SS villa on the lake."

"Go on."

"That didn't surprise me. What *did* surprise me was that Greta Heiss was *also* connected to Heydrich."

Collin thought about that. Not being an expert in history, he didn't know what to make of it. Ziggie Einbaum had revealed some of that information also. "Yes, so?"

"Now, the *first* wife of Joseph Stalin—the Russian communist dictator who murdered an estimated thirty million of his own people—and Reinhard Heydrich's *father*—who was a music teacher—were also connected."

"That sounds like quite a coincidence. Is it relevant to my case?"

"I'll explain. Stalin's brother-in-law, Alexander, lived in Germany and probably Austria as well for about a year. He studied music under Heydrich's father. This connection between a honcho of the Final Solution and Stalin has never been documented before."

"What's the significance?"

"Listen, Stalin's first wife—the sister of Alexander—is said to be the one who helped introduce the young tyrant to Bolshevism. She also influenced him in other ways. This is supposed to be a direct quote from Stalin himself at her funeral: ' . . . *This creature softened my heart of stone. She died and with her died my last warm feelings for humanity'*." This wife, whoever she was, perhaps drove Stalin to later kill millions of people."

"What are you suggesting?"

"Guess *where* Stalin's brother-in-law studied music?" asked Childress.

" You tell me."

"*Teufelheim*—that's what binds Heydrich, Heiss, Troost, and Stalin together." The professor paused. "Specifically, Teufelheim Castle is where Alexander took his lessons. Alexander had quite an influence upon his sister—quite a talented fellow . . ."

Collin digested that, and it went down like week old herring. He then heard something strange in the background at the other end of the call. He listened carefully as Childress continued. " . . . Alexander was also said to be a great scientist, and instructed his sister. Young Heydrich, also an accomplished musician, had taken music lessons in the castle as well. Later, the SS used the castle as their mystical getaway."

"What else?"

"I dug up more facts. It seems that Greta Heiss and Troost . . .well, I don't know how to say it . . . "

"Just spit it out."

"Dr. De Gise—they appear to be the *same* person. It sounds crazy, I know."

Not that crazy, Collin thought. He almost mentioned what was also on his mind—that his wife Dara could be the double for both women. He still couldn't quite grasp what Childress was trying to tell him.

"Dr. Childress, can you put it all together for me? I'm very tired."

"This is weird—even supernatural."

"What?"

"Does the symbol of a triangle with a circle at one point and a dot at its other two points mean anything to you?"

Collin rose from his desk. "Where did you see that?"

There was a long pause on the other line.

Collin turned off the music. He sensed a growing desperation in the professor's voice. "If you found other evidence, tell me!"

"You know that photo of the woman you gave me. You asked me to find out if anyone in my historical research resembled her. I found two old photos—almost a hundred years apart. I then put them with the photos of Troost and Heiss. Did you say that photo you gave me of the woman was taken six months ago? I'll tell you, all . . ."

The other line went dead.

"Are you still there, Childress?"

He was gone.

What had happened? Maybe it's a bad reception area. Collin called back, but all he got was voicemail.

Collin mulled over the strange conversation. He didn't quite know what to make of it. It didn't enhance his cool any, that's for sure. The Professor had found something that obviously had shaken him up pretty bad. He thought he knew what the professor was going to say, but he put that horrendous thought out of his head for now.

Collin needed sleep. He'd talk to Childress first thing in the morning. The last important step in the development of the vaccine would begin tomorrow, right after the critical gene splice—the all-important process of recombination. Collin knew that he must have a clear head.

After all, countless lives were at stake.

CHAPTER THIRTY-THREE

Georgetown College, Wednesday morning, March 28:

Professor Charles Childress sat at his desk in his faculty office located on the fifth floor of the college's Faculty Office Building. He quickly pulled out an envelope from the drawer and stuffed a piece of paper into it. He sealed it with shaking hands, and hurriedly labeled it.

The window behind his desk lay wide open, and though a frosty morning breeze blew the other papers off his desk, he barely noticed. His bloodshot eyes darted fearfully around the room as if he suspected an armed intruder to appear at any second. Unshaven, hungry, and thirsty, with his wrinkled dress shirt open at the collar with no tie, he looked to be in desperate straits.

When he placed the envelope on the corner of his desk, he startled. He glanced over at the locked door to his office. He thought he had heard the knob rattle.

He rose slowly from his chair, and inched toward the door.

Hearing another noise behind him—this time a rustling sound—he spun around.

Where had it come from?

Maybe it came from the closet? He saw nothing out of the ordinary, except for a sheet of paper whirling above his desk. He realized, with some relief, that it had only been the wind playing with the papers again.

As he resumed his progress toward the door, he heard the rattling again.

He could see the doorjamb had been loose near the knob, and that reassured him. The pressure difference in the room—caused by the open window and the gusts of wind—had shifted the door back and forth against the metal latch—creating the annoying sound.

That's all it was. He let out a deep sigh of relief.

Then, fear had gripped him anyway. Childress knew that his secretary would be arriving an hour late that morning. He hated leaving the office empty during business hours. It didn't matter.

This was, after all, an emergency. He would leave immediately. Strange things had been happening to him all night.

Then, he heard a faint hissing sound coming from the closet.

Could it be the old heating pipes on this unseasonably cold morning, he wondered? He ran to the closet and threw open the door. It's nothing, he reassured himself, just like the other noises.

He scanned the inside of the closet, and his weary eyes fixed upon the long black object resting on the shelf. It moved. That's strange, he thought.

My God, it's a snake!

He froze.

The serpent raised its shiny, diamond-shaped head as the ebony skin—with the tiny yellow triangles—slithered and undulated toward him, as if it were floating.

Childress' gaze fastened upon the bright yellow eyes that seemed to have human intelligence, but no human capacity for mercy.

The vertical slits in the eyes slowly expanded and then contracted as they sized him up. The snake opened its wide mouth—displaying two, very long and curved fangs.

The viper struck in a flash. The teeth clamped onto his neck. Childress stumbled back and fell to the floor, writhing in agony, screaming as the blood gushed from his neck onto the linoleum. The creature released its fangs, and then slithered back to the closet—disappearing from sight.

Childress slowly got to his knees, his vision blurred. After great effort, he got to his feet.

The professor jammed his hands over his ears. His face contorted. The shrill noise that filled his head was deafening—splitting his eardrums. His thoughts collided with the evil sound.

Stop it! Please, make the noise stop! Oh please.

He turned, staggering in the direction of the open window. The snake—gone—nevertheless still controlled him, commandeering his willpower. Only that beast could stop the terrible noise.

It had to end—that's all Childress cared about—*make the deafening noise stop!*

140

He stumbled, but he had almost made it to the open window. When his eyes fixated upon the merciful means of escape, joy came to him. All he could think about was ending his torment, and the cool, refreshing air wafting from the window.

The belfry in the campanile rang nine times.

Collin strode through the quadrangle that was bordered by the University's brick buildings. The quad had filled with students pre-registering for classes.

He walked briskly through the crowd, looking up at the five-story faculty building where Dr. Childress's office was located. His window faced the quad from the corner of the fifth floor. Collin noticed that, unlike the other windows in the building, it was wide open on this very cold morning.

The chilling wind rushed around Collin like a plunge into arctic seas. Very strange weather, thought Collin. He buttoned up his brown overcoat and quickened his pace over the cement walkway.

From the corner of his eye he noticed—for a split second—a bulky, dark object moving overhead from the fifth floor.

He saw one of the students point. He looked up.

There was Childress at the window. He waved to the students like an intoxicated fool. Even from this distance, Collin noticed the blood running from his neck.

The big black man crawled out on the ledge of the window.

At first, a few of the students screamed, then fell silent and motionless, peering up at the strange figure crammed against the side of the tall building, greeting them—with an empty smile—as if he were on a float in the Tournament of Roses Parade.

Collin just stood there, looking up at the horrific event in total disbelief.

Then, Childress dove onto the cement from sixty feet—head first.

Collin darted backward. He had judged correctly. The body landed in the spot where he had just stood. After he heard the splat on the cement, he saw that Childress lay only three feet from him—in a pool of blood.

His body had bounced a couple of feet, like a tennis ball, when he had landed.

141

Collin couldn't look away, even though the sight of the cracked skull and the enucleated eyeball gripped him with nausea. The arresting sight blunted the shrillness of the students' screams, as though the sense of sight had overwhelmed the others.

The professor lay motionless on the ground for what seemed like an eternity.

The poor man's intact eye—resting in the lifeless skull— glared at Collin.

In the glint of its numbing, fish-eyed stare, there appeared to be a warning.

CHAPTER THIRTY-FOUR

Northeast of Bethesda, Maryland, Later that Wednesday morning, March 28:

"We did it. We really did it!"

Frank Seaton was a bit tipsy as he strutted about the main lab, champagne bottle in hand, filling the glasses of the reveling white coats that had donned funny hats—just like during New Year's Eve. *Happy Days Are Here Again* played over the speaker system.

A large banner on the wall proclaimed: "RECOMBINATION IS HERE!"

A table had been set up with a huge chocolate cake, plastic utensils, a coffee urn, and bottles of bubbly. Collin sat at his desk in his white lab coat, staring at the cake from across the room. After a couple of hard hours gene splicing that morning, he had finished.

Childress had died a horrible death, like the others. But, life had to go on, thought Collin. He knew he was in the middle of something horrible. His sense of doom was heavy indeed. But, it was just a feeling, and surrounding him in the lab was evidence of his groundbreaking scientific achievements. His pride made up for a lot of bad things.

Stephanie sat across from him at her desk, wearing her usual Redskins varsity jacket, carefully studying the people in the room. They were the only two not drinking. Collin had never seen Frank drink alcohol before, let alone guzzle it in the laboratory.

"Why don't you have a glass, Doctor De Gise?" Frank asked as he stood over him, swaying. "Just a tiny one!"

Collin glanced at him. "Too early, Frank. Maybe later." He winked at his daughter. Stephanie giggled.

Many of the staff came up to Collin to shake hands. There had been many dead ends and setbacks during the two years, and then the final disaster with Dr. Astaire-Adams. Then, there had been Gordon Givens' horrible death near the parking lot. These hadn't been the only deaths during the project, but they were the most dramatic.

Collin couldn't help but think about Astaire-Adams during the celebration as he looked into the distance and through the glass wall. The Firehouse had been a necessary evil, he concluded.

The Dante button will never have to be used—thank goodness.

Collin marveled at how soon after the torching of the Fridge, it had been brought back to its pristine condition. It's as though the tragedy with Astaire-Adams had never happened. Then, he saw Dr. Stanley Chu marching toward him, his face glum as usual.

No one had been sadder—then more livid—about the untimely death of his colleague than Chu. Collin knew that there would be trouble ahead.

Chu stopped about two feet from Collin. He glared down at him. "I saw your log, Dr. De Gise. I don't like it. The splicing today had no strict controls!"

"Get off it Stanley. I used the standard controls. It went flawlessly."

"Also, no one else signed the log. Stephanie helped you."

"As Director, I'm exempt—."

"—That's only a technicality!"

"Nevertheless . . ."

Frank Seaton, overhearing Chu as he chatted with revelers, turned his head toward Stanley and scowled. "Ah come on, Dr. Chu."

"I'm sorry Frank, but I have a duty to the public. We must maintain the integrity of the program."

Collin waved Chu away from him, and then pointed at Frank Seaton. "That's the man to bitch to."

Stanley Chu looked at Frank Seaton. Frank just shrugged.

Chu was determined to have more procedural rights with the final virus. "Someone needs to mind the store. I demand auditing authority."

Frank threw up his hands. "All right Stanley, anything you say!"

Stephanie sat up in her chair and took note of Frank's response. So did Collin. It was an unusual step, thought Collin, but not a big deal. After all, Stanley Chu had a security clearance, and was fully credentialed.

Chu had also been trained in safety procedure. Collin could see why Frank Seaton didn't give a damn, though. If Chu wanted to butt his head in during these last couple of days of the vaccine project, no harm done. What could he do, after all? At most, he'd file a negative report and it would probably be round-filed by Frank.

One of the staff appeared at Collin's desk. "Sir, it's the First Lady on line one."

Frank and Collin exchanged looks. Stanley Chu's lips formed an O.

"She wants to congratulate you, Dr. De Gise," said the staffer.

Collin knew he had better take that one.

Shonda Rice O'Neal was not only the money tree behind the project, but an important one. She also protected Collin from the encroachments of the germ warfare crowd. That effort hadn't ended with the death of Gordon Givens, by any means.

Collin saw the phone dial on his desk light up. He lifted the receiver. Mrs. O'Neal's soft but determined mid-western voice came over the line.

"Collin?"

"Good morning, First Lady."

"Congratulations."

"Thank you."

"Three days to go, right?"

"Yes."

"Then it grows fast, right? Then we have the vaccine at work for the children?"

"Yes, very fast. Stephanie helped me with the calculations on the final solution media."

"Then, we keep changing it, right?"

"The master virus and vaccine? Yes, we come out with different serotypes to combat the mutating strains of the wild viruses in Africa."

"Wonderful. Another Nobel Prize—for both of you—you and Stephanie! How about that?"

"Well . . ."

"You've done the human race a great service, Collin. The children of the world thank you. You've reached your potential. You don't know how much."

"You're very kind, Mrs. O'Neal."

"Goodbye."

Collin then realized that Dara hadn't called him during his moment of triumph. She used to call him all the time to wish him well. Those days were over, he realized.

His thoughts left his wife and went back to his great achievement—his, and Stephanie's.

"What are you thinking, daddy?" Stephanie walked over to his desk and put her hand on his shoulder. "What are you thinking?"

"I'm thinking what a great feeling it is to be at the helm of scientific milestones that will change our world. But, it wasn't without cost."

CHAPTER THIRTY-FIVE

Georgetown, The Black Peacock, Late Wednesday morning:

"I've located a very interesting painting, darling. It should be here soon." Lilith had on one of her black smocks with the oriental collar. She wore a scarf around her head with patterns of the moon and stars on it. Despite her strong sense of theater, Collin knew she was frightened.

Collin shuffled past the piles of old oil paintings in her loft, settling upon a particularly interesting one of a cathedral consumed in flames. He held it up for Lilith to see as she sat behind her desk doing paperwork.

She eyed the piece. "The East European stuff's larded with forgeries."

As Collin took a step, his shoe almost crushed a Prussian landscape. Dressed in a navy blazer and woolen pants, he was too warm for comfort again. It seemed like his body temperature was always a bit higher than what was normal.

"Watch your step! You crush it, you buy it." Lilith held up a completed order form. "My distributor found a religious piece. He claims it's nine hundred years old. There's a certain woman in it. " The piece of paper shook as she held it.

"And you're just dying to tell me she has red hair, aren't you?" Collin's eyes met Lilith's for a fleeting moment. He knew that Lilith's agenda wouldn't go away.

"I saw a picture of it on line—it's hard to see anything much."

"Let me see it then on the computer." Collin browsed for another painting.

Lilith's sharp eyes darted over her reading glasses. "No, I want the real thing. It's a big painting, too."

Lilith rose from her desk. She marched over to Collin and helped him rummage through the musty old pieces. As she did, she dwelled upon the series of strange and violent events that they had just discussed in detail over coffee. She thought that Collin had been backsliding due to the euphoria of his success with the project. She accused him of ignoring the danger signals inherent in what he had just described to her over the last hour. Ever since the Greta Heiss discovery, Lilith had gone from skeptic to hanging judge.

"How about the sharks in the tank?" She held up a painting for his approval—shaking it in his face. "How about Childress?"

He glanced at the piece and shook his head. "I don't think so." She plopped it back down on the pile.

She grabbed another particularly dark and gothic picture. "Frau Troost and Greta Heiss; that's too much to be just a coincidence."

Collin shook his head at the piece. "No sale."

She held up another. "How about this gruesome one of angels wasting a sinner? What about the fact that they're both from the same town as your wife? Aside from the fact, of course, that they're both dead ringers of her too."

"I'm not buying yet."

"You don't like angels with bloody swords?"

"Forget the paintings. I know you're not really trying to sell me anything Lilith, except that there's something supernatural going on—ever since Greta Heiss. That's just what it is—a coincidence—so far at least. No dice."

She plucked another out of a pile. "What about Barry Bledsoe and the assassin? What about Gordon Givens and Carmen? What about Dr. Astaire-Adams? What about all the rest of it? And, there's always the weird triangle, of course. "

He looked at her gravely. "Right."

"Is that all you can say?"

Collin took the painting from her and put it down.

He looked down at the floor. "I'll be back on medication again soon. How much of this is in my mind, I have to ask myself."

"Oh Collin! You're no crazier than I am." Lilith smiled.

"That's what worries me." Collin then broke out in laughter.

Collin had no rational explanation for what was going on. He only knew that sometimes in life strange events are clustered to give them the aura of abnormality. Moreover, he knew his history of delusions and paranoia, so he had to check himself when considering wild theories. Maybe he had gone too far in the condemnation of his wife. Deep down, he knew there was something to what Lilith was saying. But, until the smoking gun was pointed right at him, he would wait until the vaccine was made, then come to some conclusions when he was under less stress.

Collin headed toward the stairs, thinking that maybe part of him still loved his wife and he hoped that somehow things would turn out. Lilith followed him.

"All right. We've played around," said Collin, "but I need something irrefutable."

"I'm still tracking down that book *Faces Behind Shadows*. You'll get it—even if I have to mail the darn thing to that stupid lab that you're camped out in all the time!"

They reached the ground floor, and Lilith left Collin to help a customer at the front of the bookstore. She blew him a kiss as she walked away from him.

Poor Lilith. She was terrified, but she hid it well, thought Collin.

The fact was, despite what he had told her, so was he.

CHAPTER THIRTY-SIX

Washington DC, Wednesday afternoon, March 28:

Collin, having just walked in and chosen his table at the restaurant, stared at the wrinkled, hand-addressed envelope resting next to his silverware. He was meeting Ziggie Einbaum for an early dinner and had arrived at the famous eatery a little early.

The envelope on the table had been addressed to him in in a trembling hand. He could see that it had already been opened, and then resealed. He opened it and emptied its contents onto his bare plate. One piece of plain paper fell out.

He examined the piece of paper. One word and four numbers had ben printed on it in longhand. Professor Charles Childress had written those characters just before he died: "SATO 1906."

Collin mulled the information over.

Sato—nineteen-o-six—what could that be? The number could be a date. It could be part of an address, I suppose. The word 'Sato' could be a place, a person, or an event, or anything really.

Whatever it is, thought Collin, I can't make anything of it.

Collin considered the circumstances. Why would Charles spend some of his last moments on earth trying to tell me this gibberish? The answer of course is that he had no time, so he scribbled a message as fast as he could.

So, who was threatening him?

The Georgetown Police Department hadn't thought that anything in Childress' death was amiss. In fact, the professor had suffered from a long history of depression. They thought it had been a "show" suicide. Childress' devoted administrative assistant had personally delivered the envelope to Collin after the authorities had "cleared it," apparently the police not thinking it very important.

As Collin sat alone in The Old Vienna restaurant near the FBI building in Washington, he turned those thoughts over. Tucking the piece of paper away in his pocket, he scanned the menu of the Austrian restaurant that had been frequented by the likes of "Black Jack" Pershing and Teddy Roosevelt.

Collin had changed into his brown cardigan with leather elbow patches, white shirt, and striped tie, and grey slacks. While waiting, he observed the restaurant's antique lamps and heavy wooden furniture that complemented the dark oil paintings hanging on the walls. Mostly pieces depicting eighteenth-century battle scenes, the grim pictures reminded him of Europe's self-destructive heritage. With the dim, chandelier lighting, the restaurant's whole atmosphere lent, in Collin's mind, a forbidding cast to the Old World charm.

Dara had chosen the restaurant, and Collin had scheduled to meet her for an early dinner at four o'clock. Her voice had been gritty on the phone, and she had said that she had something "imperative" to tell him.

He could guess what that was. She would be leaving him, he thought with some sadness. Despite recent events, he still felt a terrible sense of loss.

Collin glanced at his watch, five minutes 'til. Unknown to his wife, he had invited Ziggie Einbaum—the Belzec death-camp survivor—to the join them. This, thought Collin, promised to be a revealing evening—just as TNT is more interesting when you put a lighter to it.

The photo of Frau Troost—the one Collin had seen in *Faces Behind Shadows*—had not been a close-up. To him, the likeness to his wife had been overwhelming, but perhaps a fluke. The same could be said of the Greta Heiss picture. Childress' comments over the phone were somewhat damning, but unclear in their significance. Maybe, Collin hoped, Einbaum won't even notice a resemblance. Maybe he doesn't even remember what Troost had looked like in the first place. Maybe he'll prove it *couldn't* be his wife.

Mr. Einbaum stood to gain from the encounter also, rationalized Collin. The old man had been interested in Dara's hometown in Austria—Teufelheim. He was even obsessed. Maybe he would obtain valuable information during the meeting, to offset the negative potential of the encounter?

Collin ordered a scotch from the waiter. Despite his rationalizations, he still didn't like the setup. The alcohol might help take the sting out of his underhandedness. He drank up.

Dara strode in. He put up his hand to guide her. She noticed it, but didn't smile. Collin's eyes traced her progress from the crowded entrance through the spacious room. The black chiffon dress, open in the back, showed off her trim athletic figure and radiant skin. As an accent, she wore the ruby necklace he had given her on their tenth anniversary. It highlighted her lustrous, red hair. He also noted the effect that a red necklace might have on Einbaum.

As she walked past the men seated near Collin's table with her forward leaning stride, she turned heads. At that moment, Collin wondered how he could ever have suspected her of anything so bizarre and hateful as what had been happening over the last few days.

She sat down beside Collin, not looking at him as she spoke. "It's been a long time since we've eaten here."

Collin glanced down at the dinner table to study her elegant hands. Her nails were painted bright red, which reminded him yet again that Frau Troost had gruesomely worn red fingernails around her neck as a souvenir necklace. Suddenly, Collin felt nauseated.

"How did work go?" he asked his wife without conviction.

"We're in the testing phase of a new weapons system," said Dara flatly. "I've got something to tell you, Collin."

"What's that?"

"It's about us. It'll hold it for now." Dara's eyes widened as they tracked something approaching her from behind Collin. "What an adorable old dear—I think he's lost," she said.

Collin turned his head. It was Ziggie Einbaum. "No, he's not lost. I forgot to tell you—Mr. Einbaum is joining us for dinner. Sorry, it was short notice."

If there had been something brutal and wicked between her and this old man, she didn't let on. Collin stood up and walked over to greet Einbaum.

Ziggie smiled broadly, not yet acknowledging Dara, who remained seated at the table—her sparkling eyes fastened upon him. Collin recognized the lively brown eyes of his dinner guest that had no eyebrows, the thin grey mustache, the dapper three-piece suit, and the slightly labored breathing. His nervous tic of closing his eyes reminded Collin of the poor man's past trauma.

Collin motioned to a space at the table, directly across from Dara, so the old man could have a full view of her. Before Collin sat down however, he wanted Mr. Einbaum to meet her up close—and to kiss her hand—with the red fingernails. Collin was sure he would do this, given his advanced age and Continental upbringing.

Collin took him gently by his arm and ushered him over to Dara. She got to her feet and held out her hand. Her expression, observed Collin, remained neutral.

As Collin stood beside Einbaum, he motioned to his wife, "Ziggie, this is Dara—Mrs. De Gise. As I told you, she was born in Teufelheim, Austria."

Dara extended her lovely hand—the fingernails bright red and lustrous under the light of the chandelier.

"It's so nice of you to join us, Mr. Einbaum." Dara smiled innocently.

Ziggie bowed his head. He took her extended hand and kissed it. He then smiled as his lively brown eyes reflected the pleasure in beholding such a beautiful woman. He didn't let go.

Collin relaxed. Studying the two closely, there was absolutely no sign of recognition from either. They appeared to be meeting as complete strangers.

Then, the old man's eyes unexpectedly smoldered. He pulled Dara closer to his face and studied her red fingernails. Collin witnessed Mr. Einbaum's eyes transforming into cinders of burning rage. The old man started to cough violently.

Dara, her eyes turning from those of a charmed hostess into the look of threatened prey, quickly yanked her hand away. She stepped back out of striking range.

Einbaum studied her face closely. He then let out a growl.

Dara looked at Collin. Collin stepped deftly between them.

Ziggie started to shake violently. Having caught his breath, he then yelled. His eyes pierced through Dara. "*Du!*"

He coughed louder. He pointed a shaking finger at her. "Butcher of Belsec!"

Collin looked around the huge restaurant. He noticed the shocked patrons. He saw that Ziggie had shifted his eyes down to the knife lying next to him on the table.

The enraged old man's withered hand quickly groped for the weapon. Dara increased her distance from him.

"Collin! He's mad!" she exclaimed.

Then, all of a sudden, Ziggie Einbaum let out a big scream as he clutched his chest. He spun and fell over backwards—crashing down on the dinner table.

He lay motionless in a pile of plates and glasses, his eyes wide but expressionless.

CHAPTER THIRTY-SEVEN

Georgetown, Later that Wednesday evening, March 28:

Collin couldn't sleep. He had awakened after only two hours.

He had gone to the hospital after Ziggie Einbaum had crashed at the restaurant, and the old man had died of a massive heart attack. He felt partially responsible for exposing him to such a traumatic situation. When Collin had finally arrived home, Dara was sound asleep.

The old man had recognized his wife as Frau Troost, and the gruesome fact haunted Collin. It pushed him to dig deeper, and fast. Is it possible that Ziggie had just recognized only the coincidental *likeness* of his wife to the Nazi officer, and that upset him enough to cause a massive myocardial infarction?

Maybe.

Collin lay in bed with his back to his wife, two feet from her. He realized that he hadn't dreamt that night. It was as if his body had taken over his real life, so he needn't live through his dreams anymore.

The information on Charles Childress' note went through his head: "Sato—1906". Unable to go back to sleep, Collin quietly slipped out of bed. He left the bedroom and walked down the hallway to his study. He fired up his computer and then went online to the search site.

He typed the following word in the search box: "Sato."

The returned hypertext displayed something about a famous football player who had been suspected of double homicide. Below that was something about the Duke of Windsor's dog in 1934, below that something about a string of comedies starring a famous comedian, and below that was a line or two about a famous nudist beach in the Bahamas.

Collin scanned through a hundred more hypertexts screen after screen, recognizing nothing that would be of use—nothing that seemed remotely helpful in unraveling the mystery of the odd information that had been left behind by Professor Childress minutes before he had died.

He tried the search in German, his fluency just good enough. Again, nothing valuable came up.

Kaiser Wilhelm's second cousin apparently had named his sailboat *Sato*, but that fact was certainly of no use. The list of historical events then displayed for the year 1906, but that offered no clues either.

Then, Collin typed in the numbers *and* the letters. His eyes scanned the long row of hypertext:

"A NOVEL IS BORN . . . "

"SAN FRANCISCO EARTHQUAKE . . . "

Nothing helpful.

The same with the rest:

"CARUSO ALMOST DIES IN SAN FRANCISCO EARTHQUAKE . . . "

"GERMANY EXPANDS ITS NAVAL FLEET . . ."

"AMERICA EXPORTS HOT DOGS FOR THE FIRST TIME . . . "

Collin, clueless, reached for his mouse to click off the site when he remembered what Charles had said about the Russian dictator Joseph Stalin. Charles had been excited about the news surrounding the tyrant. Collin wondered if a clue lay buried with Stalin.

Scrolling down the screen, he saw little about Joseph Stalin. He clicked past three more fresh screens. This was useless too, he lamented. Then, he came upon a strange name and the words "Russian bride."

Maybe this is it?

"AKATERINA IVANIDSE—RUSSIAN BRIDE MARRIED IN 1906 TO . . ."

Collin's heart raced. He knew that Childress hadn't known about the birthmark, but he may have seen a close-up photo of Stalin's wife that matched the photo of Dara he had given him— *matched too well.*

Collin punched in the hypertext and it immediately brought him to an online encyclopedia. In the first paragraph, he read the following words: " . . . Akaterina Ivanidse, first wife of Joseph Stalin, who was said to have indoctrinated the young Georgian about Bolshevism, was also reported to have 'broken his heart' when she died of typhus in 1907. She and Joseph Stalin had married in 1906 . . . "

He remembered Childress had told him something similar.

He found what he had been frantically searching for when he came to the fifth paragraph of the online history "'Stalin's first wife was also known as Sato'."

So, this is what the word "Sato" meant on Childress' little note—Joseph Stalin's first wife!

He rapidly typed in the search box the full name "Akaterina Ivanidse" with the added parameters: "Joseph Stalin," "photo," "Sato," "1906," and "wife."

He got back twelve entries, all grainy, black-and-white images shot at long distances from the female subject. Most of them also had a young Joseph Stalin in them, so the central figure in the shot was Stalin, and not Akaterina—or Sato.

A large, close-up photo of Dara's face then stared back at him—dressed in Russian clothes of the 1906 period—her eyes clearly visible. The photo was labeled "Sato—1906". The scarf that partially obscured her forehead failed to conceal the familiar, sparkling eyes. Chillingly, this woman looked just like Dara.

Collin centered the arrow of his mouse over the left eye of the image.

Collin zoomed in on the left eye. He zoomed in again. Then he did it again. The round iris—the part of the eye surrounding the pupil—filled the screen.

There he saw it—the definitive marker.

The birthmark—the black dot—was at six o'clock in the left eye, just like Dara's. Only one in ten million could have that mark.

They have to be the same person!

Collin just sat there for what seemed like hours, but really was only seconds. He had found his unshakable proof, and in that instant, his life had dissolved.

Who is this woman I'm married to?

He thought again about Dara and their loving life together. How they made love and had raised an innocent daughter together.

Then, he thought about Frau Troost and her gruesome, fingernail necklace. He thought about Ziggie Einbaum's little daughter way back in 1943—and her tiny painted fingernail that had been torn out with pliers. He thought about the souvenir necklace that probably was his wife's.

He also thought about the millions of innocent people who had been murdered by Joseph Stalin, whose brutal persona had been influenced by none other than his mate.

And what about all the tragic deaths that have been happening now?

Collin then bent over his waste can and vomited.

CHAPTER THIRTY-EIGHT

Georgetown, The Black Peacock, Thursday morning, March 29:

"Well, I don't know who she is darling. But it seems that she's not a nice person. Put these together with Frau Troost, and it's not exactly a model for *Little Women*."

As Lilith studied the printed images of Greta Heiss and Sato, the poised tone of her patrician voice started to sound uneven.

A blustery morning with high, cold winds, the worst seen in decades, pilloried Georgetown. Collin could hear the branches pound against the bookstore's stained-glass windows as they sat at Lilith's desk up in the loft.

Earlier that morning he had stopped in briefly at the lab to see that everything was all right, got back on the highway, and headed for his meeting with Lilith at the bookstore. Collin found that the solitude in his car, notwithstanding the poor driving conditions, helped him think through the nightmare that had become his life.

Lilith picked up the blow-up image of Sato's birthmark—the tiny black dot in the iris of her left eye at the six o'clock position. She held it up to the light.

"How rare is this birthmark, Collin?"

"Rare."

Collin then reviewed the visual evidence against his wife.

He handed Lilith the aerial view of Teufelschloss Castle that he had printed off while on the web. He put his diagram—drawn in pencil on a piece of notebook paper—on the desk for her to compare with the shot of the castle.

The triangular diagram also reproduced the figure that he had seen in one of Dara's paintings in the greenhouse and that had been on the cover of *Faces Behind Shadows*. Charles Childress had also alluded to the symbol.

"Look at the outline of both images, Lilith—they're identical."

She looked from the castle photo with the turrets to the triangle—back and forth.

"I see what you mean, precious. So?"

"So the castle is the landmark in the little town in Austria where both our First Lady and Dara grew up together. Consider what the town and the castle connect: Joseph Stalin through his wife, Sato's brother; Greta Heiss—the early atomic experimenter in Nazi Germany who contributed significantly to the development of atomic warfare; Frau Troost—a Holocaust murderer; the SS honcho Reinhard Heydrich—another bad boy; and the President of the United States through the First Lady, the President being the most powerful person in the world."

Lilith put down the images and studied the stained-glass window in the distance, the banging of the branches against the glass now louder. "What is the exact significance of the strange triangle?"

Collin's eyes narrowed as he considered his answer. "I think it's a symbol—of a holy shrine, so to speak. It represents the geographic focal point of a dark force. Sort of like how the manger, the baby, and the Three Wise Men in Bethlehem represent the opposite."

"*Dark force*—what are you saying exactly?"

Collin leaned forward and put his hand firmly on Lilith's shoulder. Lilith's eyes fastened upon Collin's.

"Look," explained Collin in an even voice, "we now know that Dara is—or *has* been—by some strange force—all three of these powerful women. Now, the question is—just who is she and what does she *want*? Who else is involved?"

Lilith's keen intelligence lock-stepped with Collin's. The fear in her eyes receded, replaced with firm purpose. "So the triangle symbol is the emblem of some kind of foul tapestry that weaves together evil events throughout history?"

"Yes. Incredibly, Dara has the ability to reappear throughout time in various roles—maybe even at different biological ages and physical forms—depending upon her objective. I have several hypotheses, but my first thought is that Dara wants—when all is said and done—*power*."

"Maybe."

"She—and whoever she may be working with want to take over the government—then maybe all governments."

Lilith's eyes flashed with recognition. "The First Lady—Shonda Rice O'Neal!"

"Exactly. It wasn't an accident that Dara spent her early childhood in that small village. She wanted to get close to the most powerful person in the world—in the future."

"That's wild," said Lilith.

"If we've already accepted certain facts about her that are hard to swallow, it's not a stretch to assume that she can see into parts of the future."

"So, as a little girl, Dara knew that Shonda Rice O'Neal was the future First Lady."

"It seems probable," concluded Collin.

"So—."

"—So she wants to be close to power—maybe to kill the President as a start." Collin observed the incredulous look on Lilith's face—her thin-lipped mouth had formed a little O.

"Yes, maybe that's what they've wanted for centuries. It's insane," said Lilith.

"No argument." Collin stood up from the desk. "Have you ever seen a symbol like that triangle before?" he asked.

Collin paced the floor, studying the oil paintings on the wall as he thought over the whole mess. "You once mentioned the man who built your home—around the time of the Civil War—Thaddeus Hawthorne," he continued. "That's what put me on to this power theory in the first place—sort of an epiphany. What if there's a connection? You know that Dara's lineage goes way back in Washington—a center of power and corruption."

"Hawthorne was close to President Lincoln—he was a big munitions man," added Lilith. "After all, Lincoln's death was a conspiracy. But, we know that Booth killed Lincoln."

"Exactly"—interjected Collin. "But *who* was Booth, really? Who put him up to it? Do you know that Booth was a soldier at Harper's Ferry when John Brown—the violent abolitionist—was hung for treason? Is that only a coincidence? Many say that is what really started the horrible slaughter of the Civil War."

Lilith snapped her fingers. She rose from the desk and bolted downstairs. She obviously had remembered something.

It must be pretty damn important, thought Collin.

CHAPTER THIRTY-NINE

Collin thought about Thaddeus Hawthorne and the Black Annex with the skylight, and how Union Soldiers had murdered him. Had the evil munitions mogul been directing Booth in a conspiracy? Dara was part of a supernatural force, maybe even a conspiracy that coveted power, and so may have been Hawthorne. Apparently, both wanted to be close to the President.

Lilith had abruptly left when he had brought up the strange symbol of the triangle, and Collin expected her to return with something that would solidly connect the Civil War munitions mogul to his wife.

His thoughts were interrupted by Lilith's return to the loft in the bookstore.

Lilith—still and silent—resembled a computer that had frozen from over-activity. She handed Collin an old photo that was obviously, considering the style of the uniforms and the grainy quality of the image, Civil War vintage. Collin studied it closely.

He saw a very tall, portly, middle-aged man in a dark suit, with a bushy mustache and sideburns, standing in front of a house that looked very much like Lilith's. A throng of women in hoop skirts looked as though they were dancing—some with their men—some with each other.

Collin remembered that at Lilith's dinner party the other night, she had told him Hawthorne had his throat cut, and then he was hung.

He continued to study the photo.

Union soldiers in the picture were grinning. But, Collin observed, it had hardly been a soiree. The massive hands of the tall man in the dark suit were bound behind him. His throat had obviously been cut. Two Union soldiers held him up.

A third held a long rope, as if it were a trophy, one end tied around a branch of an overhanging oak tree, the other end formed into a hangman's noose.

Collin swallowed hard.

"This is—."

"—Yes—Thaddeus Hawthorne—Lincoln's weapons mogul, an inventor of one of the early repeating rifles. It increased the casualty rate in the Civil War tenfold. I meant to show you this the other night at dinner, but I thought it was too gruesome."

"So, is this what you had remembered?"

Lilith wrung her hands, sitting back down at the desk. "I'll show you on the photo." Collin took a seat next to her.

"See the Union soldier holding the noose?" She pointed to the spot on the picture.

Collin studied the lean, dark Union soldier in the photo. "What about him?"

"That is Captain Rotberg."

"Who" asked Collin?

"This photo was taken a few years before the Lincoln's assassination," explained Lilith. "Rotberg was the officer who was with Mr. and Mrs. Lincoln in the Presidential box the night that he was shot."

"Are you sure it's the same person?"

"Yes, I checked," said Lilith.

"And?"

Lilith's voice rose with excitement. "He was engaged to the daughter of a Senator who often socialized with the Lincolns. The Senator had been lobbying Lincoln to use an early form of chemical warfare—using a laboratory in which he had a financial interest —but Lincoln turned him down. That night at Ford's Theater, John Wilkes Booth attacked Rotberg also—with a dagger." Lilith tapped the desk to emphasize her point. "But—."

"—Maybe it was a setup?" concluded Collin.

"You decide. The other soldier in the President's party— the one who was supposed to be protecting Lincoln outside his Presidential box in the theater—walked off guard. He was never seriously punished. *Why not?* Here we have two strapping officers, and two duds. Of course, Rotberg had been wounded by Booth's dagger, so maybe that explains his inability to help the President."

"Nevertheless its suggestive," said Collin. "After all, Booth was more than just a malcontent; he advocated slavery and even genocide—a man with an evil agenda." Collin shook his head. "It's hard to know what those Union soldiers in the photo were really up to. But, you remembered something important?"

"Yes. Look on the edge of the photo Collin, next to the buggy carriage. Do you see something familiar?"

Collin studied the part of the photograph far off in the corner. Two Union soldiers held up a banner while some others stood at the periphery with their arms grimly folded. The diagram on the banner stunned Collin. In the old Civil War era photo, on the banner held by the Union soldiers, Collin recognized the hateful triangle—with one small circle at one point and a dot at its two other points. It was the emblem of the wicked castle again.

Collin just stared at the image—speechless. Was the symbol on the banner their flag, or were they mocking a false idol? That is what Collin wanted to know.

"So, what now, darling?" asked Lilith. "Let me get this straight, dear. Are we to go off half-cocked just based upon an ageless theory of lust for power—all based upon a few old photos and a silly triangle?"

Collin considered the question carefully. "Einstein was supposed to have said that the simplest theory that fits the facts is the best one. I know this is a stretch. But, you know the same facts that I know. Do you have a better explanation? The fact is that this dark symbol of the triangle now connects Dara with Hawthorne, a current President's wife, and maybe the murder of a past President—a century and a half earlier."

Lilith was lost for words. She finally spoke. "That, and a lot more. It's fantastic, isn't it? However, I can't say it's surprising. We're dealing with a clever lot. They don't leave a trail, Collin. Where's Dara now, anyway?"

"I left her sleeping early this morning. I snuck out."

"Get her out of your home! Or, *you* leave her and stay at my house—you and Stephanie both!"

"The last thing I want to do is tip Dara off," said Collin. "For now, I think Stephanie's safe. She doesn't figure in this. I'll put a tail on Dara."

"Is that all?"

"Do you have a better idea?"

Lilith shook her head.

"I want to know what she's doing, who's she's doing it with, and where she's going. Then, we'll take the proper action." He wondered about the dangers and hoped that he had been right about his daughter.

Collin studied the banner in the photo again, lost in thought.

"Lilith, the first time I'd ever seen that weird triangle was on the cover of *Faces Behind Shadows* a few days ago in this bookstore. The next time was on my wife's painting. Before, I wanted to know who Dara really was. Now, I also want to know what she really *wants*."

"And until you drew it on that piece of paper, I had only seen it in this photo—about a year ago."

"We know that Dara might be connected to Thaddeus Hawthorne," added Collin. "The Union soldiers in this photo look like they're making an example of him, and the triangle symbol represented what they were trying to destroy. But, maybe Rotberg and the rest might have really been in cahoots with Hawthorne, and wanted to silence him, not punish him. I wonder if my home is also involved some way in all of this. After all, Josiah Sanford was a nasty kind of guy and died almost the same way."

"Maybe."

"Dara wants power. She must be talking to somebody. Who?" Collin asked.

"Good question," said Lilith.

"That's the kind of question a good private detective could answer."

CHAPTER FORTY

Washington DC, Later that Thursday morning:

"Spider Torres, private dick." Torres chucked in a vulgar way as he extended his hairy hand to Collin. "I always like to say it that way—especially to the broads."

Collin studied the face of the detective that he had hired to spook Dara. He didn't like him, but the man had come highly recommended by Lilith and had the reputation for getting results.

"Let's walk," said Torres.

He waved toward the promenade by the water, the gold rings on his fingers sparkling in the late morning sun that had just broken through the clouds.

"I need this work done rather quickly, Mr. Torres." Collin had suggested that they meet at the entrance of the Jefferson Memorial. They strolled around the perimeter of the Monticello-inspired structure and the lovely, tranquil waterfront.

Collin's explanation for the job was marital problems. He couldn't tell Torres the real reason why he had hired him. If he had, the man would think him insane.

"You said on the phone that your wife is hosing around?"

Collin, somewhat taken aback by such blunt language, dug into his bag of clichés.

"We've grown apart—she doesn't understand me. I want you to follow her. I must know who it is. If you can, tell me also what they *say*."

Collin found the man's appearance—considering the enormity of the task—somewhat unsettling. Short, heavy, and balding, with a heavy mustache and a turned-backwards baseball cap, the detective hardly inspired confidence.

"Any dude in particular?" Torres got right to the point

As they wandered around, Collin enjoyed the smooth lines and lovely symmetry of Jefferson's monument.

"Not exactly." Collin moved closer to the water, where there were fewer people. He pulled a large manila envelope out of his coat pocket and gave it to Torres. "Three photographs: the first is Frank Seaton—a man I work with; the second is Dr. Jonas

Bridgestone; and the last is my wife, Dara. They're yours. Let me know if she meets up with these two men."

Torres studied the photos as they walked. "Screwing *two*, huh? She's a live one."

Collin ignored the off-color comment. "Their names and descriptions are on the back." He stopped along the promenade next to the waterline, observing a couple of ducks fighting over a piece of floating popcorn.

"I want to know if she meets anyone . . . *famous*." Collin noticed that the detective's dark and skeptical eyes widened with his last word.

"'*Famous*'—like who?"

"A politician maybe. The spouse of one, perhaps."

"Got any in mind?" Torres looked around, then down at the water. His eyes tracked the ducks as they paddled by. He spit his gum in the water.

Collin thought about the poor ducks eating that gum. The urge to toss Spider Torres into the drink and feed *him* to the ducks gripped Collin. His old, aggressive impulses seeped in more and more, he had noticed. "Let me know, that's all."

Torres stashed the photos in his pocket.

Collin wanted to leave. "Anything else?"

"That's it."

"Time is critical."

"When we talked coin—I forgot to mention the twenty percent bonus. Bills go out weekly."

Greed didn't disqualify him, thought Collin. He wanted results, and fast.

"Fine." Collin couldn't take much more of the uncouth Mr. Torres.

"We've got a deal then?" asked Torres.

If he found something bizarre, figured Collin, he lacked credibility to outsiders—*perfect*. "Yes."

"You'll hear from me pronto," said Torres.

Collin walked away for a few steps. He abruptly stopped, spun around, and instructed the detective. "One more thing, don't contact me at work. Don't call me at home, either. Call my cell— anytime—understood?"

"No problem."

Collin didn't like Mr. Torres one bit—but that wasn't required.

CHAPTER FORTY-ONE

Georgetown, Thursday afternoon, March 29:

"Look at her eyes! For God's sake Collin, look at the eyes!"

"I've been looking at those eyes for twenty years." Collin had never heard Lilith evoke the Almighty before, but he could see how this old oil painting would establish a precedent.

"So, she had a hand in this too," commented Collin. They stood three feet away from the tormenting image.

Lilith's fingers were clamped onto Collin's shoulder as she huddled close to him, almost grafted to his side like a Siamese twin. Their eyes burned into the canvass of the nine hundred year-old painting that had finally arrived from her supplier.

"Calvary Hill—the Crucifixion of Christ," said Collin. He recognized for the first time a pattern emerging that went beyond governments and the life of the President. But, it wasn't enough to change his primary theory.

They stood in the loft at the bookshop. Lilith pointed her finger to the area just over Christ's bloody crown of thorns. A black snake lay on top of the right arm of the T that formed the famous cross—to which Jesus had been nailed. "Look Collin, the snake's eyes are yellow—like the one you saw."

They cautiously inched closer to the piece as if the painting were a source of contagion. "I noticed that too," answered Collin. The young woman in the painting was what really enthralled him. "It's probably *her* all right," said Collin. "Radiant green eyes—red hair—the aggressive, forward tilt of her posture. Red heads must have been pretty scarce over there."

The young woman in the painting wearing the white toga, standing under Jesus Christ, smiled radiantly as she looked up at him—as if in a Fourth of July parade. The Roman centurion next to her had a smirk on his face.

Collin moved toward the paining until his nose was an inch from the canvass.

Lilith looked on. "What else do you see?"

He pointed to the small, faint, grey sliver in the corner of the piece, just visible in the evening sky. "That's the moon, isn't it?"

"Yes, I think it is."

Collin, leaning forward, put his finger next to the sliver. "That's the moon, all right." His finger traced the moon's outline. "See the orange hue around the edges—the painting's very old—it's almost worn off. The moon looks half full."

Lilith slowly moved closer to the painting. "The orange glow of the half-moon."

Collin looked back at her. He nodded. "Exactly."

Collin grabbed Lilith's hand and led her quickly down the stairs to the newspaper rack. They almost ran into several customers browsing the in stacks of books.

"Look in the *Post*—front page," he said.

Lilith picked the folded paper off the shelf. She opened it. She displayed it to Collin. On the front page was a color photo of the moon—from the previous evening. It was nearly a half-moon. There was a faint orange glow around it. The headline read: "'Strange Lunar Glow Maxes This Saturday Night'."

"Just like in the painting," concluded Lilith.

Collin whispered softly. "So this Saturday night there'll be a half-moon—and with the orange glow. They said it's global warming, but . . . "

Lilith slowly looked up from the paper. "It may *not* be global warming."

Collin realized exactly what else would be happening that Saturday.

Recombination of the Vampire Virus would be complete, and consequently the remote chance that a rogue gene would produce a Super-Virus. But, thought Collin, the chances of that are next to zero. The chances of a mistake like that escaping from the lab are also next to zero. However, what if these were done on purpose? *Maybe we just scooted from government conspiracy to— ? Have the stakes risen dramatically?*

He also knew that the viral project was vital to humanity. Nothing could be allowed to interfere with it, especially a fantastic theory that, although plausible, is yet unproven.

Maybe it's time to prove it?

Collin sat down on the stool next to the magazine rack. "My God, is it possible?"

His energy drained out of him as he slumped into a listless funk.

Lilith stared down at him. "Of course, the vaccine project—the Vampire Virus. You work with dangerous strains of that thing. Could that be connected to all this?"

Collin looked up at her. "We'd better find out for sure—and quick. The final virus emerges Saturday night."

Lilith dashed over to the cash register and grabbed a small brown box from behind the counter. She pulled Collin out of his chair and led him back up to the loft, carrying the package with her.

They stood at her desk.

"Open the box," she said, her eyes wide with excitement.

She threw it on the desk as they took a seat opposite the Crucifixion painting.

"My distributor sent it with the painting. The old parchment was sewn into the back of the frame. He found the picture in an ancient mausoleum in Jerusalem—in a Black Annex."

Collin's ripped off the top to the box. He pulled out a wrinkled animal-skin with writing on it—the letters looked to be in Greek. Beside that was a yellow piece of paper—a very old, handwritten English translation.

"This English translation looks relatively recent, maybe early nineteen-hundreds. The parchment with the Greek writing, rather, is ancient."

Collin read the translation aloud. It chilled him:

"Armies of Darkness sew plague and destruction, as the End draws near, ye witness the strange glow of the moon, when man and beast shall fear."

Collin stood up and walked to the Crucifixion painting. He studied the eyes of the snake resting upon the cross. "Thousands of children are dying each day from that bloody virus. We may be next. The vaccine project is good—I *know* it is." Collin turned around and looked at Lilith. "Nothing—but *nothing* comes before that until I know exactly what's going on. Think of what we have

171

to lose." Collin began to sense that the meaning of his whole life's work might be on the line.

"So?" said Lilith.

"We need to know exactly who Dara's talking to. I hope our detective is better than he looks."

Collin waved the piece of paper with the translation. "It's also high time that I go back to my home and search for a skylight."

CHAPTER FORTY-TWO

Georgetown, Thursday evening, March 29:

Collin searched inside his house while Dara was away working, but found no passageway to a Black Annex. The next solution was to find the skylight, which, he figured, would probably be on the third floor—forty feet above ground level. A skylight meant a secret room, and a secret room in Sanford Manor more likely than not meant a Black Annex. That probably would, based upon Lilith's story at her dinner party, reveal a clue of his wife's heinous plan.

But, as far as he knew, his house didn't have a skylight.

An old playroom on the top floor, used as a storage space, offered a grimy window big enough to view the roofline. Peering through the glass, Collin saw a rickety ledge below. He forced open the rotted sill, advancing his long legs through the opening.

His sneakers made contact with the soggy wood of the ledge, bowing under his full weight. He crawled out the rest of the way, wincing at the long drop to the patio cement below. As he looked around, he couldn't see a skylight along the roofline. Much of the gabled roof wasn't visible from that vantage point anyway.

Unfortunately, the roof inclined sharply toward its summit about twenty feet from him, with many steep peaks and valleys between. He also noticed many holes in the decomposed cedar shingles. Fooling around up there to find a skylight looked dangerous, and a broken neck wouldn't help his mission. He returned to the playroom, determined to find the passageway from the inside of the house.

He considered City Hall. He called their recording, and blueprints only went back a hundred years. Collin remembered that Dara always worked very late on Thursday nights. That was critical, since he must hurry and find the secret worshiping space before Dara returned home from work. Then, he remembered the chanting that he had heard about a year before from the master bedroom.

What if the strange sound hadn't been a dream? What if it hadn't been Carmen praying, or her eerie, religious music? It could rather have been Dara in the Annex—worshiping the moon through the skylight. In that case, decided Collin, there must be a passage near the wall behind the bed, just above the master bedroom on the third floor, which leads into the Black Annex. It's the Annex he wanted, not the skylight.

The passage must be here in the playroom!

Collin noticed a tall china cabinet standing against the wall. It looked empty. It had been moved there recently, since a rectangular, lighter-colored space, about the same size as the cabinet, was outlined on the grey wall next to it. Collin dashed over and moved the piece of furniture, revealing a large air-vent, with a wire mesh, at about chest level.

An odd place for a vent, he thought. In any case, no ducts connected to the third level. Collin ripped out the mesh and saw that the opening was deep and wide, leading sideways behind the wall and past the same wall that bordered the master bedroom below. Collin, in his black sweats, after fetching a flashlight from his study, climbed through the mysterious opening.

After walking about ten feet in a crouch, the beam of Collin's flashlight moved over the walls of a small enclosure. He turned his light on high beam and inched along the wooden floor toward the interior of the room.

The enclosure enlarged into a hidden alcove.

Red, white, and black colors dominated. A sign hung on one wall. Written on it, he saw the hateful symbol: a black triangle with a dot at the tip of two angles and a small circle at the tip of the third angle.

Collin knew for sure he was standing in the middle of the Black Annex!

A poster hung next to the sign, the kind that could adorn the wall of any tourist agency. It featured the Austrian village of Teufelheim with its gothic spires. The demonic castle, in aerial view, towered over the little town. Its two turrets had the familiar stone roofs, with the third turret having a cylindrical wall with no roof, running from the ground to the open sky. Hence, as he had realized while viewing a similar image on the net, it resembled— from above—the strange triangular symbol.

Crimson peacocks patterned the black wallpaper, with the images featuring the eyes on the tails. The skulls of Rams' heads hung over the wallpaper. A large, silver pentangle had been painted on another wall.

As he moved the flashlight around the room, Collin discovered a large wooden table, with a red tablecloth and chairs around it. The cloth was decorated with a black pentacle—a pentangle circumscribed in a white circle. Collin cringed as he realized that the pentangle was the traditional sign of Lucifer.

Black candles, with a black chalice, rested on the table.

Several bizarre oil paintings hung from the walls. One featured Romans in red togas and gladiators with swords and armor, each crouching upon one knee, their hands clasped in invocation. The sky in the picture displayed dark clouds—except for a clear opening that allowed the light of the half-moon to break though.

An orange glow rimmed the moon in the painting.

Then Collin saw it, fixed to the wall.

He pointed the flashlight. As he inched toward the object on the wall, he saw that a black curtain lay over it. It was about six feet long and four feet wide. When he reached it, he ripped it back.

What he witnessed confirmed his worst fears.

He felt ill. It told him exactly what Dara had wanted all along, and what the Dark Army desperately sought.

Collin's eyes scanned the demonic banner that filled his vision, as he ran the beam of his flashlight over the chilling words that ripped through him like shrapnel.

"COUNTDOWN TO ARMAGEDDON: Jesus of Nazareth Crucified—Year 0; The Black Plague—1334; Seven Years War— 1756; The Repeating Rifle Patented—1860; Dynamite Patented— 1867; Joseph Stalin Born—1878; Adolf Hitler Born—1889; Chlorine Gas Chemical Warfare Initiated 1915; Spanish Flu Epidemic—1918; Atom First Split in Berlin—1938; Prototype V-2 Intercontinental Missile Invented in Nazi Germany—1944; Nazi Holocaust Completed—1945; Atom Bomb Blasts, Hiroshima and Nagasaki—1945; Modern Computer MANIAC Perfected—1952; Watson-Crick DNA Double Helix Discovered—1953; 'Mike' H-Bomb Test Successful—October 31, 1953; Cuban Missile Crisis— October, 1962; Khmer Rouge Cambodian Genocide—1975; 9/11

*Terrorist Attack; Molecular Manipulation and Computer DNA
Remodeling Perfected—2003 . . . "*

There was also a last entry on the timeline.

Collin read it carefully. He had confirmed what he wanted
to know.

*"Vampire Super-virus unleashed through vaccine project
near Washington DC—year unknown—Dawn of Armageddon."*

*It was Armageddon, not power, that Dara and her Dark
Army desired!*

That last, dark milestone instantly transformed Collin's life
into an evil void, knowing that his very existence, his marriage, his
scientific talent, and all his good works had been nothing more
than an evil manipulation by Dara and the Dark Army over
centuries past. The whole process had been a violent,
technologically driven, and desensitizing subversion of history that
had been spun—unknown to him or almost anyone—for thousands
of years.

Collin felt that there was a lot of good in the world worth
fighting for—*killing* for—if need be, and if forced to, he would
indeed battle the dark forces arrayed against him. The whole world
wasn't as pure as his beautiful flower—the Royal Catchfly—but
it's worth saving. He realized that this discovery had made his life
take a right turn at breakneck speed, with the cost of failure rising
exponentially.

He looked up at the skylight where the moon and the
orange halo were clearly visible.

By Saturday evening, the day after tomorrow, the
completed half-moon and the full, orange glow would shine in the
evening sky, and the catastrophic Super-virus would be poised to
destroy everyone. Someone in the lab had concocted that
horrendous organism and was poised to unleash it upon the world.
Collin felt that he knew exactly who that was: Frank Seaton.

Armageddon had been what Dara had wanted, not world
power.

Collin vowed that he'd destroy her plan—and her too if
need be.

CHAPTER FORTY-THREE

Collin, stunned by his discovery of the "Countdown to Armageddon" in the Black Annex, made his way to his greenhouse, almost as if he were in a daze. Not only was Dara not human and consumed with dark intent, her plan was to destroy civilization through subversion of his talent and work. It was incredible, but true.

Collin rummaged through his greenhouse. He could see the moon shining through the glass ceiling with the hateful, orange glow. He walked the rows of perennials and annual blooms with his watering can, sprinkling the potted soil as he waited for Dara to arrive home.

He knew that could kill her outright, but, he asked himself, would that stop her plan? Moreover, killing someone like that may not be simple. Remorse and sentimentality now had little to do with it, for Collin knew what she was and what she wanted.

He marveled at the ingenious plot that had been unfolding for centuries, and the powerful, dark, guiding hand that had authored it, weaving together scientific and political "assets" to produce the perfect vehicle and time for total devastation. Years ago the government had recruited him into an elite, international corps of commandos due to his scientific prowess and aptitude for rarified game theory—war games that is. He couldn't have hatched a more effective plot to destroy mankind.

He picked his vibrating cell phone out of his pocket.

"Lilith."

"Did you find it?"

"Yes—Black Annex all right—and the solid proof I needed."

Collin looked around him to make sure that he was alone.

"Dara's after the virus. She's using me—and Stephanie—to get it. Her goal is Armageddon. She's not working alone, of course. I'm pretty sure who it is in the lab that's working with her—it's our administrator."

"*Faces Behind* Shadows is on its way. You'll have it soon. It may give us more vital information, darling, about all the culprits and what to do. "

177

"I know what to do. I'm pulling the plug on the vaccine project. I'll try that first. Stephanie will stay with you. She's packed. She's on her way to your house in a taxi. Now that I know what Dara is after, Stephanie can't live at home. She's an expert on the virus, and she may be a target too."

"Fine. What else?"

Collin put down his water can and picked up his weeding fork. "We have until Saturday evening until the Dark Army can get their hands on the Super-virus."

Collin hesitated talking on his cell, but he didn't see a way around it, and he was too tired to try. He needed to talk to his ally. "This virus will be much more dangerous, of course. One way or another, it must be stopped."

"How can you stop it now?"

Collin looked over at the door of the greenhouse. He knew that at any second Dara would be walking through it.

"It won't be easy," whispered Collin.

Collin walked over to his potting desk and arranged the plants. "Be careful, Lilith. She may be on to you. She considers you a threat. Me too." He spotted his prize flower—the five-pointed Royal Catchfly. He caressed it fondly.

Hearing the door to the greenhouse open and close, he kept his back to the entrance. He slipped the phone back under his coat as he turned it off. He sat down at the desk.

"In the end, sugar, I'll defeat you, you know that don't you? You, and whoever you're working with." Dara's voice was soft and self-assured.

Collin didn't turn toward her, but continued to tend the majestic flower in front of him. He couldn't stomach looking at her.

"You know, drones may be the perfect delivery vehicle for the virus. Too bad that Gordon Givens wasn't as stupid as you thought," replied Collin.

She remained silent.

"Maybe you'll win. We'll see, won't we?" Collin added.

"*Everything* depends upon it, isn't that right?" she asked.

"Yes." He could hear her light footsteps on the fine gravel as she slowly moved closer to him, halting behind his desk. He didn't care that he couldn't see what she was doing, since he knew that he would be safe at least until the Super-virus was complete.

"What about Stephanie?" she asked.

"You tell me."

"I don't know you anymore, Collin. I'm not sure I ever did."

"I'm pretty good at routing weeds in my garden, love."

Collin tended to the Royal Catchfly—its red blossoms giving him his sense of purpose. He adored its arresting, five-pointed, star pattern.

"Where did you hide it?" he asked her.

"What?"

"The triangle painting—the one with the two dots and the circle. Your dark emblem."

"You're mad—literally. You need to get back on your medicine again."

"Maybe, but it doesn't matter."

He could hear from her footsteps that she was now pacing back and forth, probably pondering her options.

"When we met—twenty years ago—did you care about me, even a little?" asked Collin. He fed his five-star beauty with fertilizer. "I loved you, you know."

"That's an odd thing to say," she answered with convincing perplexity. "Anyway, that's all gone now, isn't it?"

Collin took his mist bottle and sprayed the Royal petals. "You tend a garden for a long time—and till the soil—you must kill the weeds."

"You're right," she responded with conviction.

Collin's tone sharpened.

"Problem is, the forces that kill the flowers are the things you can't even see—they're invisible." He held the Royal Catchfly up close to his face, studying it from every angle. "Take viruses, for example. Then, you just have to take them out."

"This is bigger than all of us," she whispered.

"Stephanie's packed and gone," blurted Collin. "Stay away from her."

There was a long pause.

"You too—pack up and get out," she said in an icy voice. "It'll be better that way."

"Yes indeed."

He turned around on his stool, facing his wife for the first time.

What he saw wasn't entirely a surprise. "You won't use that."

Dara held a pistol in her hand. It was trained right at his heart. Collin noted that her hand shook. He stood up from his potting desk and walked up to her.

She looked down at the gun, and then lowered it.

The fact was, moments before *he* had considered killing *her*. There had to be far more to this plot than his wife. Killing her might not defeat the plan, and besides, it might not be as easy as killing a weed. He could wait.

Dara put the gun in her purse. She was wearing a stunningly attractive red dress with her turquoise earrings. "I suppose I won't use it."

Such a beautiful facade, mused Collin. "We have nothing more to say to each other," he blurted.

"I'll say it again." Dara's eyes burned with resolve. "In the end you'll lose."

CHAPTER FORTY-FOUR

Northeast of Bethesda, Maryland, Friday morning, March 30:

"I called you into my office because, Stanley, you were right all along," Collin lied. Collin sat behind his desk in his enclosed office at the laboratory, his eyes fixed upon the yellow bowtie of the troublesome FDA bureaucrat occupying the chair across from him. Both men wore long white lab coats with dress shirts and ties.

Collin felt as if he were starring in some surreal, science-fiction movie. He knew the consequences of killing the project and of the loss of the vital vaccine he had been working so hard on. The responsibility weighed heavily. However, there was no alternative to his next move.

"The master virus is compromised," explained Collin. "The possibility of a dreaded rogue gene is real. I'm pulling the plug on project. I have the authority under the charter."

"This late? How can you be sure? Our jobs are on the line now."

Conning Chu would be difficult.

Collin's strategy was to use Chu as a club to beat Frank Seaton. Collin had made a plastic model of the part of the DNA of the virus that had been altered using molecular manipulation. He picked it up off his desk. "See this part of the model here, Stanley? The red part—we inadvertently substituted the wrong nucleic acids."

Stanley leaned forward in his chair. "What about the failsafe procedures?"

"A technical computer failure isn't covered by those."

"Where's Stephanie? Let's get her in here."

"She's not involved. *I* goofed. It's my responsibility." Collin threw the model back down on his desk. He looked into Chu's skeptical eyes. "Besides, now that we're in recombination, she's on leave. I have a call into Frank Seaton about all this."

Chu sprang up from his chair, his posture stiff. "Dr. De Gise—this is highly unorthodox procedure, although I share some of your concerns."

Collin stood up too. "You've been aching to nix the project all along, Dr. Chu. Now's your chance."

Chu's eyes shifted to the model, then back at Collin. "Maybe you're right—Dr. De Gise. This rogue virus—or even the possibility of one—must be stopped. We'll have to regroup." Chu nodded eagerly as he spoke.

Dr. Chu held out his hand to Collin, and Collin took it. Then, Chu marched out of the office, slamming the door. Collin sat back down behind his desk, folded his hands, and pondered the situation.

It had been too easy. Chu might be doing an end-run instead.

Frank Seaton promised to be much more difficult. Chu, who knew the ropes, would make a beeline straight to Frank Seaton to dump the problem on him. In fact, Collin expected Frank to be banging on his door any second.

Collin also knew full well that his life hung by a thread. Even though the Dark Army needed his expertise, maybe even for a long time, he was expendable. Many had already died at their hands, and he could be next. But, he must carry on anyway.

"Close the project down? Not on your life!"

Frank Seaton stood over Collin's desk, his eyes blazing. It hadn't taken him long to barge in. His hyperventilation fogged his stainless steel, square-rimmed eyeglasses. His military-like attire— tan pants, olive shirt and grey tie with a silver clip—gave him the appearance of a drill sergeant. So did his odd stare.

"That just isn't going to happen."

"Have a seat Frank." Seaton took the same seat that Dr. Chu had occupied only minutes before.

Collin forged ahead. "The project's compromised," explained Collin. "We have a rogue virus on our hands. I'm going through standard channels to have the project shuttered—at least for a while."

A tiny bit of spittle formed at the corner of Frank's taught lips—the man literally frothed at the mouth. "You haven't the authority to do that. I call the shot's around here. This is a Government-funded project." His fist pounded Collin's desk. "Do you understand that?"

This reaction just confirmed in Collin's mind Seaton's probable complicity with Dara's plot. "Technically, true. Real world—it's not so simple, Frank. If a Super-virus escapes, millions may die in weeks—*here* in the USA."

"No dice. I won't be bamboozled—."

"—Then, there's always the Scientific Committee, of which I'm the Chairman. I'll call it into emergency session."

"Over which I have veto power," added Frank.

"True, then there is always the press, DHS, and the Surgeon General. In fact, I'm scheduled for a follow-up TV interview on Public Television this afternoon—live."

"You'd be violating—."

"—Then of course, there's always the ear of the First Lady . . ."

Then, Frank Seaton took a left turn.

"Dr. De Gise, I understand you're tired. I understand that you've been under quite a strain lately, haven't you? The rumor-mill has it that you've been having marital difficulties, and that you may have *other* concerns."

With the word "other," Frank stopped and locked eyes with Collin.

Of course, realized Collin, Frank was playing the "nut" card. Frank knew that Collin had been seeing a psychiatrist. He didn't know much more than that, but that might be enough.

What if he and Bridgestone, both old Navy vets, had been comparing notes?

Collin sat silently as he waited for the rest of Frank's monologue.

"Dr. De Gise, I know you've had issues with your *health* in the past. I sympathize with that, really I do. But, I can't let that get in the way of our successful project, can I?" Frank leaned back in his chair, putting his hand to his chin. "Why did Stephanie take leave?"

"She's feeling more anxious. I guess it's the stress of the project."

Frank nodded as if he fully understood Collin's explanation. If he didn't believe the excuse, his manner didn't betray it. Collin realized that Frank wasn't going to allow him to close down the project so easily—not without a lot more trouble.

Frank could play hardball, too. He had other options, good ones.

Collin recalled that the Foundation Charter had a "loony clause" embedded within it. It stipulated that in the case of a Scientific Director losing the "mental capacity" to participate in the project, he could be jettisoned immediately.

Collin therefore decided upon a different tack.

"I see your concern, Frank. I forgot to see how things look from a managerial perspective. Perhaps I *am* a bit tired. Maybe I got ahead of myself."

When all was said and done, Collin knew that Frank had the upper hand—at least through ordinary channels. He had to be careful. Otherwise, he might find himself out on his ear with no say whatsoever. The problem was, time was very short.

Collin decided that he might have to unleash public opinion instead.

Frank rose from his chair. He smiled and leaned over the desk, paternalistically patting Collin on the shoulder. "That's the ticket." He straightened his tie. "I'll call up the Scientific Committee for Monday—then we'll talk it over with our colleagues. I'm sure we'll fix whatever's wrong. I don't think the omega gene will be an issue."

As Frank headed for the door, Collin's watchful eyes trailed him.

Frank stopped after he opened the door. "By the way Collin, give my best to Stephanie. I hope her new medication works for her."

The epiphany shot through Collin like a point-blank Colt 45.

Frank Seaton and Jonas Bridgestone had definitely been spying on him. How else did Frank know about Stephanie's new medication if Dr. Jonas Bridgestone hadn't given him a detailed account of Collin's privileged clinical notes about him and his family? Aside from Collin, Bridgestone had been the only one that was supposed to know about the new medication—not even Stephanie had been told yet.

Maybe they are part of the same dark team, concluded Collin.

There was something else that was bothering Collin. He was suspicious about what Frank had just said about the "omega" gene—the gene essential to the accidental transformation of the Vampire Virus into the Super-virus. Frank, supposedly not a techie, used that piece of scientific jargon too easily.

Frank must be the one who is secretly trying to splice in the rogue gene! Maybe the wily administrator had been more scientifically trained to accomplish that task than he had let on?

Frank had to be the mole within the lab. It fit the facts. He had always been the most gung-ho about the vaccine project, no matter how bad the risks.

Then again, Frank and Bridgestone could just be spying on him together for the US Government, couldn't they?

Collin thought not. He had to be right. His mind was clear enough to know that.

One thing for sure—Frank Seaton wasn't going to let him kill the project.

CHAPTER FORTY-FIVE

Washington DC, Later that Friday Morning, March 30:

"So, before you were all hot on this vaccine project. Now—all of a sudden—you're out to kill it. Is that right Dr. De Gise?"

"New technical issues that deal with safety—."

"—What about the thousands of children bleeding to death in Africa?"

Collin was back in the PBS station for his second, live, televised interview.

Priscilla Korn had replaced the deceased Barry Bledsoe as the host. Korn—a blustery, pinkish, overweight woman who wore muumuus and wielded a thunderous voice like a battle-ax, burned hardball questions at Collin in rapid succession.

"What if that sucker finds its way over *here*? What do we do then, Doctor?"

"I understand your concern. What if a Super-virus escapes from our lab? Consider that . . . "

The producers of the TV program—wanting to look tough on terrorism and not cowed by the violence during the last telecast, insisted upon continuing with the second part of Collin's interview. Moreover, they had wanted a different "feel" to the show. They wanted more viewers. They wanted a televised slugfest.

So, without bothering to wait a respectable period in deference to the departed Mr. Bledsoe, they retreaded the program as *Capital Hot-Seat*. Priscilla Korn, unlike Bledsoe, had a reputation as a crusty radio-talk-show pro who craved controversy.

Collin had considered not doing the second interview. Then, he had realized that there was no better way to torpedo the project than to go on TV and terrify the viewers with portents of doom. "What we have is a *rogue* virus on our hands—a potential Super-virus. It's alive. It's potentially much more deadly than the wild Vampire Virus."

"That hasn't been verified."

"It doesn't need to be—you're looking at the Scientific Director."

"According to an unimpeachable source it *does* need to be verified."

"Who?"

"Frank Seaton—he texted me ten minutes ago. He runs the show in the lab."

"Seaton's not . . . "

That bastard, thought Collin. Frank Seaton had gotten to her. He had forgotten that Frank had set up the interviews in the first place. The interviewer went on about the importance of the vaccine, and how risk is inherent in scientific research. She sounded just like *he* had during the previous program!

"Like I said, the new virus is too dangerous," said Collin.

This buzz saw sitting across from him was no slouch. She was smart, aggressive, and informed. Priscilla Korn was the kind of journalist that would stop at nothing to discredit anyone who disagreed with her—even a distinguished scientist. She was the junkyard dog of cheap journalism. Seaton and the rest had probably paid her off.

"The epsilon gene during molecular manipulation is very close in its nucleic acid sequencing to the dreaded omega gene," he droned. Unlike Bledsoe, he knew that she had no scientific credentials. "Without a technical background, it's hard . . . " Collin thought that he could try an end run around his surly host by snowing her with technical mumbo jumbo.

"Let's cut through the bull, Doctor. This isn't really a scientific issue, is it? Priscilla then fluttered one eyelid at Collin. It looked suspiciously like a wink. Collin wondered what she was up to—blackmail perhaps?

Is she warning me with a wink?

"This is science and nothing else," insisted Collin, ignoring her threat.

The interviewer smiled. "Haven't you been going around making some rather strange statements, Doctor De Gise?"

"What do you mean?"

Priscilla leaned forward in her chair, playing to the audience that was assembled in the rows of seats below her. "Meaning, Dr. De Gise, that you think there's some kind of evil conspiracy going around, right?"

The loaded question dazed him. Collin wondered what exactly Frank Seaton had told her. After all, Frank had been conferring with Jonas Bridgestone. "Who is your source on that?"

"Well, *Doctor*." She used his title repeatedly like she was smashing cockroaches with a hammer. "I can't divulge my source. So, it must be *true* then, you don't deny it?"

"Deny what?"

"You think that the viral project is a satanic plot!"

Collin looked at her, and her face this time was stone. He glanced down at the dimly lit audience, noticing that there were three heavily armed guards standing in the first row.

Something about the audience was strange, thought Collin.

Rather than a diverse set of scruffy students like last time, they were all middle-aged white men in business suits. They sat with their arms folded—expressionless. Many wore sunglasses.

"'Plot'" is a strong word." Collin groped clumsily for the right word.

"Well, *you* choose the word then. You think that people are plotting to use your virus to destroy the world."

Priscilla looked down at the audience as she smiled broadly, waving her hands upward, as if she were a symphony conductor. Collin then heard guffaws and chuckles come out of the first row.

"I think the virus is too dangerous."

"You think there's a plot to destroy civilization! You're a scientist, and you want to disrupt the vaccine project—the savior of thousands—maybe even millions of children—all for a nutty conspiracy theory!"

Her ground-glass voice echoed throughout the studio as she pointed her pudgy finger at Collin. "Isn't it true that you see a psychiatrist?"

"No, well, not for this—."

"—You mean not for the *Devil's* conspiracy that you've been raving about." Now the belly laughs rolled over the studio like a tidal wave.

Priscilla giggled too. "You signed a release with your employer—and you signed one here too. I'm within my rights to ask you these questions. After all, the public's health is at stake. *My* life may be at stake. This virus in Africa is spreading."

188

"This discussion is really getting us nowhere." Collin removed his lapel microphone. He realized that he was clearly doing himself harm.

"Isn't it also true that your wife's suing for divorce because of this paranoid plot you've cooked up?"

"How dare you—."

"—Haven't you been having her followed?"

"How did you know that?"

"So it's true then? Isn't it also true that you are on anti-psychotic drugs? Isn't it true that you're paranoid? Isn't is true that you're delusional?"

"No! Well, I'm not on any now—"

"My God! You're *off your meds*!"

"You're a disgrace to journalism."

"No wonder you're a nut case!" Priscilla grinned at the audience.

Collin looked up at the large studio screen standing next to the set. The last time he had been in the studio, it displayed horrific slides of dying African children. This time, it displayed the large image of a walnut.

The audience roared with laughter. They were taunting Collin, making the loony sign with their thumbs jammed in their ears with their fingers wiggling in the air.

Collin stood up. He spoke, but his voice was drowned in the audience's ribaldry. He glanced at the faces of the men in the front row—contorted and grimacing in laughter.

Priscilla stood up too. She had thoroughly discredited him. Her round, mirthful eyes locked on Collin. "Know what I think, Doctor?"

She pointed at the screen.

"I think you're nuts."

Collin stomped off the set.

He thought he had really stepped into it this time.

As he departed, he heard the audience roar with laughter.

He now realized that there was only one person he could talk to who might have the power and the will to order the vaccine project halted.

He was on his way to convince her.

CHAPTER FORTY-SIX

Washington DC, Friday afternoon, March 30:

"Tell me one thing, Collin."

"All right."

"Why?"

"You have to trust me, First Lady."

"No I don't."

She pushed back her thick hair. Her soft, flawless skin flushed. "Why have you disgraced yourself, your profession, the project? I trusted you."

"I'm sorry."

Collin noticed the slightly ajar door to the tiny meeting room. A Secret Service agent showed through the crack. "The risk of the vaccine now far outweighs the benefit."

"Don't hand me that scientific crap! Your fly unzipped on PBS—now CNN's playing it. I know all the gory details from other sources, too."

"All right."

Collin put his hands on his lap. "You also talked to Dara, didn't you?" Collin wasn't sure he wanted to go there just yet, but the question had slipped out.

"Damn straight I did." Shonda Rice O'Neal's mascara started to run as the tears rolled down her cheeks. Her sternness melted. "She actually could tell me very little."

"I can't tell you *everything*, Mrs. O'Neal." Collin looked at the crack in the door.

He leaned forward on the cream-colored, cloth couch. He pulled a pink tissue from the Kleenex box sitting on the small walnut coffee table between himself and the First Lady. He then stood up and gave it to her as she reclined in her easy chair.

"What's everybody telling you?" he asked softly.

She unfolded the hankie and wiped her nose, answering his question. "You've gone off your rocker. Everyone thinks you're absolutely barking—that is—except the conspiracy nuts. They're swamping the White House with obscene calls of support," she offered in an unsteady voice.

Collin took his seat.

"Do you think so too?" He looked out the huge jet's oval portal, and could see the sun's yellow rays play with the shiny metal on the gas truck. Air Force One must need a lot of fuel, he mused.

She studied him closely with her lovely grey eyes. "I don't know what to think, honestly."

Shonda, scheduled to give a speech at the United Nations in New York City in just three hours, and about the new vaccine, glanced at her diamond-studded gold watch. "We take off soon, I don't have much time." She straightened her nubby, pink-wool dress with the black trim.

The dress seemed oddly familiar to Collin, but he couldn't place where he had seen it before.

"I need your help," he pleaded.

"Look Collin, just tell me what the hell's going on over in the lab—and what's going on in your head." She wiped her wet face with the tissue, and then smiled at him disarmingly. "You need to trust *me*."

"I need six more months. The virus isn't ready."

Collin felt the vibration from the powerful jet turbines as they turned over in preparation for the flight. "I'm making changes—to make it safer. You'll have your vaccine. One thing for sure, Frank Seaton's got to go."

"Why?"

"Let's just say he's dangerous." Collin frisked the First Lady's reaction with his gaze. The comment didn't seem to faze her any. He relaxed a bit. "He may not be the only one."

She leaned toward him as if to share a moment of intimacy.

"Tell me about this *plot* theory you have. I don't like second-hand information." She shook her head. "Someone said something about a *demonic* conspiracy? *Lord sakes!* You don't really believe *that*, do you?"

Collin desperately needed results, and not talk. He didn't have much time. "I believe the live virus—the organism that we derive the vaccine from—may have been compromised."

Shonda Rice O'Neal poured herself a glass of water from the onyx carafe lying on the table. "And?"

"*And*, that means a potential catastrophe beyond imagination."

He could see in her eyes that she was weighing the possibilities. "Go on."

Collin could sense in her manner a small measure of sympathy, but no more.

Telling her about any part of what I've discovered about Dara and the Black Annex over the last couple of days will only make things worse. I must close the damn project down! I can't do it from a lunatic asylum.

"And, First Lady, it's possible that it's *not* an accident, that's all I can say. It's possible that the organism that might escape from the lab will kill millions. It'll kill them *here*—not in Africa. Even the President might be in danger. That is what I think, and I think nothing else."

Collin recognized that he had gotten very used to telling fibs.

The First Lady nodded understandingly, showing no sign of fear.

"It's no secret that you've been working hard, Collin. You've had marital problems, too." Collin and Shonda exchanged knowing glances. "Dara told me, of course," she continued. "She also admitted that you're under a great strain. She's been telling me for some time that the job has changed you. She says you are hanging around with some woman who thinks she's a witch. Frankly, I think Dara is a bit off, too. Does she see a shrink also?"

"No." That seemed like a question from left field, but he could understand why she might ask that. Collin wished that he could tell her all about her childhood chum. He restrained himself instead. "Well, let's just say the project has been a terrible burden to her too, First Lady. I think Dara is not who we think she is."

Shonda Rice O'Neal smiled warmly. Collin felt that he had her complete support. "Yes Collin, I also know how Dara can be sometimes. She's a very intense woman."

"Yes."

"Tell me Collin, do you really see a psychiatrist?"

Collin was dazed by the question. He suddenly felt like he was sitting on quicksand. "Well, yes I do."

"What's his name?"

The conversation had taken a bad turn, thought Collin. "Dr. Jonas Bridgestone."

"I understand you're virtually done with the vaccine project. The rest is practically on autopilot, right?"

"Yes, more or less."

"How many children do you think the vaccine will save—and how quick?"

"We *had* estimated three million in the next six months."

"And, less likely to spread to other continents?"

"That's what we had calculated, yes."

"This rogue gene you've been talking about—the Super-virus—is it as bad as all that?"

"Worse."

"Collin, I have to say goodbye. I see from the yellow light above your head that we have twenty minutes until take off. I have a speech to memorize, after all." She pulled a sheaf of papers out of a nearby drawer.

"Do you approve of my plan then? For the lab," asked Collin.

"I'll have to get back to you on that, Collin dear. You know, retirement isn't that bad. You can rest on your laurels."

All of a sudden, the cracked door swung wide open, and a tall, husky agent took Collin by the arm and escorted him off the jet, down the steep metal steps, and onto the tarmac of the airport.

Before Collin left the agent at the deserted gate, the burly man pulled Collin by the arm to draw him near.

"Next time, Doctor, when you want to speak to the First Lady, you contact *me* through the general White House switchboard. Do *not* call her social secretary on the private line. Ask for Agent Bradley."

"But . . . "

The agent cut him off as he winked at Collin. "—Got that? Have a good day."

Then he abruptly left without a handshake or a good-bye.

Collin felt as though he had just had an ice water enema.

CHAPTER FORTY-SEVEN

Northeast of Bethesda, Maryland, Later that Friday afternoon:

Collin entered the security code to the front door of the main laboratory in the little box on the wall next to the entrance.

To his surprise, it opened.

Considering the result of the disastrous TV interview with Pricilla, and disappointing meeting with the First Lady, he had expected a lockout. Shonda Rice O'Neal had obviously thought that Collin might be insane, and she had to get out from underneath her decision to place him as the Scientific Director of the project. After all, thought Collin, she had her position and her husband to protect.

Yet, Frank Seaton hadn't switched the code. Security had generally been lax at the lab, the entry codes inadequate, and in this instance, the inattention to detail had played into Collin's hands. Consequently, he strode to his desk unimpeded, with his mind consumed by the catastrophic Dante button that had been installed underneath it.

Activating the button would destroy the Super-virus behind the glass wall—and everything else—dashing the hopes of Dara and her Dark Army at least for the foreseeable future. At the present that would be overkill, Collin had decided. The black lever at the entrance of the glass wall would be a better option.

Rotating the black lever before pulling it would torch the contents of the entire Firehouse, including the Super-virus, but not the main lab, resulting in few deaths. He could smash the glass box in which it rested before anyone could stop him, then activate the fire jets. As Collin strode to the door of the glass wall and the black lever perched upon it, he saw, thankfully, only three staff members at work in the adjunct lab area.

Burning them to cinders would be regrettable, thought Collin, but this chance had presented itself and must be seized. He might not get another. It was the hardest thing he ever had to do in his whole life—murder three colleagues in cold blood.

As Collin neared the glass-enclosed box containing the black lever, he glanced around the main lab area. No one seemed to notice his presence. He felt as if his body were in slow motion, his fingers itching to yank on it. Then, just as he reached his objective, he saw security guards dashing towards him. He felt a strong hand clamp around his arm. It halted him dead in his tracks.

A security guard had stopped him. Stanley Chu then intruded into his field of vision. Collin lunged for the glass box that housed the black lever in a desperate attempt to break away. Another guard tackled him to the floor. Two other armed guards then piled on.

Collin, pressed to the tile floor by the weight of the men, noticed other staff looking over at the scuffle. A crowd of white lab coats formed around the melee.

Collin could see Chu from the bottom of the pile. His expression was icy. "Dr. De Gise, upon Frank Seaton's authority, you are hereby terminated from employment at the lab."

Chu nodded to a guard that had remained standing. "Please escort Dr. De Gise to the front door after you help him off the floor. No charges will be pressed as long as he doesn't attempt to return."

The other guards climbed off of Collin. They helped the Nobel Laureate to his feet, leading Collin gently by the arm to the exit. Arresting a famous scientist was not what Stanley wanted, Collin knew. The bad publicity would harm the project.

Stanly Chu accompanied them to the door. "Your desk will be cleaned out and the proper belongings returned to you in due course," reassured Chu. "You may *not* return. You'll be arrested if you do, " added the contentious FDA bureaucrat.

Collin tried to jerk his arm away from the guard again, to no avail. "Where's Frank, Dr. Chu?"

"He's on important business, Dr. De Gise."

Chu and everyone else halted at the door. Collin had blown his chance.

"Dr. De Gise. It pains me to do this," mumbled Dr. Chu. His voice softened. "I didn't volunteer for this duty. As a federal officer—and this being essentially a federal project—I was ordered to do it." Chu held out his hand to Collin. "We expect you back when you're feeling better."

The guards released Collin.

Collin ignored Chu's handshake, contemplating his precarious situation as he marched out the door. Banning him, and branding him as a lunatic had been a much more effective option for Frank Seaton than a direct confrontation. Frank had won this round.

What Collin couldn't quite understand was why Frank Seaton had installed the Dante button and the black lever in the first place. It seemed that the last thing he would want is to destroy the viruses—under any scenario. Then, the reason hit him, and it had been obvious.

Seaton, Dara, probably Bridgestone, and the rest of the scum weren't world-class scientists in the field of molecular biology and genetics. They had no way of knowing whether or not the Super-virus would work. If their plan went bust, or the Dark Army were exposed, what better way to destroy the evidence and all the witnesses than a fiery inferno?

It was ingenious, really.

Collin had no hard feelings toward Chu. The man was only doing his duty.

But, now he'd have to do his. Collin had tried the peaceful way, now he'd have to resort to violence.

CHAPTER FORTY-EIGHT

Washington DC, Later that Friday afternoon:

The afternoon sun had pushed the dark clouds away. Collin figured he still needed his detective to tail Dara. It was even more vital now—knowing what she wanted—in order to plan and execute his next move.

"Tell me what you know," said Collin as Torres rowed the boat in the Tidal Basin.

Collin could see the first pink blooms of the cherry trees next to the Jefferson Memorial. The detective, obsessed by secrecy, had insisted upon discussing his findings while rowing around along the waterfront of the famous Washington shrine.

"Dara met with Shona Rice O'Neal—the First Lady. They met in a swanky restaurant in DC—on the patio," explained Torres.

Collin unbuttoned his long brown overcoat as he sat facing Torres in the bow of the boat. The detective rowed strenuously in his New York Jets windbreaker and faded jeans. Collin studied his shaking hands and darting eyes. His private detective had the jitters, thought Collin.

"Dara and the First Lady knew each other as children, Mr. Torres." Collin wondered if Torres secretly carried a microphone on him. In fact, he really didn't know if he should be discussing anything with the man—but he needed information.

The detective's restless eyes shot around, making sure that another boat wasn't near. "Why didn't you tell me?"

"Tell you what?" asked Collin.

"That you're connected."

Collin just shrugged.

The detective stopped rowing and unzipped his windbreaker. A bead of sweat formed on his forehead.

"Your wife and the President's wife don't seem to like each other much."

Torres pulled out a large manila envelope. He handed it to Collin, and then resumed rowing. "The photos are in order. Take out the top one first."

Collin removed the first photo. He saw a color image of Dara with Shonda Rice O'Neal. The First Lady was pointing her finger at Dara—her trademark cat sunglasses and sixties hairdo clearly visible.

"I saw them arguing. No, they were *snarling* at each other," said Torres.

"What were they arguing about?"

"Don't know—I couldn't use my little directional microphone—too many Secret Service agents around to get close. I was lucky to get anything."

Torres guided the boat closer to the shore. "I clicked off the photo of them near the restaurant as they stood on the sidewalk—the picture you're holding. I got lucky with the telephoto lens buried in a rolled up magazine—a quick side-shot."

Collin studied the image closely. Whatever the argument had been about, thought Collin, it hadn't been trivial. *Maybe they had been arguing about the use of the Vampire virus?* "All right, what else?" asked Collin.

Just then, a couple of tourists with cameras rowed by them. They were about ten yards away. Torres steered the boat away, furtively glancing to see where their cameras were aimed.

"The next one's a doozy," Torres said, looking around nervously.

"What's with you anyway, Mr. Torres? You're nervous."

"Pull out of the next photo in the stack and see." Torres guided the yellow rowboat toward a narrow canal in the distance. "I'm ready for a long vacation." The canal had a U-shaped, Japanese-style bridge running over it.

"Look at the picture, Doc. See what the ball and chain's up to."

As Collin examined the second photo, the sun that reflected off the water irritated his eyes. "Dara's behind her car, fooling with some boxes. So what?"

"Look at the blurred sign in the background—above the roof of the car."

"Army Surplus," read Collin out loud. "I see. She bought a gun then? What else?"

"A Colt forty-five; a detonator and plastic explosives too, probably long expired. It's legal in in small quantities in some states; also, a gas can and fuel with an igniter."

"What's she doing with those?" Collin's question was addressed to himself, not Torres.

"Is she a pyro?" asked Torres. "Is she out to dust the First Lady? Does she know how to use this stuff? Does she want to use it on *you,* Dr. De Gise?"

"Her dad was in military demolitions. She grew up with guns." Collin glanced at the narrow bridge about fifty yards ahead of them. "I don't know what she has in mind, Mr. Torres."

Collin could see that part of one rail on the bridge was missing. The red arches of the bridge rose to a point about five feet above the water. "Where did she take these weapons?"

"To *your* house," answered Torres. "She stashed them in the greenhouse in your back yard."

Collin wondered who Dara's target was.

It could still be the President, or the Congress, or any symbol of power. He doubted they were meant for him. The fact that the Dark Army planned to unleash the Super-virus didn't preclude other smaller acts of violence as a preliminary or a rear-guard action, he figured, or maybe a decoy.

She could also be planning to hit the First Lady, thought Collin.

Killing any White House luminary would be a good distraction. It would take the media attention away from a spreading pandemic.

"There's two more photos in the envelope," said Spider Torres as he started to wheeze from the strain of the oaring. "I told you to bring the cash. I want it—all of it—as agreed. Plus, my bonus—got that? I'm traveling."

Collin reached under his coat and pulled out a fat envelope. He gave it to Torres.

The detective stopped oaring and counted the bills.

"This is *leave* pay, Doc, and *hazard* pay. After this meeting, I'm on extended holiday."

"Where are you going?"

After stashing his cash away, Torres resumed oaring. "I have a little place outside of Mexico City. I'm taking my honey and losing myself. Tonight I'm gone—I already have the plane tickets."

"What did you mean exactly by '*hazard* pay'?"

"Let's just say that—if I tell anyone what I meant—the men in the white coats might pound on my door."

"Why?"

"Before we get to the rest of the photos—I want to tell you something."

Collin nodded. "Go on."

"There's a man involved—one of the men you gave me a picture of."

"Yes." Collin thought that it was probably Frank Seaton.

"Dara met him a couple of times. I couldn't get a shot or a sound bite, but he hugged her when they met. She hung on his every word. She looked very upset—"

"—Dr. Jonas Bridgestone?"

"—Yes. Tall—dark hair and beard, looks like Abe Lincoln?"

"That's him."

Collin looked into the sparkling water. The pierced eyebrow, spying on him with Frank Seaton, both gung-ho on the project, asking a lot of technical questions about the virus, it figured more than ever about Bridgestone, thought Collin. "All right. What's last?"

"Pull it out—look." Torres stopped rowing to search the water behind him. Seeing nothing out of the ordinary on the horizon, he turned back toward Collin who had the next photo in his hands.

Collin examined the image of Dara—standing on the edge of the street, outside The Black Peacock—stooping behind the top of her car. She was spying on someone about twenty yards away—but that someone or something was out of the field of vision.

Torres' voice raised a note. "I got that one this morning. Your wife's been tracking this same young lady all day. I caught her following her three times over the last twenty-four hours.

"Who is the young lady?"

"Take out the last photo."

Collin slipped it out of the manila envelope. He already knew.

Torres noticed Collin's reaction: " Take it easy, Doctor? Well, she's not exactly a young lady—kind of a funny kid."

Collin swallowed hard.

The image of the short green hair, the dark eyeglasses, and the Redskins jacket grabbed Collin.

"One time in particular, your wife had approached her real close," offered the detective. "She had just put her gun in her purse. I saw her load it. I think she meant to use it on this sweet kid."

Collin's eyes flashed at Torres as the detective averted his eyes from his murderous gaze. "It's our daughter."

How *could* she? But then again, the creature that was Dara wasn't human, and titles like "mother," "daughter," and "husband" had no relevance, thought Collin.

Dara must sense that Stephanie suspects something, concluded Collin darkly.

No wonder Dara and Stephanie had been at each other's throats.

Stephanie now faced direct slaughter from her "mother." Collin knew he must do something massive, and quick.

Dara would have to be dealt with.

Collin's pacifism vaporized like spittle on a red-hot grill.

CHAPTER FORTY-NINE

The air had turned nippy.

The late-afternoon sun drenched the skyline with brilliant yellow and orange hues. Collin wanted desperately to conclude his business with the detective as soon as possible and rush back to protect Stephanie and Lilith from Dara's harm.

Just then, Collin noticed another rowboat coming uncomfortably close—about thirty yards off starboard.

Torres checked them out too. A frowning young man, dressed in an army uniform, rowed the boat. A thin woman with long, auburn hair, and wearing a bright red dress, sat at the bow. She chattered in a loud, scathing voice. She pointed her finger at her companion as their boat glided rapidly in the water.

Collin heard the woman shout. She seemed angry with her companion.

Torres glanced over at them, biting his lip, narrowing his eyes. He tried to row away from them. Then, oddly, laughter came from the strange rowboat. Collin observed that the couple in the boat kissed. They had a lover's spat, he surmised. Or, maybe that is what he was *supposed* to think.

The rowboat then got even closer.

Maybe they were really spies, thought Collin.

"That boat's getting too close, Mr. Torres. The occupants seem too theatrical to be genuine."

"Don't tell me my job, Doctor."

"I need to get back."

I'm taking the shortcut," blurted Torres. "I'm done with this assignment."

"As you say, Mr. Torres."

The close encounter with the suspicious boaters, not to mention the other incidents of violence during the last week, and now the threatening photo of her with her mother, made Collin realize he had to keep a close eye on his daughter—who may be in imminent danger. Moreover, she could be of great use to him in destroying the project. Exposing her to the additional danger was the last thing he wanted. But, if Dara succeeded in her dark plot, then his daughter's life wouldn't be worth a damn anyway.

Stephanie had the advanced computer expertise to eliminate the essential digital programs and memory from the lab's hard drives and the off-site servers. At a minimum, their destruction would set the project back years. Children would die in the meantime, he knew, but it was better than the *world* dying.

As Torres oared quickly toward the bridge, Collin continued to plan. He boiled the whole thing down to two operations. Their logic of them screamed into his consciousness. In a strange way, the two action-plans even titillated him.

First, he must neutralize the imminent threat to Stephanie. The second operation, which would be enhanced by the first, would be—in military jargon—decisive. His only ally was his trusted friend, Lilith. He was thankful for her, at least.

The Dark Army must be defeated. That meant he would have to infiltrate the lab, and he knew precisely what to do.

Collin—who'd been lost in thought—looked around and saw it would be dark soon. The strange rowboat had disappeared.

Spider Torres stopped rowing long enough to grab a piece of paper out of his pants pocket. He handed it to Collin and resumed rowing.

On the paper was a photo that shook Collin to his core.

"I forgot to give you that. Consider it a freebie."

"Where did you take this photo, Mr. Torres?"

"At a restaurant—a few hours ago." Torres scanned the water in the distance to make sure no one was following them. "Why? Do you know the woman in that picture talking to your wife?"

Too stunned, Collin didn't answer.

Collin saw that the woman in the photo was calmly showing Dara pictures—probably the same ones he had given her.

Deception, betrayal, and anger raced through Collin's mind. Had she been one of the Dark Army all along? Is she Dara's surrogate?

This woman is looking after my daughter!

The woman in the photo was none other than Lilith Green.

CHAPTER FIFTY

Collin, initially stunned, had recovered.

Aside from Stephanie, he now faced the world alone. Worse, Stephanie seemed even in greater jeopardy. He must get back to Lilith's house quickly.

Then, a lost thought found its way back through his mind.

Collin needed to know the reason for the steely detective's sudden bout of terror.

"Torres. What was it that you saw that shocked you so much? You talked about hazard pay and making a quick getaway to Mexico." Collin, leaning toward him at the rowboat's bow, made hard eye contact with the detective. "What's given a seasoned pro like you the jitters?"

Collin noticed their rowboat entering the canal, gliding under the narrow Japanese bridge. It was the short way back to the boat dock and the parking lot.

Torres' eyes met Collin's as he slowly worked the oars, but he remained silent. He started to shiver.

"Tell me, damn you!"

"It wasn't just one thing, Dr. De Gise." His face blanched.

"Then tell me the most important one."

"I saw something. I'd never seen anything like it. In all my days of hunting, I never saw anything like that.

"What?"

Spider Torres froze in silence.

"I've got to know. Tell me!"

"I saw a creature sir, a snake. Not just any snake. It took over my . . . *thoughts.*"

The boat moved below the middle of the bridge, under the broken rail. Torres then gasped as if he had just inhaled a huge piece of sirloin. Collin glanced up to the bridge.

What Collin saw was beyond terror. He tried to scream but lost his voice.

A big black snake dropped from the bridge onto the seat next to Spider Torres.

It stood on its slimy end—upright, glistening in the sun's orange rays, pointing its diamond-shaped head at the hapless detective. It vibrated and hissed, displaying two luminous yellow eyes with vertically slit pupils.

It was the same damn type of snake all right, thought Collin. Torres's eyes welded to the snake's powerful gaze. Locked in—the man was unable to look away.

The snake rotated its head, turning its yellow gaze upon Collin.

Its eyes now locked onto his. Collin tried to look away, but couldn't. As the snake rotated its head back toward Torres . . .

Torres sprung up from his seat, staggered back, and fell over the bow of the rowboat into the turgid water. The serpent shot after him, disappearing over the edge of the rowboat, brandishing its curved fangs.

The screaming man thrashed in the water as Collin looked on, stunned. The viper's fangs ripped at Torres' throat, then clamped around his fleshy neck. In an instant, Spider Torres stopped moving, sinking to the bottom of the murky water.

The snake disappeared as fast as it had appeared.

Collin carefully stood up in the boat and looked around. No bystanders were visible. As far as he knew, no one could place him with Torres, except the curious couple in the rowboat—and they were long gone. He doubted the detective had told anyone about his meeting Collin there.

Collin jumped out of the boat and into the chilling water, swimming for a deserted, grassy spot up the canal where he could lose himself along the Tidal Basin. He would then circle back to the parking lot.

He noticed the sky as he swam to shore, it being almost sundown. He didn't have time to report a body to the authorities. If he did, he would probably be detained. He could have none of that. After all, he would be very busy during the next twenty-four hours.

Collin's blood was up. The violence on the rowboat had given him a taste for more.

CHAPTER FIFTY-ONE

Georgetown, Friday evening, March 30:

"Stephanie will be home any time, precious. My God, we've been though hell, haven't we?"

"Never heard you use the word 'God' before, Lilith. How inspiring."

"Unprecedented times, my dear. I never thought a Crucifixion scene would turn my spine to jelly, either."

"Where is she?"

"Stephanie?"

"Of course."

Lilith looked at Collin uncertainly. "I'm not sure, darling. Maybe she walked to the corner store. Collin, you have a killer's look in your eye."

"You're supposed to be looking after her."

"Sorry dear, she left without telling me."

"I see."

Collin considered the long list of casualties during the last week. Maybe he would make Lilith another one. He wondered where Stephanie had been.

"What's the name of that store?" asked Collin.

"Village Market," Lilith answered.

Lilith heaped Collin's plate with spaghetti and garlic bread, then poured him a glass of wine. "Want me to call and see if she's been there?"

He drained his glass. His face felt numb from drowsiness. "I'll do it." Collin called the grocer and was told that she had indeed been at the market within the last hour, and that she said she would be walking back home after she visited a friend who lived nearby. Collin didn't know who that could be, so he let the matter drop for the moment.

Lilith served herself a portion of pasta and sat down at the end of the dinner table, catty-corner to him. She eyed Collin's black woolen robe, running her hand over his bulky sleeve. "I love that robe—it's so soft. It's too big for me—are you comfortable, dear? I'm very sorry if I've done something to upset you."

Collin looked up at the bare, cranberry-colored walls in Lilith's Spartan dining room. He shifted his bloodshot gaze to her inscrutable, tea-colored eyes. "You have some explaining to do, Lilith."

He wondered which photos Lilith had shown Dara.

"All right, what is it?" Lilith removed her hand from his sleeve.

Collin just shrugged.

Lilith wore a black blouse and jeans, with some kind of strange necklace that had a silver bauble at the end—the eerie charm looked to Collin like a half-moon. It triggered more suspicion—and hostility.

"Do anything special today, Lilith?"

"No, nothing at all. Tended the bookstore in the morning with Stephanie—then came home." She smiled at him as she patted his shoulder. "You look tired, my boy. Rest. You need to regain your strength. Now tell what is bothering you so."

Collin was thinking of the duplicity with which she had rewarded his friendship, and the trust that she had violated. The rage welled up within him, routing his advancing fatigue.

He noted the knife sitting next to his plate, and the compelling urge to drive that blade straight through her neck. Then, he might torch her whole damned, wicked house.

But, the dark urge was momentary. His best friend deserved a hearing despite the damning photograph that had been supplied by Spider Torres.

He could be way ahead of himself, he thought. "Who's the friend that Stephanie went to visit?" asked Collin.

"As I said, she walked to the corner store for something. I'd don't know about any friend, darling. She'll be back soon."

Lilith poured him more wine. Collin had carefully smelled the wine before he drank the first one. It had seemed normal, without a trace of poison. Collin wondered if she was telling the truth about Stephanie.

"What's wrong, Collin? Let's have it."

Lilith rested her face upon her hands. She studied him closely. "I know you're worried. So am I. At first, I told her not to go. She sneaked out before I could stop her."

Collin nodded.

"*Faces Behind Shadows* is paid for." Her hand returned to the sleeve of Collin's robe. "It was sent special delivery to your work directly from the source—it should already be there. Not to your home. Dara will be watching closely."

"Yeah, I caught her looking through my stuff too, and Stephanie's."

"The book's addressed to you. Your workplace mail router will probably put it on your desk."

"Probably—that's what he usually does." Collin just stared at her, saying nothing.

There was a long silence.

"Do you have something else to tell me?" Collin asked.

Her eyes burned into his as they shed their neutral quality.

The urge to harm her shot through Collin's mind again. That is, if he *could* kill her. He wondered how someone would kill the recruits of the Dark Army. Could it really happen by slitting their throats with a dagger from the Holy Land and then burning or hanging them? It would have to do, he supposed. He had heard that method around that very dinner table from Lilith herself—therefore it might now be unreliable, he realized.

Then Collin wondered, if Lilith were guilty, why would she have mentioned the Dark Army at all—or the Black Annex for that matter. So much didn't add up.

"All right. You know that I met with Dara—don't you Collin?" That wasn't so much a question as an accusation. Lilith's eyes grew cautious. "What are you thinking? I don't like the look in your eye, dear."

Collin recalled his history of paranoia—another layer of smoke-and-mirrors and uncertainty that he had to contend with. There could be an explanation for her meeting with Dara—and not telling him about it.

Collin reached into his robe pocket and threw the photograph Spider had taken that morning onto the table in front of Lilith. The picture of her confiding in Dara—the enemy—will shake things up a bit, he thought.

Lilith picked up the photograph from the table and studied it gravely.

"I see the detective is earning his fee—unless *you* took it." As she spoke, her eyes remained on the picture. "I wanted to talk to her. I don't blame you for following me."

"Dara was tailed, not you. Let's have it. Why did you want to talk to her? Why didn't you tell me about it? And where the hell is Stephanie?"

Tears streamed down Lilith's face. She trembled. As she did, Collin got angrier.

He thought that her reaction was just what he would have expected from an artful, devious enemy. However, as he clenched his fists, ready to do damage, the words that gushed out of her mouth like a dam-break had somehow rang true.

They were from the heart—a *human* heart. It reminded him of his five-pointed flower—too pure to fake. Besides, maybe he was seeing enemies everywhere, he thought.

"Tell me the truth!" he demanded.

"The truth. I'm sad," said Lilith.

"Why?"

A tear rolled down her cheek. "Your photo makes me look ten years older."

Collin's jaw dropped, and then he grinned. He burst out laughing, the tension release being huge. He didn't stop for one full minute.

Lilith cracked a smile as she wiped her eyes with a napkin. "I showed Dara the photo of the Nazi bitch. I told her that we were on to her. I love you Collin, I swear. Like a son I do."

Her words swept over him like a warm and gentle breeze. "You, and sweet Stephanie. She's so helpless. I told that slut if she hurts one hair on Stephanie's head—or yours—that I'd cut her tits off!" Lilith's eyes took fire.

Collin reluctantly accepted her story. It seemed too loony to make up.

Collin's voice was soft and mirthful. "You really told her *that*?"

"Yes I did, precious." Lilith wiped her tears with her sleeve. "Dara didn't deny anything—it was strange. She said the photo was just a trick. Then she just stared at me, and walked away. What nerve!"

Collin nodded. "Not exactly a wilting violet, are you precious."

Lilith smiled.

Collin did have some lingering doubts. He could choose to trust Lilith or not, and so he did. Besides, he needed an ally. "Lilith—you should've told me that you wanted to confront her."

"You wouldn't have let me meet her."

"True," agreed Collin.

"It was harebrained, impulsive, I know."

"True," agreed Collin again. "By the way, Torres is toast—"

"She got to him?"

"Probably."

"What are you thinking about?" asked Lilith.

"Stephanie—I hope she's all right. I hope Dara hasn't gotten to her yet. I found out that Stephanie's in more danger than we had thought. Dara's stalking her with a weapon."

"Collin, you have to do something!"

"Oh I will, I will. I will indeed."

CHAPTER FIFTY-TWO

Georgetown, Sabbath morning, March 31:

At six o'clock in the morning, Collin awoke without an alarm. The sun's rays had just started to creep into the blackness of Lilith's spare bedroom. He slipped out of his covers, put on his dark slacks, khaki shirt with a deep pocket, and thick, black leather belt. Reaching into his front pocket, he felt something soft. He pulled out the crimson flower—the five-pointed Royal Catchfly— forgetting that he had put it in there the night before for good luck.

Collin looked in on Stephanie as she lay sleeping soundly, buried in her quilted covers. Collin and Lilith had waited anxiously for Stephanie's return the evening before. He had gone looking for her but couldn't find her. She had finally arrived at Lilith's house about nine o'clock in the evening from her trip to the corner store.

Stephanie had indeed visited a friend, and thought nothing of making Lilith and her father sick with worry. In fact, she had greeted them cheerfully when she arrived home. She had always been thoughtless in that way, he remembered.

Collin quietly left Lilith's house to meet, as they had planned the night before, at The Black Peacock bookstore. Exactly what she had wanted to discuss with him he didn't quite know. It might have been something about *Faces Behind Shadows*—some details that her distributor was supposed to have texted to her that morning.

Her texting at times was unreliable, so she may have missed some of the message. According to Lilith, the book would almost certainly shed more light upon Dara's specific plans, and the precise identity of whom she had been working with.

Collin turned onto Caine Street in his old, red beamer and then raced toward Able Street. He noticed a strange glow over the roofs of the houses and the buildings in the distance. He could smell smoke, and sirens sounded in the far distance.

Collin saw that Lilith's bookstore had been submerged in a huge ball of fire, and was surrounded by flashing red lights and a glut of police cars and fire trucks. A patrolman waved him to the side of the road that had been blocked off with orange cones.

Collin pulled over, jumped out of his car, and ran up to the officer—who put up his hand to halt his progress.

"Did the owner get out all right?" he asked the officer. Collin could see that the bookstore was mostly gone—a charred heap except for the remaining flames that shot up through what was left of the second floor and the roof.

The policeman waved him away. "Get back."

"I know the owner."

"I *said*, get back!"

"Please, she's a good friend. I saw her a few hours ago." At that moment, half the charred ruins of the building caved into the sidewalk, leaving a cloud of dust and ashes.

"You did, huh?"

The stout cop pointed over to a group of police and firefighters standing in front of the burnt-out heap. "All right. Go on. Introduce yourself to Lieutenant Espinosa, the brown suit over there."

Collin dashed up to a youngish man with a steely, composed expression and sharp, inquisitive black eyes. His green tie clashed with his plain, brown suit.

"Lieutenant Espinosa?"

The reflection from the remaining flames lit up Espinosa's round face like a Japanese lantern. "Who are you?" The Lieutenant wrote on a notepad without looking at Collin.

"Dr. Collin De Gise, a close friend of the owner of the bookstore. Her name's Lilith Green. Is she all right?"

The cop sized up Collin. "Let's see some ID."

Collin fished his wallet out of his back pocket and displayed his driver's license.

"All right. Did she know anyone who might have wanted to do her harm?"

"No," he lied. "What do you mean, '*did*'?"

"This is strictly off the record at this point. One fireman managed to get in for a few minutes. He found a charred body next to the entrance. She's dead."

Collin's legs almost left him. For the first time in many years, he thought that he was going to cry. Then, a dark thought shot into his head. What if she had been lying all along?

What if the charred body hadn't really been hers, but some other victim of the Dark Army?

Collin forced that horrendous notion out of his head. He had to gain control of himself. *Lilith was my friend.*

Espinosa's eyes nodded toward one of his officers standing a few meet away. "We found *this* next to the body." Espinosa waved for the other cop to come over. "It may serve as identification."

"Let's have a look at it," said Collin.

The uniformed policeman walked over to them with an envelope in his hand.

"Naturally," continued Espinosa as he took the envelope from the officer, "at this hour of the day you'd might expect that the body would most likely be the owner."

Collin observed closely as the Lieutenant poured the contents of the envelope into his hand. He held the bauble up to Collin's face. "Ever see this before?"

Collin felt his stomach drop to his shoes. His eyes welled up. "That's—hers—Lilith Green's—the proprietor of The Black Peacock bookstore." Collin felt guilty for having ever doubted her.

It was the silver half-moon charm that Lilith had been wearing, burnt around the edges.

Lieutenant Espinosa looked down at the ground. His voice had shed its gravel quality. "I'm sorry." His eyes searched Collin's. "We'll get a final ID on the body when it cools down." He then held up what looked like a melted cell phone. "Oh, we found this too, lying next to her. I'll tell you right now—off the record—we've not ruled out arson."

Collin, not surprised, said nothing.

"Please write down your phone number and address in case we have any further questions."

Collin strode back to his car.

He then thought about that little cell phone Lilith always carried around with her.

She had texted him frequently about almost anything. Half the messages he had fumbled due to his intolerance for silly gadgets.

If she had known that the wildfire had trapped her in her building, she might have texted him before she died. As she lay on the ground coughing and gasping for air, she really had no one else to say goodbye to, thought Collin. She also might have had more information about Dara.

It was just a feeling—a hunch.

Collin jerked open his car door, sat down behind the wheel, and removed his cell phone from his glove box. He carefully pushed the buttons to retrieve the information.

The words came up on the little screen:
"READ BOOK.
PRAY. FIND GOD.
GET THEM!
SORRY, LOVE, L."

Collin trembled. He broke down and sobbed. He crashed down upon the curb and let the dam break completely. He felt weak when the sobbing finally stopped.

Rage burned through his body like a terrible disease.

Lilith's words echoed.

"Get them!"

With pure pleasure, vowed Collin as he wiped the tears from his eyes. Besides, he had his daughter to protect. Dara was going to have an early morning visitor.

CHAPTER FIFTY-THREE

Collin pulled his car up to the curb two houses down from his home, so he would make as little noise as possible while entering his property.

The sun had just risen over the homes in his neighborhood. From the lack of frost on the grass and balmy feel to the air, it promised to be an unusually warm day. According to the car radio meteorologist, a record high temperature was expected.

Dara had mentioned to Collin several days before that she wouldn't be working that Saturday. Collin therefore expected her to be home and in bed. He knew she slept in when time allowed.

He dashed to the greenhouse to search for Dara's stashed weapons—the ones that Spider Torres had told him about. After hunting in drawers, behind pots, and under shelves, he found nothing. He plucked the thinnest nail out of his tool chest and hustled over to the garage, peeking though the window.

Dara's black Lexus was there, almost assuring him that she was in the house. He headed over the lawn to the back door entrance, then jiggled the nail in the keyhole and unlocked it, gaining entry.

Collin quietly ascended the back stairs to the hallway on the second floor. He tiptoed into his study, noting that all the doors along the corridor were open except the one leading to the master bedroom. He quietly unlocked his closet.

Opening his hidden compartment, he inventoried the lethal menagerie: the flamethrower and attached canister with fuel; the curved ceremonial dagger; his modified, M110 sniper rife with a British infrared telescopic sight; and his Beretta 0.40 caliber revolver with ankle holster. He made sure all the weapons were in serviceable order, and then carefully placed them within two canvas duffle bags that had been resting on the shelf.

Collin picked the dagger out of one of the bags, slid it under his belt and shirt—over the small of his back—and crept very quietly to the master bedroom door with the bags slung over his shoulder. He placed the bags of weapons on the hallway floor and gently tried the knob—it was unlocked.

He slowly opened the bedroom door and peeked in.

It wasn't dark inside—the curtains hadn't been drawn. He glanced over to the bed. There he saw the tanned back and lustrous, red hair of his wife as she lay quietly.

She eerily lifted her hand above her head, greeting him.

"I've been waiting for you."

An electric tingle danced within Collin's gut.

"I thought I'd heard you at the back door," she added softly.

He inched toward her—dazed by her beauty.

Dara rolled over in bed to face him—poised and smiling—and then sat up, holding her hands out to him. Her intense eyes locked onto to his like guiding lasers onto a target. Her soft skin glowed apricot blush.

No one on earth looked better nude, thought Collin. It's going to be a shame to slaughter her.

Collin sat down gently on the side of the bed, running one hand through her hair, and placing the other behind his back. He slowly removed the dagger from under his belt and furtively slid it between the box spring and the mattress.

CHAPTER FIFTY-FOUR

Dara, sitting up in the bed naked, drew Collin closer to her.

She searched his eyes. "I've always loved you in my own way. Stephanie hates me. I can't change that."

She ran her perfectly manicured nails through his hair. "You don't need to be involved in all this," she reassured him with a faint smile. "Just do your work."

She kissed him on the mouth, and then unbuckled his belt. She removed his coat and shirt, running her wet mouth down his chin and over his chest, and then going lower.

"I'm trusting you Collin." She looked into his eyes. He could just make out the strange birthmark on the iris at six o'clock.

"We have each other," she said. "I think I know how things are now."

He let himself be seduced.

As she ran her hand over his crotch, he heated up. It wasn't only her looks and voice and the memory of the sweet life they had built together with their daughter that had an aphrodisiac effect upon him, but also her power and craftiness—qualities in her that attracted him. Like a connoisseur of rare wines, Collin could only get a real high if he had the best—and she was the best.

She had to be. The Dark Army had seen to that.

Collin tugged the covers away from her breasts and ran his fingers over them. Dara closed her eyes, savoring the sensations, and pulled the soft quilted covers completely away. She crawled out of bed. She undid his shoes and doffed his socks.

As she did so—turning her back to him—she knelt on the floor with her smooth, V-back and rounded, firm bottom facing him in full view, the rays of the morning sun highlighting the downy, apricot tone of her flawless skin and body.

Thoughts of Lilith and all the others that had paid with their lives darted though his mind. They splashed around in his consciousness like small bails of water on a bonfire, dousing the flames just a bit while the whole conflagration raged out of control. Then, he noticed her bright red fingernails.

As he felt himself grow, he deftly moved his hand under the mattress . . .

Like a flash, he thrust the dagger straight through her neck—running her clean through. He yanked it out, and from behind, ran the blade over her throat almost severing her head clean off.

Dara thudded to the floor into a pool of her own blood. After hitting the ground, her head had twisted back toward him, so it rested upon her torso backwards, with her eyes still wide with shock. Collin just sat there for a minute, looking into those frozen, dying eyes.

He noted something he had not expected in their appearance: a hint of true love.

CHAPTER FIFTY-FIVE

As he stared down at the corpse of his wife, Collin wondered if she was really dead—or just acting. He felt her wrist for a pulse—nothing. Well, by mortal standards anyway, she was stone dead, he thought. Even in a bloody death, she stunned him with her loveliness.

Though evil and inhuman, no one could ever convince him that she hadn't loved him just a bit. About that at least she had spoken the truth.

Collin quickly buttoned his slacks and fastened his belt, and then grabbed his khaki shirt off the bed. As he did so, he dislodged the silk pillow propped against the headboard.

There at the head of the bed lay Dara's Colt 45 revolver, ready for duty.

Collin, sniper-rifle assembled and slung over his back beside the flamethrower canister, pulled the trigger on the fire wand. He marveled at the powerful spray of fire that thrust against the walls of the hateful Black Annex. He loved torching the sinister banner, "Countdown to Armageddon." Then, he ran to the bathroom downstairs and quickly cut his hair and shaved his head, just as in his old photo hanging in the closet with his commando chums. He then doffed the red beret that had sat on the closet shelf.

He was ready for duty.

He rad outside and torched the exterior of the house, glad that Dara's body would burn too. Standing in the back yard next to the rear facade of his home, he watched the huge house as it burst into flames. Collin grabbed his duffel bags and tore down the driveway toward his parked car on the street. As he threw his gear into the back seat and jumped in behind the wheel, he felt a powerful hand clamp onto his shoulder and swing him around.

A burley young man in his pajamas—a neighbor—had grabbed him. Collin punched him in the solar plexus, sending the man onto the pavement. He jumped into his car and sped off. Racing toward the corner, he glanced in the rear view mirror.

He saw the towering inferno that had once been his beautiful home. His neighbor, who had regained his footing, shook his fist at the departing vehicle. Collin expected that the man would be calling the police very soon, along with the Fire Department.

He had talked to Stephanie not an hour before on their cell phones. It was time to bolt over to Lilith's house and get her. He wanted to support Stephanie in her grief about Lilith. The news about her mother's fiery death will be hard for her to accept, and that would have to be delayed until the proper time.

Collin planned to hide out until nightfall, and then pursue the rest of his second operation, having just completed the first action. He knew he couldn't stay long at Lilith's, for the police were sure to search her home, especially when they found out Stephanie had been staying there too. They would figure the father would not be far away from the dutiful daughter. Nevertheless, he should have a couple of hours until they would be on to them.

As Collin drove through Georgetown making his way to Lilith's house, he thought about using Bridgestone's cabin as his hideout location until late in the night. He still had the key. The gaunt psychiatrist had told him he seldom used it. Even though the shrink had probably been recruited into the Dark Army, surmised Collin, it's unlikely they would assemble there—during their "holy" day of Armageddon.

Collin drove through the neighborhoods of Georgetown—ever vigilant for police cars. He worried about one item that couldn't be easily dismissed: how would he effectively neutralize the huge jumble of computer memory concerning the molecular manipulation of the master virus, so the Dark Army couldn't reconstruct the Super-virus. Moreover, much of the technical information rested on servers outside of the lab, which only his daughter knew how to erase.

Collin had tried desperately to keep his daughter out of this mess. But, the fact was he needed her. He had told her that. Characteristically, she instantly recognized that fact. Collin hadn't told her about Dara's impending death or about her complicity with the Dark Army and their plans for world destruction. He just told her that her mother had illegally tried to steal the virus and use it to harm innocent people. He dreaded the fact that eventually he'd have to tell her about Dara's grisly death.

He was proud of her. Once his daughter had realized Collin's dedication to his action plan, she insisted upon helping him. She had a sense of duty, and knew right from wrong. He loved her for that.

CHAPTER FIFTY-SIX

Stephanie had secretly met Collin a few hundred yards from Lilith's home, on the corner of Caine and Able streets. She jumped into his car and they sped away.

"Daddy, a policeman was looking for you at Lilith's house!"

"Lieutenant Espinosa?"

"I think so."

"I'll take care of it, love."

She looked at his red beret. "What happened to your hair? And that hat!"

He grit his teeth. "Reinventing myself dear—some people will feel my pain." Collin's voice went soft. "About Lilith . . ."

Stephanie, glum, looked out the window. "I'm all right, daddy."

Collin then pondered his situation as he drove toward the Maryland countryside.

Lieutenant Espinosa, trying to figure out who may have murdered Lilith, would soon be trying to figure out who killed Dara and torched their home. One person neatly connected those two horrific events, and that was Collin. There had been an eyewitness for the second crime. As to the first, Collin had suspiciously been the first early bystander to show up at the arson of the bookstore.

The hard-nosed Espinosa would believe that Collin had flipped his lid, and perhaps that he had even kidnapped poor Stephanie. Finding out that his daughter had been staying with Lilith would only intensify his search.

Collin thought Stephanie needed a little more background information. He explained as he drove that Dara had somehow— probably through Frank Seaton—substituted the omega gene for the epsilon gene. The Super-virus would therefore emerge late that very evening.

The Super-virus would then be passed to terrorists.

As Stephanie looked out the widow studying the signs that bordered the on-ramp, Collin told her that they would not be seeing much of Dara for a while. In his conclusion, Collin emphasized to his daughter that the viral project naturally must be scuttled. This may anger many people.

Collin felt that his daughter had taken the incredible news rather well. He had thought she would break up in tears. Instead, she just sat in the car, not saying a word, looking at the passing countryside. The poor girl was probably in shock, he surmised.

"Daddy, I sensed that mommy had turned bad. I didn't know why—I didn't know what to *do*." Stephanie wrung her hands. Collin reached over to the passenger seat and touched her shoulder. "I know love, I know."

"Where are we going now?" she asked.

"We're staying at Dr. Bridgestone's cabin until late tonight."

"I don't like that place."

"It's not for long." He motored up the interstate toward their hideout.

"I don't like that place," she repeated.

Stephanie's relentlessly analytical mind then grasped the essence of Collin's dangerous task ahead. As usual, it was as though she could read his mind. "You can only erase the molecular modeling files on the server one way. It takes three passwords that I've got hidden in my desk. It's tricky. The other stuff's easier."

"If I absolutely didn't need you, I wouldn't ask you. This could be dangerous, pet."

"Yes. I know."

He must explain in general, Collin thought, how they would accomplish his second operation. Afraid that she might panic, he wouldn't tell her about the Dante button under his desk unless that proved to be totally necessary. This action plan involved rather the black lever and incinerating the Firehouse, and all the ghastly viruses with it, including the dreaded Super-virus. Then, the Dark Army would be left with nothing.

"When the police catch you with me after we're done, you knew nothing about our plan—you got it? I *forced* you to come with me. After all, I'm a raving lunatic, right? Keep your mouth shut. Do you understand?"

Stephanie nodded.

"We'll be all right," he added. He glanced her over at her as he drove. As usual, she wore her old jeans, a Redskins varsity

223

jacket, and a dirty shirt and sneakers. He looked at his wrinkled and dirty clothes.

What a pair we make, he thought.

"Stephanie, I need to tell how we're going to sneak into the lab and exactly what we're going to do when we're in there . . ."

He went on to tell her about the secret passage under the road next to the laboratory, and the hidden entrance in the toddler-park. He explained that only he and Frank Seaton knew about the secret way into the lab, and he hoped that Frank wouldn't have had the opportunity to mention it to the authorities. The police were bound to interview him eventually.

"We'll hide out in the cabin and then drive to the little park," said Collin.

"Will the police get us?" Stephanie asked.

"I hope not. Bridgestone's cabin is probably under the radar. He shouldn't be using it tonight, either."

"I'm scared daddy."

Collin looked at his daughter.

"You're not alone, love."

CHAPTER FIFTY-SEVEN

Maryland countryside, early Sabbath afternoon, March 31:

"We're almost at the cabin."

As the sun shone on the rolling hills just east of the lab, Collin raced his car along the winding country road to Dr. Bridgestone's country retreat. He and Stephanie had just stopped at a drive-through burger joint for a bit to eat and a bathroom break. Collin had washed his face in the men's room, noticing how much he seemed to have aged in the past week, with heavy bags under his eyes and some grey stubble on his chin.

He looked over at Stephanie who was fast asleep in the passenger seat. Just short of the long driveway to the cabin, he stopped at a sharp turn, driving just off the shoulder to hide the car in the surrounding forest. The turn in the road, higher in elevation than the cabin, overlooked the rustic hideout nestled among the trees.

Collin removed a pair of binoculars from the glove box and strode to the edge of the shoulder, where he could see the cabin below through a clump of trees. It was about a half mile away.

His commando training and combat experience in the Middle East was useful in appreciating the situation. The elite task force to which he had been assigned specialized in advanced technology and game theory to neutralize as many human assets as possible as fast as possible—in any manner possible.

To Collin's consternation, Bridgestone's white Range Rover sat empty at the end of the driveway. He'd expected the cabin to be deserted. Since he now knew that Bridgestone was probably part of the Dark Army, Collin decided that he would have to take him out and hope that he had driven there alone. Bridgestone wasn't married, and to the best of Collin's recollection didn't have kids, so family members shouldn't be present.

Regrettably, thought Collin, anyone found with Bridgestone would also have to die.

Collin decided to wait until Dr. Bridgestone returned to his car from the cabin and then hit him there with his sniper shot. With the caliber of the rifle and its high velocity, it would be effective at that distance. Once at the cabin, Collin could search the house for an accomplice.

He quickly returned to his car and grabbed the rifle—with accessories—out of his trunk. He rapidly assembled it, mounting the scope, the optional infrared attachment, and the silencer. He slung it over his back. He then also removed the Beretta revolver, the ankle holster, and his curved Middle Eastern dagger and threw them in the back of the cab for quick access. He kept the small binoculars in his coat pocket. Peeking in at Stephanie, he saw that she was still asleep.

Dear Stephanie, he thought. She had no idea of the probable carnage that was about to occur, and no clue about the deadly weapons that he had acquired. Just as well, he decided.

Collin dashed back to his vantage point, lying among the needles and bark with binoculars in hand. He readied his rifle, placing it in the pine needles close to him. He scoped the front door and the side-entry of the cabin below, it still being light enough. Collin observed that the sun had started to set behind the trees.

A strange sound jolted Collin into action.

He rolled just in time. The tall man's heavy boot—which he had just glimpsed out of the corner of his eye—had barely missed his head.

Collin jumped to his feet, and the attacker—the young man in the army uniform that he had seen on the rowboat—crouched in a fighting stance. Collin circled, taking the measure of his opponent: six-two; two hundred pounds; cat striking position; agile and well built, and his eyes ready for battle—not good news for Collin.

Then the intruder charged.

Collin quickly turned to his side, backhanding him to his temple, and followed through with a sweep to the legs. The sweep missed, but the punch had connected—dazing his opponent.

Collin's attacker advanced again.

A spinning back-kick to Collin's stomach sent him down on his knees, gasping for air. Collin regained his feet quickly. He circled his opponent and fired a connecting sidekick to the ribs. They crunched nicely.

The young assailant grabbed his side in agony. He hyperventilated. A broken rib probably had pierced his lower lung, thought Collin, and the overwhelming pain had temporarily paralyzed him.

Instead of attacking, Collin observed him. He didn't appear to be armed. The man in the army uniform slowly dropped to his knees about five feet from Collin. He spit out blood.

Collin slowly advanced, wondering if he might be able to interrogate the intruder. Surprisingly, the assailant rose, reassuming his fighting stance.

They again circled each other, only this time slower and with less fluidity. Their savage eyes met. This time Collin planned to finish him off.

As Collin circled, he confirmed that the man before him was the man in the rowboat, the one with the moody young lady in the red dress. They had been spying on him and Spider Torres after all. They—no doubt—had been put up to it by Dara and the Dark Army.

He charged Collin again, this time launching a series of front kicks and thrusting punches as his opponent quickly retreated. Collin followed up with a palm strike to the throat, feeling the hard trachea crumble under his hand. The man hit the ground hard, rolling and thrashing, grabbing his swelling neck.

Blood and edema slowly closed his airway as he chocked and spat blood. He lay in agony. Collin could hear the growls and curses becoming fainter. He slowly ran out of oxygen. This time the man in the uniform didn't get up.

Instead, he died.

Collin fell back to the ground, sweaty, and drained of every ounce of energy and strength. He was out of shape, he lamented, the soft life having robbed him of his thunderclap delivery.

Lifting his head off the ground, he noticed that the fight had taken him about ten yards from his rifle, which still rested upon the bed of pine needles next to his beret . . .

"Now, get up on your knees. Slow—real slow. Then put your hands on your head—now!"

It was a woman's voice, thought Collin—and a familiar one.

Collin didn't need to turn and look at her—it was the dead man's querulous female companion—the young woman in the rowboat with the red dress and auburn hair. He'd recognize that shrill voice anywhere.

She must have a gun, he figured. He slowly rolled over and got on his knees. He looked her way, and then she came into his view. She did indeed have a pistol, and it pointed right at his head—not ten feet away. It was the young, auburn-haired woman in the rowboat all right.

"Easy madam, I get along with everyone," said Collin softly.

"Shut up. One more word and you won't have to worry about that."

Clear enough, thought Collin.

He figured that he was as good as dead. He had killed their matriarch—his wife Dara—the icon of the Dark Army. The minions were hopping mad.

Now, it's my turn to die.

CHAPTER FIFTY-EIGHT

Collin, on his knees, looked up at the young woman with the pistol.

"This won't be hard," she said to Collin as she held the gun pointed at him.

Collin saw her take aim. There seemed no way out. In a moment, he'd die.

Suddenly, he heard a click as he felt tiny droplets fly onto his cheek. He glanced over at a fir tree. There stood Stephanie, his sniper rifle in her hands, crying.

The rifle hung by her side, pointed down. She dropped it.

Collin looked back to where his would-be executioner had been standing. The woman lay there motionless, her head crimson mush. Collin wiped the blood-spatter from his face and neck with his sleeve.

Hysterical, Stephanie rushed to her father, who rose to embrace her.

"Daddy, I'm glad I killed her!"

Collin looked over at the body again.

"There, there, love" he reassured her as he gently stroked her hair. "I'm not too broken up about it myself." She managed to smile. He was still proud of her.

Collin heard a car motor turning over in the distance.

That must be Bridgestone leaving the cabin!

He rushed over to the rifle, picked it up, and sprinted to the clearing in the trees overlooking the cabin. Collin then fell to the ground, putting his eye to his telescopic lens. He sited the bearded head of Dr. Jonas Bridgestone within the crosshairs of his scope.

Collin, his finger on the trigger, hesitated. He had misgivings about taking out Bridgestone, but they were fleeting. The target was almost certainly in cahoots with Frank Seaton, and had been passing on information about his mental condition to Collin's enemies. He had asked nosey questions about the project, and wore that little ring over his eye. Had that been some kind of secret insignia of the Dark Army?

The target through the windshield of the Range Rover was available.

Moving his field of vision slightly, Collin saw that the psychiatrist was alone. Just as the Range Rover started to move, Collin pulled the trigger. Bridgestone's chest came apart in an explosion of flesh. Collin had been off the mark just a tad, but the outcome was the same. Bridgestone had been neutralized.

Bridgestone's rolling car hit a tree. The impact broke a headlight.

Collin rose from the ground, strung the rifle over his back, and ran to the two bodies, pulling them by their ankles to a hiding place under the trees. He covered them with branches and leaves.

Collin had frisked the bodies—glad not to find cell phones. That meant that the intruders hadn't had the means to alert backup, at least in theory.

The authorities might be on their way to the cabin right now, reasoned Collin, but he doubted it. The young woman and man he had just killed were probably working with Bridgestone, not the police. But again, that was just a theory.

While looking around for branches, Collin had noticed something down the hill—a small road leading west—in the direction of the toddler-park and the laboratory. Located about a quarter-mile from the cabin, it promised to be handy when they were ready to make their way to the lab around midnight. By that time, no one should be around the park or the lab.

Collin dashed back to his daughter to console her. As it turned out, she looked remarkably composed considering her ordeal. Not a bad shot at that, either, he mused. She had killed the female accomplice with surprising dispatch. Those expensive weeks of archery and rifle basics at the swanky summer camps when she was a kid had paid off.

Then, he realized the trauma that it must have been for his daughter to kill someone, no matter how calm she looked. He took her by the hand and led her back to the car, picking up the rifle along the way. They got into the car and headed down to the cabin. She was silent.

She must be in shock, Collin thought.

He wondered if anyone might be waiting inside the cabin to ambush them.

It could just be that bastard Frank Seaton.

CHAPTER FIFTY-NINE

Maryland countryside, Evening of he Sabbath Moon, March 31:

Collin searched the cabin thoroughly for Dark Army accomplices, half expecting to find Frank Seaton inside. Instead, the hideout was deserted. He hadn't slept more than a couple of solid hours in the last several days, and it was hard for him to concentrate. Thoughts intruded into his mind that alarmed him, and as the death toll mounted, the whole violent mess took on a surreal quality.

All he found of any significance in the cabin was Bridgestone's brown suit-coat and a pistol lying on the table in its shoulder holster. Since Bridgestone, a busy psychiatrist, often carried scheduled drugs with him, Collin thought nothing of his gun being there. The doctor was the type of man that would wear one, and be ready to use it without hesitation.

However, the coat looked too small to be Bridgestone's, and why had he left the gun on the table and not carried it?

Collin put Stephanie in a bedroom where she crawled under the covers, shaking. He stole a few moments to soothe her the best he could. As she fell asleep, Collin lovingly stroked her hair. "Get more rest, dear," he whispered almost as a lullaby. "Your life will change, I promise." Dead to the world, she remained silent.

Closing the bedroom door behind him, he rushed outside to his car sitting in front of the cabin. He drove it into the carport that was located on the side of the cabin hidden from the road—under a clump of trees. He strode to the Range Rover that rested against the big tree—its blood-spattered windshield shattered from his sniper's bullet and its one headlight smashed. Eerily, its motor was still running.

Collin looked up at the moon. The half-moon now complete, it radiated down from a clear, black sky—the orange halo bright. He knew that very soon the Super-virus would complete its morphogenesis in the adjunct laboratory. Then the Dark Army would unleash it after a very short growth period.

Collin strained to open the driver's door of the Range Rover but it was jammed. Instead, he dashed to the passenger side, pulled Jonas Bridgestone's cold body out of the front seat, and threw it on the ground. He dragged the body behind a pile of logs, covering it with loose dirt and needles.

Collin raced back to the car and got behind the wheel, feeling the congealing pool of cool blood on the seat underneath him seeping through his woolen slacks. Determined to get the car out of sight from the main road, he drove it to the side of the house.

Looking into the forest ahead of him, he then noticed the entrance to the small service road that wound through the hills—the same one he had noticed from the highway above the cabin . . .

Collin kicked and thrashed as the oxygen left his body. As he struggled, his foot kicked through the shattered windshield. His throat felt severed from his head as he reflexively grabbed the strangling object around his neck and desperately tried to yank it free from his throat.

In the split second that thrust his life into the balance, he felt the strap tighten around his airway—the vice-like force coming from the back seat. Someone had been hiding there all along, waiting for him.

Collin kicked out the rest of the windshield as he thrashed around, his vision slowly fading to grey from lack of air. He brought his legs down onto the carpet flooring of the car, just below the console.

He knew he had about ten seconds maximum until he would pass out—and then a few minutes more until he would die.

Collin then heard the welcome sound of the assailant grunting—thus locating the exact position of his executioner. As the attacker strained to tighten the belt around Collin's neck, Collin determined that the sound had come directly from behind and slightly to his left of the driver's headrest.

Collin thrust his left thumb backwards past the headrest and into the eye-socket of his assailant. He felt the squish of the eye enucleating. A primal scream of pain blasted from behind Collin as the strap around his neck loosened.

It had loosened just enough for him to wedge his hand under the choking belt, thus relieving the pressure on his airway.

Collin, sucking in a gasp of fresh oxygen, broke away. Thrusting his feet forcefully into the carpet and punching his right hand down into the upholstery, he catapulted backwards up and over the front seat and into the back seat of the car, his hands ready to devastate the most opportune target.

That happened to be a man's exposed throat.

Frank Seaton must die—the tantalizing thought shooting through Collin's frantic mind as he moved in for the kill. It's got to be Frank. Collin's powerful hands gripped the tracheal cartilage and squeezed. He felt the firm tissue in the man's neck dissolving in his hands.

Cough, gasp, thrash, kick, squirm, groaning, weakening flails, stillness, quiet, then limpness—the assailant dutifully went still—and then lay there dead.

To make sure he was gone, Collin switched his death-choke to a vice-arm headlock, and strained with all his might. He felt the upper cervical bones separate widely in the neck—and then heard the telltale crunch.

Collin sat there stunned, panting, and looking down at his victim. Although tired and somewhat shocked, he felt elated—and very *alive*—more than he had been in years.

He felt fortunate about the way these people had died— quite ordinary—he thought, considering their purported dark powers. Maybe they weren't part of the Dark Army after all, but hired underlings instead—flunky sub-contractors, as it were. Collin then got a closer look at the dead man's face after he turned on the light in the cab.

It wasn't Frank Seaton after all!

Collin continued to study the body, the eyes of the dead man still wide open. He knew that man. He had seen him recently. Collin frisked the body, and rummaged through the pockets of the rumpled brown slacks and tanned dress shirt—nothing.

Then, Collin finally recognized the round face.

The revolver inside the cabin was undoubtedly this man's and not Bridgestone's. Collin figured that he had surprised his attacker as he was trying to sneak away in the car. The man had quickly jumped into the back seat to avoid detection when he heard Collin approaching. Therefore, the ambush against Collin in the cab had probably been spontaneous.

Collin realized that the man he had just killed was Lieutenant Espinosa of the Georgetown Homicide Division. Collin was stunned. *Was this cop responsible for Lilith's murder and the torching of The Black Peacock?* Suddenly, the net of the Dark Army seemed much wider to Collin.

Whoever Espinosa worked for, Collin knew that his backup wouldn't be far behind.

CHAPTER SIXTY

Maryland Countryside, Later that evening, March 31:

"Don't go daddy, please, give yourself up. The police think you're crazy—you said so yourself. They won't hurt you!"

Stephanie sat at the table across from Collin as he reassembled his rifle parts, cleaning each with an oilcloth. Their faces lit up like jack-o'-lanterns as candlelight flickered on the bricks in front of the cabin's fireplace.

"We'll be leaving soon. It'll be completely dark, and the lab will be deserted." He looked through the lens to make sure the scope wasn't fogged. He activated the infrared option. "Love, if you knew the whole story you'd understand."

"I'm going too, then."

"I can't let you. This is more dangerous than I thought."

"You need me. You can't do it without me!"

"I know."

"Lilith would want us to stay together."

Collin knew that she was right.

"All right" said Collin—his voice softening. "Poor Lilith. She said a book will be waiting for me on my desk at the lab." Collin thought about Lilith and felt guilty about her death. Then he remembered that he wasn't going to go into the mess about the Dark Army with Stephanie. It was true, though, Lilith would have wanted them to stay together—and finish the job—and to destroy all the computer files.

"Book?" asked Stephanie. "What book?"

"Never mind—it's a long story."

Stephanie reached across the table to take her father's hand. He kissed it.

Collin left the table with his fully assembled rifle slung over his back, and went outside to the check the perimeter of the cabin. Hopefully, there wouldn't be any last minute intruders.

As Collin walked toward the carport, he heard a car engine humming in the distance. He looked up at where the highway was winding in hair-loops down the hill. Collin saw a string of about a dozen metallic objects descending toward the cabin. The cars rolled toward him, their engines in neutral and the headlights doused to escape detection, using the moon's glow as a source of light. He heard the reverberating sound of choppers approaching a short distance away—their red and green lights gliding over the trees.

Just at that moment, Collin's hands started to shake. He squeezed each hand with the other very hard in an effort to stop the shaking, and it worked. He could feel, under the extreme stress, his manic-depression kicking in—a sign that ordinarily would have been treated with new medication.

He took a moment to close his eyes, take a deep breath, and externalize his fear and dread. Action would settle him down, he realized. The violence and murder ahead would calm his self-doubts, and he would treat the coming combat as cognitive-behavioral training—sort of a medicinal computer game where methodically extinguishing lives didn't matter, but objectives did.

Collin glanced up at the deafening noise of the choppers overhead, recognizing a helicopter raid. The choppers moved swiftly, as ropes fell from their open side-compartments. Then, they hovered over the treetops. Commandos slid down the ropes. Glancing up at the approaching cars, Collin saw them drive rapidly toward him, their motors roaring, their headlights now on.

They were at the turnoff of the long driveway to the cabin.

Collin sprinted to the front door and fetched Stephanie out of the cabin, leading her quickly to the carport where his car was parked. He put her in the passenger seat, and climbed to the top of the low-lying carport, using it as a bridge to scramble onto the roof of the cabin.

He crouched, scanning the perimeter.

Collin aimed his rifle. He figured that if he killed a couple of the insurgents, that would hold off the rest for a little while longer, buying time make a clean escape. Peering through the infrared telescopic lens, Collin sited a human target just under one of the helicopters. The commando had just made it to the ground, lowering from the tether. The target wore plain clothes—no uniform at any rate—suggesting they were not SWAT or US Armed Forces, but clandestine troops.

They probably were minions of the Dark Army, surmised Collin.

He squeezed the trigger, and the head of the commando in the scope vaporized.

He panned the riflescope, dispatching three more insurgents in the same manner. He then unloaded his magazine into the glass of one of the choppers, aiming for the likely location of the pilot's seat.

Hearing the shattering glass, Collin knew he achieved total penetration of the glass cockpit with his high-velocity rifle, even though the chopper glass was nominally bulletproof. The chopper careened off below the tops of the trees. Collin heard the crashing sound between the trees and observed the far-off glow of the ensuing fireball.

He replenished his ammo. He swung his rifle toward the end of the long driveway, aiming for the first car in the string of vehicles approaching the cabin. Collin discharged a dozen rounds in rapid succession, the first going through the windshield on the driver's side. The rest of the bullets riddled all quadrants of the target.

The first car caught fire and exploded. The flaming wreckage blocked the progress of the cars behind it, just as Collin had planned. Collin sprang to his feet, slung the rifle over his shoulder, and jumped down to his waiting car.

He sped down the front yard to the emergency road behind the cabin, racing in the direction opposite of the cars that were jammed on the driveway. Stephanie, sitting in the passenger's seat, reassuringly smiled at her father. Bless her heart—thought Collin—she had put up a brave front.

Collin took the hairpin turns at sixty miles-per-hour. In spite of that, he saw a black jeep in his rear mirror gaining on them. The jeep must have joined the road at a point different from the other cars.

Two gunshots exploded through Collin's back window. Collin looked over at his daughter, but Stephanie hadn't been hurt. He swerved along the narrow road's shoulder as he pushed Stephanie down to the floor with his free hand. She would be safer there, he thought.

A chopper appeared, flying overhead, firing shots down on them. One blasted through the roof of the car, ricocheting within the cab. It nicked Collin's arm.

He swerved the car to the opposite shoulder, just missing a row of trees along the slope of the road. Collin punched the pedal and raced faster, his car almost skidding off the road into a steep embankment.

Suddenly, the car in the rear-view mirror disappeared, and so did the choppers. Collin sped past a gas station, and then slowed down. He was reaching the outskirts to the nearby town—and relative safety. They were very close to the laboratory, and the little park across from the lab where the entrance to the secret passageway lay.

Collin heard sirens in the distance. He expected the police at any time, so he sped up slightly. At last, he sighted the little park about a quarter of a mile down the road. At this hour, it would be deserted.

Collin saw the half-moon though the windshield, its bright orange glow reminding him of how little time they had, and what lay in store if he failed.

Everything they cared about would be destroyed.

CHAPTER SIXTY-ONE

Northeast of Bethesda, Maryland, Evening of the Sabbath Moon, March 31:

Collin and Stephanie parked a few blocks from the toddler-park across the road from the lab building, and walked the rest of the way. They darted between trees and bushes to avoid detection by unlikely bystanders or police.

So far, no police had followed them to the lab, and there were no signs of the Dark Army.

Once in the park, Collin and Stephanie searched the grounds frantically to find the hidden entrance to the passageway that led under the road and to the lab's basement. Collin saw a shiny new manhole buried within the bushes. He pushed past the plants and crouched over it.

"Why would anyone put a manhole here? This must be it. Here, help me."

Stephanie held his penlight as Collin heaved up on the heavy lid, throwing it sideways. A trapdoor lay underneath.

"That's it all right!" Collin pulled his red, emergency-passage key out of his pants pocket.

"Are you sure, daddy?" His daughter was trembling as she stood over him in the dark with the small flashlight. "It looks like part of a sewer. Let's get out of here!"

"This is it." He felt for his gun in his ankle–holster, making sure it was ready.

"Hold the light on the keyhole there—on that little door."

After some fumbling, Collin thrust the key into the lock of the door.

He turned the key. It unlocked. Collin pulled hard on the handle and threw the little hatch wide open. Taking the light from Stephanie, he crawled down into the dark opening until he hit the floor of the tunnel, about six feet from the surface. It had a cement lining.

Climbing out of the opening, he helped Stephanie through the door, guiding her as he shined the powerful but small light on the dark entrance. Collin climbed down through the opening and closed the hatch behind him.

He and Stephanie huddled within the forbidding, dark tunnel. Collin's light proved just enough to find their way along the musty, cement enclosure. It was almost high enough for Collin to stand up, but not wide enough for them to walk side-by-side.

"Just stay close to me." Collin placed his hand reassuringly upon his daughter's shoulder. "I have the light. I'll go first. If we run into anything, I'll be on top of it."

Stephanie nodded. Her hands shook. Collin could see in the narrow beam that she was terrified.

"We'll advance *cautiously*, but steadily, all right?" added Collin. "The tunnel's short, so that's the good news."

"I can't move, daddy."

He looked into her face. "Honey, yes you can. Trust me."

Stephanie nodded.

Collin started to creep through the hundred feet of dark, concrete passage in a slight crouch, with Stephanie following him close behind. All of a sudden, the glow of the dim, low-voltage, emergency lighting activated—detecting their motion. Collin put away the small flashlight.

He looked back as he advanced, making sure that Stephanie was close behind. He stepped on something that moved under his foot. He glanced down at the ground, but whatever it was, it had fled.

He could hear it slithering.

Hissing noises came from somewhere ahead of them.

Then, the hisses turned into screams, with a shrill, almost human quality.

Collin saw the glowing, yellow eyes on the ground in front of him. He stomped on the creature, feeling it crush beneath his shoe. It moaned.

Collin knew what it was, and it terrified him.

"Stephanie!"

"Yes, daddy."

"Faster—stay close. Close your eyes. Don't stop—no matter what. Here, grasp my hand firmly."

Collin faced three huge, black snakes lying on the ground about ten feet in front of him—blocking his way. He felt

241

something drop on his back and crawl down his shirt. Reaching behind him, he grabbed the slippery serpent by its tail and swung it hard against the concrete wall of the tunnel—smashing its diamond-shaped head.

The same shrill scream echoed throughout the passage.

He quickly turned back toward Stephanie—she was just behind him. He grabbed her hand again and dashed to the end of the tunnel, bulling his way through the danger.

"Stay close—don't let go!"

Collin's eyes met the small, glowing yellow eyes of the closest snake in front of him—rising from the ground—poised to strike. Letting go of Stephanie's hand, he quickly pulled his Beretta revolver from his ankle holster and fired.

The impact of the bullet cut it in half, with its head starting to devour its tail.

The gunfire reverberated throughout the tunnel with a deafening explosion. The second creature came at him, its two fangs ready. Collin quickly let off a couple of more rounds. He obliterated the creature—as the third snake was almost at Collin's feet—rising on its tail to eye level.

Instead of striking, the serpent, for some reason, just closed its yellow eyes and froze. Collin wasn't sure if the viper was still alive or not.

Maybe I hit it with a stray bullet, wondered Collin?

"Just plow through to the end—fast! We're almost there!" shouted Collin.

Clutching Stephanie's hand, he pulled her swiftly past the remaining serpent with one hand while he held tightly onto his gun with the other.

Collin could see the end of the tunnel ahead of him. He also saw more yellow eyes glowing in the dim surroundings. The hisses were getting louder as he moved ever faster. He was nearly out of bullets.

Worse—with the police close on his tail and having probably figured out where he was heading—he was nearly out of time.

Finally making it to the end of the passage, he put his gun away.

Collin and Stephanie were safe—for now anyway.

CHAPTER SIXTY-TWO

Collin and Stephanie scrambled to the end of the passageway, arriving at the second trapdoor. Collin frantically tried to unlock the door with his red key. The hissing sounds behind them grew louder.

He fumbled with the lock.

The key didn't fit. Collin turned around, looking past Stephanie. The black, glistening vipers slid on the ground towards them. He jigged the key—it finally slipped in. He turned it. The cylinder didn't budge.

Collin strained, turning the key with all his might. He feared that he might break the key off into the lock. He jiggled it as the hisses intensified.

"Hurry daddy!" Stephanie huddled close behind him.

Then, the cylinder turned. The hatch unlocked.

He thrust it open. Collin pushed Stephanie through the door as the snakes poised to strike. Once his daughter was safely out of the tunnel, he quickly squeezed through the opening. He felt a snake wrap around his ankle and managed to kick it off, bolting the door behind him.

Taking the penlight by one hand and Stephanie by the other, he led the way through the dark basement to the stairwell, where he turned on the lights. They had finally made it into the interior of the laboratory, and Collin was relieved when he saw that there didn't appear to be any more snakes. Now, it was on to the back door of the main lab on the second floor—via the stairwell.

Collin raced up the steps with Stephanie in tow. He abruptly halted. "Not much time left—you all right?"

He placed his hand upon his daughter's shoulder, breathing heavily as the sweat streamed down his face.

"Daddy, you're bleeding!"

Collin's arm—where the bullet had grazed him—was covered in blood. It trickled down his forearm to his hand. He wiped his hand off on his shirt.

"I'm all right. It missed the main artery."

He looked at his daughter. Although tired, she was unharmed. Not a bead of moisture stood on that sweet face, he was relieved to see.

"The building should be empty." Collin glanced at his watch. "Interior security doesn't make rounds for another hour."

Collin looked up the drab, grey stairwell. "You sure you're OK?" He gazed at his daughter tenderly.

Stephanie didn't respond. Collin thought she must be terrified. He shook her but she didn't budge.

Collin studied his daughter gravely. "I'll go on alone. This might get dangerous. You can go back to the basement and wait for me."

"No daddy." Stephanie had suddenly regained her resolve.

"All right, let's get to it. Use your emergency destruction codes to wipe out the stored information on the computer servers. Destroy the rest of the files. Then, as soon as I engage the black lever on the glass wall—you get the hell out of the main lab—the same way you got in. You understand?"

"I'll wait for you."

"The whole adjunct lab area behind the glass wall will incinerate, and the Super-virus with it. When I'm done, I'll be right behind you. We'll meet in the basement. Maybe we won't have to use that damn tunnel again to get out of here. "

Stephanie grabbed her father's hand. "I'll wait for you *in the lab*."

"No."

"But—."

"—But nothing! Don't forget, *I* did all this—understand? You never say a word to anyone about it."

"Daddy—."

"I *made* you come here, understand? After all, I'm crazy. Remember that. I took you hostage."

Stephanie trembled at the sound of her father's stern instructions.

"Don't worry, honey. I might even turn myself in when we're done." His voice became very gentle. "Everything will be all right."

Exhausted, the two continued up the stairwell. He ascended the steps, his mind on fire with colliding facts and emotions.

The infamous Firehouse—their objective—was two floors above. They had only a few minutes, Collin figured, to destroy the recombined Super-virus before the SWAT team—or the Dark Army recruits—arrived. Collin believed the building had internal and external monitors that he had never known about, whose alarms would connect directly to the authorities.

He also knew that Frank Seaton, the mole for the Dark Army, would have something up his sleeve. Given Collin's public obsession about halting the vaccine project, it wouldn't take the police long to figure out that he was headed for the lab. Frank Seaton might even have told them about the secret passageway into the lab. He would protect the Super-virus at all costs. Time was therefore precious.

"Daddy, I can't make it anymore." Suddenly, Stephanie sat down on a step in the stairwell. "Give yourself up, *now*, please."

She sobbed. "They might kill you if you don't!"

Collin knelt before her and stroked her hair. "If you don't come with me, I'll just have to manage myself."

He helped her off the step, leading her up the stairwell with him.

She froze on the stairwell again. Collin stopped and put his arm around her, his voice desperate, "We must do this—*everything* depends upon it."

"I don't know if I can." She leaned back against the wall of the stairwell.

"You *can*—I know my daughter." Collin jauntily winked at her. "I'm going now—and not stopping until I'm done. For the last time, let's get on with it."

Stephanie nodded. "I'll be right behind you."

"That's my girl." He smiled at her. "Let's nail this thing!"

He raced up the stairs. "Try to hurry!"

Collin rushed up the steps, trying to get out of his mind the dangers that still faced him, and Stephanie's fading resolve. He wondered why Frank—up to his eyeballs in the dark conspiracy—had not disabled the secret passageway. Only he and Frank had known about it—and the Dante emergency button located below his desk.

Maybe Frank hadn't had the opportunity?

As they reached the landing on the second floor, they stood next to the secondary entry door to the main lab. Collin saw the entry-code box on the wall. His heart dropped to his shoes.

He'd forgotten. Naturally, having been fired and denied access, his code would have been invalidated. Stephanie's code also probably would have been cancelled if they suspected she was with him. Collin punched in his primary security code.

The thick metal door remained locked.

Stephanie stood right behind him. She observed him fooling with the code box.

"What's the matter?" She moved to his side.

"The damn entry code's been disabled," Collin grumbled.

He had, in all the excitement, forgotten this last obstacle. After all this, he and Stephanie had been locked out of the main lab for lack of a simple code, and denied access to the organism that was ready to destroy the world.

Unless he found a way into the lab, the Super-virus would live and the Dark Army would achieve its catastrophic objective.

CHAPTER SIXTY-THREE

"What's your primary code?"

Stephanie told him.

Collin punched the numbers in the box on the wall beside the door. Again, the door remained unlocked.

"It figures. Frank Seaton not only invalidated my code, but he also invalidated yours as an automatic precaution."

Collin pounded the wall in frustration. Then, he snapped his fingers. "Bet they didn't change your *individual* code—the code for emergencies. What is it?"

Shaking and breathing hard, Stephanie tried to think. "I . . . don't remember!" Just then, the sound of distant sirens coming from outside the building cut through the absolute quiet of the stairwell landing.

Collin glanced in the direction of the offending sound, then at Stephanie. "Please, try to remember!"

"I think—I think its one-three . . . I don't know, its been too long since I've used it!"

Collin turned toward the heavy metal door and tried keying in more numbers.

He thought that he might be able to figure out her code from his disabled number. He knew that the six-digit code used the last four of the social security number at the end. He knew her social—and the second number in the series was usually a three—the "emergency numeral." The first number was probably a one, a five, or a seven. If they had given *him* a one—then hers was probably a five or a seven.

He keyed in the five—nothing—then the seven—it worked! The door buzzed. He threw it open.

They were in the main lab.

Collin turned on the lights and activated the emergency lockdown button. He heard a set of loud clicks throughout the main lab. This automatically disabled all exterior entry codes. Now, the only way into the lab from the outside would be to bash in the three-inch-thick metal doors, or to implode the walls—and both would take time.

Then, sirens and tire screeches—penetrating even through the ultra-dense, NASA-developed plastic windows—signaled to Collin and Stephanie the arrival of the SWAT team. Collin had only minutes to destroy the Super-virus before he would be taken into custody. He looked out the window and could see the half-moon—its strange, orange halo clearly visible.

He knew what that meant, and he knew what he had to do, and how fast.

Collin's eyes scanned the lab.

He saw the two huge metal desks. His desk, with the catastrophic Dante button underneath, had a pile of mail stacked upon it—and a postal package the size of a book. The human resources manager probably had not had time to clear his desk yet.

Collin quickly recalled that there were two old books Lilith had tried very hard to get from her distributors that would help unravel the mystery of the Dara's sinister plot, one was *His Dark Army*, which seemed hopeless to find, and the other she *had* found, *Faces Behind Shadows*, the book that kicked-off the whole struggle with the photo of Frau Troost.

He also remembered that Lilith had mailed him *Faces Behind Shadows* before she died, and had sent it to the lab to avoid Dara finding it. Lilith had desperately wanted him to study that book. It seemed moot to him now—he had his solid plan and he knew all the facts that were necessary to destroy the Super-virus—the critical mission at hand.

Therefore, ignoring the book on his desk, Collin's gaze shifted to the glass wall and the Firehouse that lay behind it. He saw the glass box on the wall, with the black lever resting inside—the lever that controlled the total incineration behind glass wall—including the evil organism incubating in the adjunct lab. There was no doubt in his mind that there lay the Super-virus.

Collin placed Stephanie in a chair about ten feet behind his desk. "It's all right, sweetie. It's all right." He patted her hand. He would give her a few moments to rest before she started her vital work of destroying the computer files.

Collin felt the icy steel of the Beretta revolver against his ankle. He removed his gun and placed it on his desk next to the package that contained *Faces Behind Shadows*.

The police now pounded against the front door of the main lab just a few feet away from them. A bullhorn was blasting, demanding that Collin release his daughter—the "hostage."

Maybe that would buy him a few minutes in negotiation time?

From the point of view of the police, the danger of the Vampire Virus spreading during a shootout would have to be weighed against the potential danger to a hostage. As he strode toward his vital target—the glass wall and the incubating Super-virus behind it—he wondered how long it would take the authorities to block the stairwells and the escape route through the basement.

Then, glancing through the glass wall, Collin noticed that something looked very wrong in the Fridge. The red and white emergency lights over the window had been activated.

Dashing the rest of the way to the Firehouse door, he punched in the same emergency code as he used in the code-box by the door. The code numbers worked again.

Ignoring the black lever on the wall for now, Collin pushed the glass door wide open and moved cautiously in the direction of the Fridge. He could see that it was dimly lit inside. The door to the cooler was closed, and considering the fact that there might have been a spill, he was relieved.

Collin glanced over at the little cooler in the adjunct lab area just a few feet away. In that cooler lay his target—the incubating Super-virus. In a few seconds, it would be burnt and gone.

Collin strode up to the Fridge until his nose almost touched the observation window. He peered inside. There was something lying on the floor—something that didn't belong there.

It was a man's body, just beyond the door.

CHAPTER SIXTY-FOUR

Dried blood rimmed the nostrils and mouth. The round, hazel eyes were still wide open—as if in terror.

The stainless steel, square frames of the eyeglasses lay there next to the corpse.

Collin recognized the frames.

He lay in the Fridge just like a slab of beef in a meat locker. On the ground, in a pool of coagulated blood, a dead Frank Seaton rested in anything but peace.

No wonder, Collin thought, that the emergency-escape passageway was still operational. A dead man can't destroy anything. Maybe Frank Seaton had been innocent all along, and was yet another victim of the Dark Army.

Collin studied the body through the thick, protective-glass window from the outside. Frank could have been accidently exposed to a virulent strain of Vampire seed-virus that had been restocked in the Fridge. Sure, but more likely, someone had exposed him purposely to get him out of the way. Just like poor Dr. Astaire-Adams.

Collin surveyed the interior of the Fridge—the green beakers resting quietly upon the shelves—all except one. He noticed one large beaker had somehow broken, leaking its evil contents throughout the cooler. That supported his theory. Such a finding would probably have been due to sabotage.

Collin exited the Firehouse and closed the door behind him. Before he broke the glass case holding the black lever—he would rush back to Stephanie to make sure that she was prepared for her critical task.

Stephanie still sat in her chair, a few feet behind Collin's desk. She was bent over, with her head buried in her hands.

He knelt down beside her. "Baby, start disabling the computers. I'm going to torch the Super-virus now."

Just then, pounding noises and shattered glass could be heard from the floor below them. An explosion boomed on the floor above. Collin figured that he had about five minutes, but no more.

"Stephanie dear," said Collin in a soft voice.

Stephanie had frozen from the threatening noises—a profound catatonic state that Collin had not seen her experience in years. She shook uncontrollably. He would give her a moment to compose herself, and then dash over to the black lever to pull it—sending the Super-virus into oblivion. Collin saw no point in mentioning Frank Seaton. It would only upset her more.

"Stephanie love—the computers . . ." Collin nudged her shoulder as he stood over her. She didn't respond. She just sat there, staring into space, shaking like a leaf in a storm.

Collin realized that he would have to destroy the computers himself, before he pulled the black lever. He decided he would bash the machines in with one of the fire axes hanging on the wall. It wouldn't destroy the servers, but it was better than nothing.

Collin moved quickly to his desk. He needed to get a special set of keys buried in his side-drawer. One key would unlock his main desk drawer and thus allow him access to all his computer passwords. He sat down and fished the keys out of the drawer. He took one off the ring.

When Collin reached into the pocket of his khaki shirt to put the key for safekeeping—his fingers felt the Royal Catchfly that he had placed there the evening before for good luck. He removed it and held it up to the light, the five-pointed, crimson flower that was his favorite bloom. For an instant, its goodness reminded him of better days. It was his reminder of all that was right with the world.

Then, he noticed the small package was missing off the desk—and the gun . . .

The voice that resonated behind him was familiar, yet strange.

"The flower's a *pentangle*—our beloved emblem. That's the real reason why you love it so, my husband. It is a five-pointed star that has always been the symbol of our Great One."

Horror gripped Collin. He dropped the flower on the ground.

The strange voice coming from behind him continued. "I have tried to redeem thee, but you remain the Apostate. It is hopeless, and the Super-virus must live."

A shot rang throughout the lab.

Collin felt something like a hot poker stick into his left shoulder. Warm blood trickled through his fingers. Stunned for a moment, he turned in his chair to look behind him, from where the voice and the shot had come.

As he did so, he felt cold steel roll over his throat—but strangely, it didn't hurt. The gush of fluid flowed down his chest, warming him.

He saw her standing there. She seemed cocky. She had confidence. She had taken charge. The shot hadn't come from the police. Stephanie had fired the gun.

The deep, alien-sounding words had come from his sweet daughter. She held Collin's bloody dagger in her hand. He realized that she had carried it with her, concealed, since they left the cabin.

Collin saw the smoking gun lying on the floor.

Stephanie's posture didn't belong to his dear child—it had transformed. She stood straight, shoulders back, and her head slightly forward, as she cautiously backed up from him. There was a cruel smirk on her face.

She had sliced deep enough into his throat to sever his carotid veins, but spared some of his windpipe. He could only speak to her in a whisper.

The thought tore into him, wrenching his very core as he asked her: "Did you say . . . '*my husband*'?"

CHAPTER SIXTY-FIVE

Stephanie's tone was harsh and with purpose. Her language impediment had vanished. He had never heard her sound like that before—*never*. After she had observed him closely, as if verifying the seriousness of his wounds, she moved slightly closer to him with the same aggressive, forward lean that her mother had.

Collin's dreams glittered through his mind. He thought about the violence, the destruction, the chanting. Then, he considered his flower that looked like the pentangle, the satanic emblem he had seen in the Black Annex. Everything started to come back to him in bits and pieces.

Losing blood rapidly from the shot wound in his shoulder, his arm, and from his throat, he tried to focus upon the hard, brutal creature that confronted him.

"Why did you call me, *husband*?" Collin swallowed a mouthful of blood.

Stephanie moved yet closer to face Collin, dropping his bloodstained, ceremonial dagger on the tile floor. She folded her arms. "Your human wife was innocent all along. I was the one in the old photographs, not her. She suspected me though, and you too. That's why she pulled away from us."

"Suspected us of *what*—?"

"—Being in the Dark Army, of course. Dara had just by chance seen my photo in some historical picture book at the Georgetown College Library, and then started digging."

"No! It's impossible—," insisted Collin.

"—It's true. Every word."

"Frank Seaton?"

"Innocent," she said, shaking her head. "I spilled the beaker on purpose. Of course, I'm immune."

"Dr. Bridgestone?"

"Innocent."

"What about his spying on me? What about the pierced eyebrow?"

"He was working for the government—with Frank." She smirked. "As for the jewelry, get with it. Men can wear pierced anything these days."

"Lieutenant Espinosa, the young service man and woman in the rowboat, they tried to kill me."

"All innocent—they were trying to protect a vital government project. They thought you were cracking up—and that you'd kidnapped me."

Collin started to breathe heavily. He was afraid of the answer to his most important question. "You just called me your *husband*!" From the loss of blood, Collin's vision started to slowly turn grey.

His daughter glared at him. "Your *real* name is *Alois*. Mine is *Klara*—not Stephanie. You're also the known as the *Apostate*. You turned against the Great One long ago, but I'd hoped you'd remember your past and come back to us."

Collin felt dizzy. "*You* killed Dr. Astaire-Adams . . . even Lilith."

"Me, or a chum. Lilith never caught on. For a Nobel prizewinner you sure catch on slow, my dear. The Professor, Carmen, Gordon Givens, Torres, all of them too," she said complacently, as if talking about a guest list to a tea party. "Good thing for me Lilith sent the book directly here, instead of to her first, she would've made me for sure."

Collin noticed the book on the chair behind Stephanie. The wrapper was off. He felt a surge of rage and tried to stand, but his legs were too weak.

"Yes, that's right, it's over there." She nodded toward the volume, *Faces Behind Shadows*. "You didn't have time to look through it that morning in the The Black Peacock. I saw you enter the store and left quickly, without the book. Dara almost caught me. Of course, I came on a day that Lilith wasn't working."

"I don't believe any of this rubbish." Collin wondered if he had indeed gone mad. Now his dear Stephanie was claiming to be one of *them*, and she was making wild statements that could only be the product of a nightmare.

Could this be a delusion?

Stephanie chuckled, nodding her head, as if reading his mind. "No, you're not crazy. The Great One shall forgive you if you repent. Get on your knees and beg Him, before it's too late! I tried to stop you from coming here, but you wouldn't listen—as usual."

The sound of the police breaking in grew louder. A bullhorn sounded, its words muffled by the wall.

"*The Great One?*"

Stephanie voice crackled. "You know who he is." Her voice softened. "You once loved Him too."

A thought inserted into Collin's mind, it was dark, and foreign . . .

"That strange name you called me?"

"You mean, *Alois?*"

"*My* name is Collin!"

"It's all coming back to you now, isn't it? I can tell."

"You're out of your mind."

Collin then remembered that Dara had asked him at the cabin if the name "Alois" meant anything to him, and he had said it didn't. He also remembered telling Dr. Bridgestone that he had mistakenly called his wife by the name of "Klara."

Bits and pieces *were* coming back to him.

She backed up to the chair, her eyes never leaving his. She knelt, grabbed the book, and walked up to Collin very close, throwing it on the desk in front of him.

She shook her head as if admonishing a naughty boy. "Were you looking for this? This will explain everything."

Collin wiped the blood from his throat. He glanced down at the book on the desk. It looked to him to be indeed *Faces Behind Shadows*. The book lay open, blurred from his loss of blood, and then came back into focus.

He saw a black-and-white photo of a man and a woman, the woman holding a baby.

"Have a closer look, my husband."

"Don't call me that!" His voice was weak.

Collin slowly stood up and his knees buckled. He felt chilled, shivering.

Stephanie pointed to the book on the desk. "Look at it! It won't do us any harm now. Our work is done—Praise Be!"

His daughter then embraced him lovingly. She kissed him on the mouth passionately with wet kisses. He started to kiss her back, and then caught himself . . .

"No!"

Collin pushed her away violently. She came back. He backhanded her hard, her glasses flying across the room. Stephanie staggered.

Collin saw the glasses shatter upon the hard tile floor, and then the epiphany struck. He then realized the real test of her identity.

As Stephanie fell, and before she had hit the floor, Collin caught her and threw her on the desk. He mustered all his remaining strength, his fist jamming against her slender throat. The room spun, his dizziness causing him to swoon.

"You can't stop us now—it's too late!" she screamed, the words garbled from the choking action of Collins hand.

"I want to see your left eye—close!"

She tried to get up from the desk and he slammed her head back down hard. Pinioning the back of her head to the desk with his right hand to make sure she was still, Collin put his head close to hers. His wounded shoulder burned with pain as he propped her eyelid open with his left thumb.

She squirmed, and then went limp, unexpectedly smiling. "Go ahead, look!"

He held her head steady as he examined her eye carefully.

Collin saw the tiny black dot—the same birthmark as Dara—at six o'clock.

That was proof that what she said was *possible*, thought Collin.

Was it really Stephanie in the old photos all along and not Dara?

Both had the familial birthmark, but had his wife been the innocent one? He remembered how much alike they really looked, aside from the odd clothes and glasses that Stephanie wore, with her died hair and weak posture.

Still, this was too fantastic and evil for Collin to grasp.

She stroked his hair gently. "Now kiss me before you die. I want you one last time."

"You evil bitch!"

"Will this help?" Stephanie started sweet-talking him in Dara's voice. She ended her torment with a faint laugh.

Collin's legs were too weak to hold him. He dropped to the floor. His vision left him for a second, and then returned. The sweat of cardiogenic shock rolled down his cheeks.

Stephanie rose from the desk and stood up over Collin as he lay bleeding upon the floor. He glanced under his desk, the welcome sight of the Dante button, which Stephanie had never known about, giving him comfort.

"All right then, have it your way." She kicked him hard in the ribs. "Get up. I'll prove it. You've always been my husband."

"You lie!"

She grabbed him by the collar and forcefully yanked him up. She seemed to have the strength of three men as Collin rose to his feet. She threw him in the chair.

"Look!" She pushed his head into the page of the book resting upon the desk.

"I *said* look!"

"All right."

Collin felt maybe the time had come to play along.

CHAPTER SIXTY-SIX

Collin's eyes, now blurry, fixed upon the old black-and-white photo. It was grainy, but plain in most details. He saw that a young man and a woman sat together, she holding an infant child. The hairstyles and dress were very old.

Collin noticed a caption below the picture.

"Read what's below the photograph!" Stephanie grabbed and shook hard. "That photo is the mother and the father of the baby—taken in eighteen eighty-nine." Stephanie pointed down at the book.

Collin could see that the father in the photo had his head turned from the camera.

"See the mother?" she asked.

Collin looked. The face was identical to Stephanie's.

"Now, turn the page." He couldn't. His coordination was gone. She turned it for him.

"Look at the man! Look at the father!" she ordered. "Who is it?"

Collin, tears streaming down his face, now didn't need to, but he did anyway. The horrible times and memories came back to him at last. All the centuries of death, destruction, lying, subversion—and rebellion, crashed down upon him.

The second photo was the same shot, but at a moment when the proud father looked back into the camera.

Collin swallowed hard. He sat stunned.

It's me!

Collin saw that *he* was the father in the photo.

He looked up at Stephanie. Her eyes were of a beast, but they oddly had a hint of love in them nevertheless.

"It's you!" She turned the page back. "Read the caption below the picture." Stephanie pounded on the page with her fist. "I *said*, read it!"

Collin snuck his hand below the desk. He tried to distract her by antagonizing her.

"No!"

"Read it!"

He read the caption out loud:

"Alois and Klara Hitler, Braunau am In, Austria, eighteen eighty-nine; proud parents of the newborn Adolf."

A primal scream erupted from Collin as the full meaning of the words gripped him. *He* was one of them too, and he had been married to his own daughter for over a hundred years, and had fathered Adolf Hitler! Likely, he'd spawned other monsters too, maybe even Joseph Stalin. He truly had been the Apostate after all.

Collin broke down in tears.

Stephanie held her palms up with her eyes closed. "You know my words are true. Hail Great One. I love Thee. The world is ours!"

Collin felt the protective cap over the secret Dante button as he groped under the table. He flicked it off with one finger. He knew what would happen in two minutes, and he would play her for a little more time.

Stephanie gloated. "I've won!"

Collin pushed the button.

He knew that soon the whole building would erupt in a ball of fire that even a volcano couldn't match.

Stephanie's voice became almost a hiss. "Let us pray. Redeem yourself in His eyes."

"Yes. I see everything clearly now, my wife. Praise-be!" he said.

Now, it all made sense he thought as he waited to be burned alive. His latent love of fire, his hidden desire to murder, his stubborn and inquisitive nature and his fixation upon the triangular symbol and the castle, the violent dreams, his fascination with the Royal Catchfly—his beloved flower that was shaped like an evil pentangle. Then, there was his preoccupation with the story of Judas, and his life pursuit as a molecular scientist.

It was all for Armageddon. And now, he had stopped it.

As he sat at his desk, bleeding to death, waiting for a fiery end, he watched his wife pray to the Beast. He tried to remember all the details of his past lives, but he couldn't. Maybe he didn't *want* to know. He knew that there was still good in him, and in the world. *That's why I'm an Apostate.*

Collin then started to laugh uncontrollably, shaking with irony. In that instant, he wondered if he would come back as a flower. He saw his Royal Catchfly lying on the floor a few feet away. He didn't care if it resembled the satanic symbol. For him, it stood for everything beautiful and good in the world. *Nothing* could pervert it.

Collin dropped to the floor, and crawled toward it.

The police had cut their way through the thick, metal door. They rushed in with full gear, guns ready. Stephanie glanced back at them as they rushed toward her, their guns trained upon Collin.

She looked down at Collin and pointed at him. "He's mad! He kidnapped me. Help me, please!"

"Freeze!" The guns pointed at Collin's head.

As his hand was about to grasp the flower . . .

The explosion was heard all the way to Washington DC. The building went up in an orange fireball—there was noting left standing. The heat was so intense it even melted the solid steel beams.

The Super-virus was gone.

Collin had won.

CHAPTER SIXTY-SEVEN

Georgetown, The Dawn of Armageddon, Sunday morning, April 1:

The middle-aged Asian gentleman in the black raincoat picked the worn book off of a low shelf and took it to the counter.

"Is this the only copy?" He handed the sales clerk the volume as she checked in her computer. His eyes followed closely the lines of her tight jeans and sweater.

She murmured the title as she glanced at the cover, sensing his roaming eyes traveling down her behind. "'*His Dark Army*'— by Adrian Pappas." She giggled, "Funny name. Yes, its the only one."

"Any other editions?"

She tapped her keyboard. "No, *sir*. It shows that the author is recently deceased."

"I knew that." He hated to be called "sir" by attractive young women.

She glanced at him uncertainly. He took back his book, treating it as a gem that might get stolen. "You haven't seen any other copies in the store lying around, have you?"

"No, sir. I haven't."

"Then it's the only one left?"

"You got it."

The man didn't like her tone. He, in fact, didn't like most people, or humans, that is. Well, no worries, he thought, he won't have to put up with them for long—there won't be any.

"I'll take it."

"Do you want it wrapped?"

"No."

He pushed his cash at her with a hint of irritation that went entirely unnoticed, and straightened his yellow bow tie.

The young girl with the tattoos and purple-streaked hair rang the register and then handed him the change. Her pat smile faded as she glanced at his face—she sensed an uncommon intensity in his eyes.

The man exited the Disowned Tomes bookstore on Caine Street with the book in hand. Due to a light sprinkle in the air, he

261

buried it in the cleft between the buttons of his overcoat as he walked to the ride waiting at the curb.

The man fondly remembered that The Black Peacock—just around the corner— had recently burned down. As he walked along the wet sidewalk, he dug his free hand deeply into his coat pocket. It was an unusually cold April morning. In fact, there had even been a few snowflakes—a truly freak event. The weather had been very odd lately, and he was one of the few people who knew the real reason why. This day was very special.

He threw open the front passenger door of the black Mercedes waiting at the curb, its muffler spewing grey billows, and slid inside. The attractive blonde woman at the wheel— dressed in tight black woolens—turned off the radio news with a hint of irritation. She didn't look at him but worked the wipers instead.

Little chunks of ice and insipient snowflakes whirled away from her windshield. The wind had grown very strong. Her powerful gaze shifted to the book.

"The last copy?" she asked.

"In this town anyway. Probably anywhere. I checked— been out of print since nineteen-ninety." He handed it to her. He took off his wet coat and loosened his tie.

"She wants the last one destroyed. I had to dig one up somewhere in Southern Iraq last year. What a place to visit." The woman turned the pages of the book. "Half my time's spent running around the globe, tracking down old, rotting photos and paintings and whatnot."

She thumbed through a few more pages, then, finding what she was looking for, placed the open book on her lap—the print face down. "Open the glove compartment. I want another look at it."

The woman glanced around furtively, as if spies might be lurking just outside her window.

Dr. Samuel Chu of the FDA always did as he was told. He was afraid of Camilla Givens despite his newfound faith. She turned toward him slowly as he removed a small box from the compartment. The package was carefully insulated in layers of bubble-wrap.

Chu handled the object as if it were a firecracker, ready to go off at any moment.

"Here it is: The *Super*-virus. I sneaked it out before the Apostate torched the lab."

"Be careful!" she admonished. Camilla Givens reverently took it in her hands. "So, the new, improved product. More lethal—more contagious?"

"With this remodeled virus—with the inserted omega gene—two billion will die, minimum. In only one year, that number will double at least. As I explained, barring any unforeseen scientific breakthroughs, *no* vaccine should be effective—it mutates too fast. There's no antibiotic on the market that's therapeutic, either." Chu smiled. He was happy with himself.

Camilla whistled, obviously impressed. "But, there's always the unexpected. What if it's a dud? We've been disappointed before."

She took her time, studying the precious cargo minutely, as if the murderous contents made the plain wrapper more interesting. "It won't be the first time. But, let's not go negative."

Chu nodded. "Yes, let us rejoice. We had some luck." As time passed, Chu felt more comfortable in his new role—and bolder and more ambitious. After all, his government connections and scientific prowess—not to mention his language skills and his ties to the powerful home country—would seem to assure him an important perch within the "Organization".

So, if it were a dud, he'd still be needed. If not, then even more.

Camilla, in a reflective mood, shook her head. "Yes, luck—and we're tech oriented now. We blend in. We're also not as *gender* biased, with women running the Dark Army now."

Camilla, very competitive, tossed a glance at Chu as if to warn him: "Be careful whose toes you tread on—*buster*."

"Or, *racially* biased *I* might add," Samuel Chu chimed in. "Have you ever seen a *yellow* Devil?"

Camilla tried unsuccessfully to beat back a smile. She then giggled. He laughed with her. She carefully handed the package back to Chu. He put it back into the glove compartment and locked it.

"Well, Collin De Gise was after all a malcontent." Camilla shook her head, as if she were talking about a winning racehorse that had gone lame. "After he turned against the Great One, ages ago, he came back to the fold—then left again. Then, he went back and forth. He was too unstable. He led a dual life with no compatibility, and each life had little memory of the other. He was brilliant, but damaged goods."

"You're right, Camilla, as always."

She pulled down the sun visor and fixed her hair in the little mirror. "Too sentimental, too non-conformist, too indecisive. I don't put down the old timers. They laid the groundwork. But now, who needs them?"

"Collin barely even knew how to text," added Chu, as if he had committed the ultimate transgression.

They chuckled together heartily.

Somewhat reassured by the shared levity—as if he'd just pet his neighbor's pit bull and to his surprise hadn't lost a finger—he spread his legs a bit and relaxed. He even inched a bit closer to Camilla. She was a looker.

Then, she got serious again. She glared at him as if he were an intruder. "What's the virus stored in—a test tube?"

"The virus? Goodness no—a climate-controlled, airtight beaker with hardened glass and stabilizing agar."

"Good. The Pentagon—and the Cuba connection—will unleash this sucker—soon."

Camilla nodded in the direction of the glove compartment as she refreshed her lipstick in the mirror. "My trips to the Bay with Gordon were productive. Poor patsy—he found me out too late. We turned a few of those prisoners. But, they're nothing like the ace in the hole we already have."

"Nevertheless, it was a great piece of work, Camilla. We've done it!"

She took the crimson volume off her lap and glanced at the page, and then closed it.

"Yep, this's the one all right." She was very pleased with herself. Camilla then put the car in gear, and sped off down the road.

The lovely woman had sat down alone on a large picnic table to a light supper of scrambled eggs and sausage. The umbrella over the picnic table had been taken down since the storm had let up a few hours before, but the portable heaters were turned up to their maximum. The rustic, California Redwood outdoor furniture, resting in the center of the Mexican tile, had been gifted to the White House from Herbert Hoover.

It was the First Lady's favorite place to have a quiet meal away from the hubbub of the executive office. The kids were asleep and her husband was off to Berlin again on Air Force One. Shonda loved a roaring fireplace on a dark, blustery night such as this, so the barbeque flame burned full blast with the grill removed. Craving the smell of the burning charcoal, she cocked her head slightly to the left side, as was her habit.

A Secret Service woman entered and placed a wrapped package on in front of her. "Here's the parcel you've been expecting, Mrs. O'Neal."

"Thank you."

The agent left. Picking up the rectangular object and stripping off the brown wrapper, Shonda Rice O'Neal held the crimson-leather bound book and examined its title: *His Dark Army*.

She opened it to the creased page, and studied it closely in the beam of the overhead lamp. She placed the old tome open on the table in front of her, and then focused her attention upon two color photos on the page. One image was a distant shot of a woman standing in the crowd lining the street of what looked like a parade route. The other was a blow-up image of the face of that same woman in the first photo.

Both pictures, somewhat blurred and of mediocre quality, nevertheless clearly presented essential details. It had been a bright and clear day in the photos, and the people in them wore early-sixties-style clothing.

Shonda's eyes narrowed as she closely studied the two pictures.

The distant shot in the first photo featured a black Lincoln convertible limousine with a small American flag attached to the side of its front hood, on a spectator-lined street in the middle of the parade route. A lovely, dark-haired young woman—wearing a pink, black-trimmed outfit with a pink, pillbox hat—sat in the back

seat waving to the crowd. A handsome young man, clutching his bloodstained throat, sat next to her, slumping forward in the seat—his auburn hair glistening in the sun.

In the background of the same photo, Shonda spotted the attractive young blond woman standing with her hands upon her hips. Her head was cocked to the left side, and the blond hair displayed a sixties flip. She was dressed in a white uniform and wore a nurse's hat. She stood on a grassy knoll, just in front of a fence.

Shonda then turned her attention to the second photo, which featured the face of the nurse in close-up. Despite the cat sunglasses, lamented Shonda, that woman in the old photo was very recognizable—far *too* recognizable, she thought.

Now, thankfully, this dangerous photo would exist no more.

The face in the photo was definitely *her face*—Shonda Rice O'Neal's—the current First Lady of the United States of America, and the shots of her had been taken a half-century before in Dallas, Texas, on November 22, 1963.

Shonda slammed the book shut and rose from the picnic table. Walking over to the roaring fire, she dropped the book in the flames and then closed her eyes. Her elegant, bejeweled hands rose palms-up to the dark sky.

"Praise be unto The Great One—the End is near. Hail Satan!"

END